R℞

P

ADDRESS:

Prescription:

A
Road to Blissville
S T O R Y

PRESCRIPTION FOR LOVE

AIMEE NICOLE WALKER

Signature: _____ Date: _____

Prescription for Love (Road to Blissville, #7)
Copyright © 2019 Aimee Nicole Walker
aimeenicolewalker@blogspot.com

SBN: 978-1-948273-13-8

Photographer © Wander Aguiar—www.wanderaguiar.com

Cover art © Jay Aheer of Simply Defined Art—www.simplydefinedart.com

Editing provided by Miranda Vescio of V8 Editing and Proofreading—www.facebook.com/V8Editing

Proofreading provided by Judy Zweifel of Judy's Proofreading—www.judysproofreading.com

Interior Design/Formatting provided by Stacey Blake of Champagne Book Design—www.champagnebookdesign.com

DEDICATION

This is for all the true crime junkies, amateur sleuths, and podcast addicts all around the world. Let us never stop learning, asking questions, demanding that justice is served.

PATIENT NAME: _____
_____
ADDRESS: _____
_____
_____

Prescription:

CHAPTER ONE

Signature: _____ Date: _____

Tucker Garrison

"DADDY, I WANT THIS KITTY," SAID A LITTLE GIRL WHO couldn't be more than five years old. She was pointing at the white cat who'd lived at the shelter the longest. His nameplate read Boris, but I'd named him The Brain because his ever-present scowl said he was plotting to take over the world and would initiate those plans at any given minute. What kind of name was Boris for a cat? No wonder he looked pissed all the damn time.

"Why not this one?" her father asked, pointing to the tiny ball of gray fluff curled up at Boris's feet. "He's younger and doesn't look so p—" The man stopped to consider his audience and chose a better word. "He looks less angry, sweetheart."

"No, Daddy!" the little girl said indignantly then crossed her arms over her chest and stomped a tiny foot sporting a glittery pink boot. "That one!" She uncrossed her arms and pointed at Boris.

"No, Jessica. I don't think he's a good fit for our home."

Jessica disagreed and demonstrated it by throwing a tantrum the likes of which I'd never seen. She threw herself to the ground, kicked her feet, flailed her arms, and screamed loud enough to shatter windows. I'd witnessed families having disagreements on shelter adoption days before, but nothing like this display.

Boris turned his head in my direction, narrowing his eyes. His expression clearly said, "I will chew your balls off if you so much as think about opening the cage to let that screaming brat touch me." The noise woke Natasha from her slumber. The tiny gray kitten stretched and ambled over to the edge of the crate to peer through the bars at the spectacle below. Then she turned her pleading green eyes on me with a pitiful expression that said, "Please don't let them take us."

"I guess I'll take the old white cat," the man said glumly.

"Nah," I said. "Boris isn't a good fit for your family."

The man hadn't even wanted to take Boris home and was only doing it to shut his tiny human up, yet he stiffened and looked offended by my response. "Is there something wrong with my family?"

"How much time do you have?" my grandmother asked as she sidled up beside me. She looked pointedly at Jessica who had started to scream even louder because her father was ignoring her. "Problems, Tuck?"

"No, Grammie. I was just explaining to this nice guy how Boris wouldn't be a good fit for his home. He's old and needs peace." Boris seemed to be insulted by the "old" comment, but I silently implored him to work with me.

"Everyone's a critic when it comes to raising kids," the man said, getting angrier by the second. I wondered if he was going to throw himself down next to his daughter and kick his feet and scream also. The image made me smile, earning a scowl from him. "You think this is funny?"

"No, sir," I calmly said, trying to diffuse the situation.

Grammie, who never gave a damn about appeasing anyone, said, "From where I stand, I don't see a lot of parenting going on. You're allowing your daughter to ruin everyone's pleasant afternoon because she doesn't like being told no. When my grandson tells you no too, you look like you're on the verge of joining her for a tantrum on the cold concrete." Ha. It didn't surprise me Grammie and I were thinking the same thing. "I wonder where she gets her temper from?"

"I don't have to stand here and be insulted," the irate man said. "I was trying to do you people a favor." *You people?*

"You're right," Grammie said. "You don't have to stand here, and I prefer if you didn't. Kindly take your child and leave. We don't need your kind of favors."

"Wait until I tell everyone about how you treated me today," he snarled.

I pointed to a group of people who had gathered around to record the scene with their cell phones. "Please do, but be sure to tell the entire story. If not, I'm sure *they* will."

"Come on, Jessica," he said, hoisting his screaming and kicking daughter in the air. "We're leaving."

"I want a kitty," she wailed as he carried her out the door.

Everyone inside the shelter shared a collective sigh of relief once the man and his daughter left. We enjoyed the blissful silence for several seconds; then, as if a movie director yelled "action," everyone simultaneously went back to what they were doing. I looked into my grandmother's twinkling, dark brown eyes that were identical to mine.

"I was going to handle it," I assured her. Grammie knew I hated confrontations, but I wasn't about to let the idiot adopt Boris because his daughter had thrown a fit. "I might not have been as blunt as you were, but I was handling it."

"I know you were, honey," she said, but it sounded a lot like she was pacifying me. She'd dubbed me the gentle giant as far back as I could remember, and she wasn't wrong. The only time a person saw the ferocity I kept hidden deep beneath my skin was during sports... or fucking. "I'm just going to return to my station since you've got everything under control over here."

They put me in charge of four crates with five cats. Boris and Natasha refused to be separated, and whoever adopted one better believe they were taking the other. I looked around the shelter and smiled at the happy, well-balanced families in attendance who were choosing their next fur friend. Then my eyes landed on the gorgeous face of a man I'd resigned myself to never seeing again. Trent Love. The first time I'd looked into his light blue eyes, we were working together to deliver a baby at the Curl Up and Dye hair salon. Trent was there getting a haircut when one of the stylists had gone into labor in the small kitchenette. The call had come over the radio when I was driving home after a long shift, and since I was both a fireman and paramedic, I stopped by to lend a hand.

There was an immediate spark between us even though we were opposites in every conceivable way. Trent with his blond hair and light blue eyes and shorter, leaner frame was a gorgeous contrast to my taller, darker bulk. The differences didn't start and stop with our looks either. He was a doctor with an expensive education, and his wardrobe probably cost more than my new truck. I was a fireman and paramedic with no college education and a penchant for faded blue jeans and old T-shirts. A few weeks after we met, Josh Roman-Wyatt, the salon owner, threw a pool party at his home to thank us for safely delivering his best friend's baby girl.

Seeing Trent lounging poolside in short black swim trucks showcasing long, toned legs and chiseled abs and pecs made me temporarily forget I was out of his league. Trent smiled and waved me over when I'd arrived. He said he'd reserved the lounger beside his for the other guest of honor. We spent the night flirting, drinking, and laughing. Trent had a sharp, wicked sense of humor which put me at ease. When he invited me on a date for the following weekend, I'd thought to myself: this could be the one. It only took thirty minutes in to our date to realize just how far out of my league he was, and it killed any hope I had of taking our night further. I liked sex as much as the next guy, but I was beyond drive-by fucking at thirty-two years old, especially with men who lived in the same tiny town as I did. If I wanted a hookup, I'd go to Vibe and find one.

Trent hadn't understood my sudden change in attitude, and I had hated upsetting him. It wasn't his fault he could afford to eat at restaurants that didn't list the prices of the food or drinks on their menu. I'd had my heart broken plenty of times, and I wasn't willing to gamble on a summer fling with Dr. Love. He hadn't given up right away, but by December, the man disappeared. One minute, he was working at the family practice in town, and the next, he was gone. I assumed he'd received a better offer somewhere else and tried my best to shove him out of my mind, but the spark he ignited inside me continued to smolder. I spent most of my free time wallowing around in regret and doubt. What if I'd acted too hastily? The man's only crime was taking me to a swanky restaurant. What if he was only trying to make me feel special?

Sometime after the first of the year, the Blissville Daily News ran an article about him working in South America with Doctors Without Borders. They mentioned he would be resuming his work at Blissville Family Medicine when he returned in March. Hadn't Grammie just made a big fuss when she flipped the calendar to March last week and saw I was the model featured in the charity calendar?

He was back! The radiant smile on his face matched the hope blooming in my chest. I was getting the second chance I wanted to prove I wasn't a dick about the differences in our backgrounds and bank account balances. I wanted to return his smile and wave him over, but I just stared at him like a deer caught in the headlights.

Trent's smile faded, and a look of determination washed over his features as he made his way across the room to reach me. "Hi," he said a little breathlessly. If I hadn't watched him casually stroll over to me, I would've thought he just finished running shirtless around town with sweat glistening all over his body. Oh, how I missed watching him jog by the firehouse. I must not have been as subtle as I thought because the guys liked to give me a hard time. *"Here comes your man,"* one of them would say.

"Hi yourself." God. *Could I be any dorkier?* "What are you doing here?"

"It's the second Saturday in March, and I'm here to find my new best friend," Trent stated.

A rumbling noise came from the cage beside me; I glanced over and saw Boris arching his back and rubbing against his cage. Boris purred? Who knew? It sounded more like a rusty motorboat, but I was pretty sure a purr was what the cat intended. Natasha rolled to her back and batted at Boris's tail and nipped at his feet. I'd been on the receiving end of her razor-like teeth and felt sorry for the older cat. He didn't seem to notice because he only had slutty eyes for Trent. I couldn't blame him. I wanted Trent to make me arch my back and purr too.

"Hey there, big fella," Trent said when he noticed Boris's blatant attempt to get his attention. Of course, my dick hoped he was talking to it. "Boris and Natasha?" he asked me when he read their names on the cage. "Can they be any cuter together?"

"I won't separate them," I said more forcefully than the situation called for. Trent arched his brow. "Sorry. After the last incident..."

"Want me to throw myself on the ground and have a temper tantrum?"

"Do you want my grandmother to come over here and spank your ass?" I countered.

"Could I perhaps choose a different volunteer to deliver the punishment?" His blue eyes shimmered with mirth. Down south, my cock started to swell from the images of Trent lying across my lap with his bubble butt in the air. Trent smiled wickedly when he saw the way I started to fidget behind the table.

"Um..." I wasn't sure how to answer him, so I changed the subject. "You really came to adopt a pet? Is that wise with your schedule?"

"Plenty of pet owners work," Trent countered with a shrug.

"Not all pet owners disappear for months at a time. Who will look after your pet when you leave again?"

"I can't say I'm never leaving the house again, but I just completed my last commitment to Doctors Without Borders." Trent cringed and said, "That sounded callous. I did commit to a set number of trips, but I joined the team because I wanted to, not because I was obligated. The town of Blissville is stuck with me now."

"I wouldn't say we're stuck with you," I countered, trying to lighten the mood. By this time, Boris was slamming his body into the side of the cage. "It's just Boris has been stuck at the shelter for a long time, and I don't want him to get attached to a human only to get hurt later."

"It's great Boris has an ally like you." Trent looked away from me to focus on the cat. I'd never seen Boris take to anyone like he did Trent. Pets had a great sense of judgment. If Boris wanted Trent, then I wanted Boris to have him. I'd live vicariously through the grumpy cat. Wait. I wouldn't be around to witness Boris curled up against Trent's chest or sleeping beside him in bed. I'd have to use my imagination.

"As much as Boris likes you, you might be able to adopt him without Natasha. She won't have a hard time finding a home." The tiny ball of fur let out a pitiful meow like she knew what I'd said.

"Don't you listen to him, sweetie," Trent cooed. He slid two fingers of one hand up high for Boris to rub against and two from the other hand down low so Natasha could see if she liked him. She immediately rolled to her back for Trent to rub her belly. "I'll take them both."

"Wait. I have to ask you some questions."

"Ask me your questions then. I've never failed a test in my life."

"It's not a test," I said contritely. "It's more like an interview."

"You need to make sure I'm a suitable owner for these precious cats. I wouldn't have it any other way. Fire away, big guy." Did he like them big? I wasn't one to brag, but I could *fill* his needs. My mind instantly turned to dirty thoughts again, and I fought the urge to fidget more as I went over the questionnaire. "Well, did I pass?" he asked once I finished.

"With flying colors. Do you want to hold them first before you commit?" I moved to the cage and placed my hand on the latch. "Keep an eye on Boris," I warned Trent. "He tries to escape every chance he gets. I call him The Brain."

"Are you Pinky then?" Trent asked Natasha.

"You've watched *Animaniacs*?" I asked him.

"Why do you sound so surprised?" Trent asked instead of answering my question.

"I don't know," I replied, shrugging. "Be ready in case Boris makes a run for it."

Trent took up the position next to me, and the smell of his body wash had me inhaling a little deeper than required. Grammie was a huge fan of essential oils, and Trent smelled like cedarwood and vanilla with the faintest hint of lavender. Damn. I wanted to run my nose along his hot body to find the places he wore the scent the strongest. I imagined pressing my nose against his pelvis, the crease of his thigh, and his pubic hair. A tiny groan escaped my throat, but I hoped it was quiet enough Trent couldn't hear it over Boris's rumbling purrs.

"Is something wrong?" Trent asked. "Do you think the cats will react badly to my new body wash?"

"No," I said. "I just tweaked my back at basketball practice the other night, and I felt a twinge just now."

"Want me to take a look at it?" Trent asked, sounding concerned.

"No. No. I'm fine," I assured Trent. "It was just a minor thing."

"The groan didn't sound minor to me."

"Do you want to meet your cats or not?" I asked, changing the subject.

"I do want to meet them."

I slowly opened the cage door expecting Boris to make a run for it, but he sat patiently and waited for me to reach for him. I handed him to Trent, and Boris cranked up his purring another few notches as he rubbed his head against Trent's chin. The old cat closed his eyes and practically melted against Trent like he'd been waiting his entire life for this human to find him. I reached into the cage and plucked Natasha up and handed her to Trent too. Natasha curled up in the crook of his arm and Boris began to bathe her ears like he was making certain she was properly groomed for her new human.

"I think we're compatible," Trent said, eyes twinkling and laughter rumbling from his chest. "I didn't bring a cat carrier or anything though."

"We have cardboard ones," I told him. "We also give you a coupon booklet for Brook's Pets and a certificate for a free checkup with Dr. Vaughn."

"That's great. Where do I pay the adoption fees?"

"At the front desk. I'll take your feline friends back while you pay the fees and get the cardboard carriers."

Boris wasn't excited about being handed back to me, but he didn't struggle or try to get away. I held the two kitties and whispered, "I'm going to miss you two most of all. You're going to a good home. I bet he feeds you fancy wet food from crystal dishes like those silly cat food commercials. You'll have custom beds with your names stitched on them, but you'll neglect those to sleep beside him at night. Lucky bastards." Boris looked up at me then, and I swear to God, the damn cat smirked at me.

"All set," Trent said, returning to me with a cardboard cat carrier. "Should I have grabbed two?"

"Nah. Boris and Natasha won't mind sharing one for the short drive to your house."

"I need to stop by and pick up some cat food for them," he said when he took Boris from me and set him inside the carrier. "We need to celebrate their first night in their new home." I handed Natasha over to Trent but not before I gave her furry face one last kiss. Trent stood there silently blinking like I'd stunned him somehow. "Sorry," he said, shaking his head. "Big sexy guy and a tiny kitten is a killer combo. They chose well for your photo shoot for the calendar. I bet that kitty found a home really quick." Trent lowered his voice and leaned closer, invading my personal space. "I bet the kitty's owner wished you were part of the package too."

"Oh man. You've seen the calendar?" I asked, ignoring his other remarks.

"Seen it? Sexy, I own it. Guess which month is my favorite?"

"December?" I asked. My best friend, Braxton, wearing red velvet pants and suspenders, had posed with a Chihuahua wearing antlers.

"Nope," Trent said emphatically. "I'll see you soon, Mr. March." *Soon?* Trent hadn't said he'd see me later or he'd see me around, which were casual ways of saying goodbye. He'd said soon. Trent's playful wink, wry grin, and devilish tone removed any doubt that it was a slip of the tongue. He seemed like a man with a plan.

I said nothing as I watched him walk away. The rest of the afternoon wasn't nearly as exciting, and I was more than ready to go home by the time adoption day was over at six o'clock. Grammie came over when I was putting on my jacket and handed me an envelope containing the coupon book and certificate for Dr. Vaughn's animal hospital.

"What's this?" I asked.

"The handsome and very single Dr. *Love* forgot to take these. He seemed eager to get back to his pets or the hunky man holding them."

"Grammie, don't go there."

"Where? I'm standing right here. I haven't gone anywhere."

"You know what I meant. Don't get your hopes up that the good doctor is going to sweep me off my feet and carry me off to his castle."

Grammie snorted. "Like he could pick you up. You must outweigh him by a good fifty or sixty pounds. I just thought you might drop these off at the nice doctor's house on your way home since you don't have plans. Maybe you can check on Boris and Natasha. I know they were your favorite pets at the shelter."

"They are my favorites, but I'm not dropping by unexpectedly like I'm doing a home check. Can't you just drop the coupons in the mail to him?"

"He could use them sooner," she countered.

"Then you stop by the man's house."

"I'm old, Tucker. I've been standing on this concrete all day long. My bones and joints ache like a son of a bitch. You'd rather me go out of my way to drop this off when you're going right by his house on the way home? Those are valuable minutes I could be sitting on my heating pad."

"You're not fooling me, Grammie. I know damn well you're going bowling with your seniors' group."

"Fine. So I stretched the truth a little. You can either bust my chops or take this envelope to the fine doctor. We both know what you want to do."

"Nothing is going to come from this, Grammie."

"Not with that attitude," she agreed.

I took the envelope from her hand and headed out the door. Even though I'd cautioned Grammie not to get her hopes up, my heart raced at the idea of seeing Trent again.

CHAPTER TWO

_____

Trent Love

"HAPPY BIRTHDAY, BIG BROTHER," MERCEDES SAID WHEN I answered the phone. "Are you doing something special to kick off your thirty-fourth trip around the rock?"

"Define special," I said, looking down at my scorched hand beneath the stream of cold water from the faucet. Four months in the field made a guy forget to use an oven mitt when grabbing the handle of a cast iron skillet. I shut off the water and gently patted it dry on the hand towel.

"I was hoping you had plans to do *someone* special," my sister teased. "You've had a long dry spell."

"How do you know I wasn't tearing my way through South America while I was gone?"

"I know you better than that. You're not a player." She wasn't wrong. While they would never name a saint in my honor, I lived a fairly dull life. "You know what they say about all work and no play."

"How are my nieces?" I asked, changing the subject. Madison, Brooklyn, and Savannah were the lights of my life. I'd missed them so much, and speaking to them over FaceTime and Skype were poor substitutes for holding the girls in my arms.

"Come see for yourself, knucklehead. We only live thirty-five minutes from you," Mercedes said dryly.

"But then Mom and Dad will know I'm home. Dad will start his passive-aggressive bullshit trying to convince me to find a more prestigious position, and Mom will blatantly try to fix me up with the first suitable bachelor she meets who swings in my direction."

"Yeah, I can't blame you for hiding out. I'd hate to be you when our parents find out you're home and avoiding them though. I almost feel like I should use this to my advantage to get something from you."

"Or you could bring my nieces for a visit tomorrow to help me celebrate."

Mercedes gasped dramatically. "And be complicit in your lies?"

"It wouldn't be the first time."

"Nor will it be the last," she added. "What time would you like us to invade your home?"

"Does one thirty work?"

"It sounds perfect. I'll check with Benjamin first."

"Do you have to tell him?"

Mercedes sighed. "He's my husband, and the father to the three hooligans you expect me to toss in the car and speed off like I'm running away with them."

"Well, that's a bit more dramatic than I was thinking, but I see your point. Since Benji is Dad's CFO, I'd hate to put him in the terrible spot of having to lie to his employer and father-in-law."

"Oh, please, Trent. Benjamin would love knowing something

Father doesn't. Don't worry about food. I'll take care of everything. I'll call you if the time doesn't work for us."

"Okay. Love you, Mercedes."

"Love you too, Trent."

My heart felt lighter after talking to my sister, even if my hand still throbbed like a son of a bitch. Boris rubbed affectionately against my leg, and my blister was forgotten. I'd just started to pick him up when the doorbell rang.

"Are you expecting anyone?" I asked Boris. *Meow.* "I didn't think so. What about Tiny Tot over there?" I asked, pointing to the plush, princess pink cat bed Natasha was sleeping on. *Meow.* "I won't let anyone take you, Boris." I reached down and scratched his ears before heading to the front door.

I didn't bother looking through the peephole because I lived in Blissville. I would imagine most people didn't lock their doors, even if violent crimes had occurred there in the recent past. Somehow, I would've been less surprised to find Jack the Ripper on my front porch than Tucker Garrison.

"Wow," I said, leaning against the doorframe. "When I said I'd see you soon, I figured I'd wait at least a day before I resorted to desperate measures to see you again."

"Desperate measures?" Tuck asked, his mouth tilting up on one corner. "How desperate?"

"Well, I wasn't going to start a fire and lure you to my house, if that's what you were thinking."

"The thought hadn't crossed my mind."

"I wasn't going to throw the cats in the tree to lure you over to save them with your ladder either," I added.

Tucker snorted. "That's also good to know." His posture was less rigid, and his voice wasn't as stiff, which I took as tiny victories. "I stopped by to—" Tucker's words died, and he sniffed the air. "What smells so damn good?"

"That would be my dinner."

Tucker's body tensed right back up. "Oh, you're expecting company. I didn't mean to interrupt," he said, taking a step backward.

"I wasn't expecting anyone, but I'm extremely happy you're here. Would you like to join me for dinner?"

"Oh, I-I c-can't," Tucker stammered.

"Can't or won't?" I waved him off before he could answer. "Come on. Have dinner with me. It's bad enough I had to make my own birthday dinner; don't make me eat alone too."

"It's your birthday?"

"Yep. Eat dinner with me, and you can make sure I'm taking good care of the cats."

"Trent, I didn't come here to give you a hard time about the cats," Tucker said, briefly closing his eyes. When he reopened them, I saw how badly he wanted to accept my offer. What could I say or do to convince him to take a chance? I fully expected him to back down, but he surprised me. "I'm not going to refuse the kind offer for dinner though." Suppressing the urge to do a victory shimmy, I stepped back and to the side so he could enter.

"Your house is really nice," Tucker said, looking around the living room.

"Thank you. I knew it was supposed to be mine the second I crossed over the threshold. I fell in love with its charm and character."

From the ornately carved spindles and arched doorways to the original hardwood floors, the house had been meticulously crafted and cared for with a lot of love. It hadn't needed much work when I bought it. All I'd done was paint it and had the floors refinished.

"I can see why." Natasha and Boris scampered through the arched doorway between the living and dining rooms. "Hey, guys," Tucker crooned as he knelt in front of them. "I miss you already." I adored seeing this big hulk of a man turn all mushy at the sight of my cats.

"It's plain to see how much you love these guys. Why didn't you adopt them yourself?"

"Between my shifts at the firehouse and my EMT runs, I don't have a lot of free time. It wouldn't be fair to the cats."

"Ever think about slowing things down?" I asked. "There's more to life than working all the time."

Tucker rose to his full height and looked into my eyes. "I find time to play basketball and softball. I have fun playing sports with my friends."

"You don't have any other kind of fun?" *Where in the hell was I going with this?*

Tucker's raised brow said he wanted to know too. "On occasion," he replied vaguely. "Oh, before I forget..." Tucker reached inside his leather jacket and pulled out an envelope. "Here are your coupons and gift certificate for a free visit to Dr. Vaughn's."

"I think you got played, Tuck," I said, fighting a smile.

He narrowed his eyes. "Played how?"

"Your grammie offered them to me, but I declined. I told her to save them for someone who truly needs them."

"My grammie?"

"She's the one with purple hair, right? At least it's purple now. I think it was blue the last time I saw her at the library. She has the same dark brown eyes as you. They're almost black. Did you know that? Oh damn. I'm rambling. You've been looking at your eyes in the mirror your entire life and know damn well they're almost black. I think I'm stumbling all over myself because I've just thrown your grandmother under the bus. Who does something like that?" I spewed those sentences so fast I was breathless. While I sucked air into my lungs, Tucker tipped his head back and laughed so loud the cats scrambled into the kitchen. "It's not that funny," I sullenly said when his laugh stretched into a length of time bordering on rude.

Tucker raised his hand and cupped the back of my neck then pressed a gentle kiss against my lips. *Whoa!* We both took stunned steps back from each other. I lifted my hand and touched my tingling lips.

"I...um didn't mean to kiss you," Tucker stammered.

I lowered my hand and smiled at him the way I did when one of my pediatric patients looked like they were ready to scream. I had hoped it would set him at ease, but he looked more anxious instead. "It was just a tiny little kiss, not unlike the little peck you gave Natasha before I left."

Tucker scowled. "You can't possibly think I view you in the same light as a kitten."

"I can't possibly know what you think about me, Tuck, because you've done your best to forget I exist."

"No," he said, shaking his head.

"No, you haven't tried to forget I exist, or no, you weren't successful?" I asked.

"I didn't try to forget you existed, but I tried to forget I cared." Tucker's voice was firm and calm, but the nervous way he ran his hands through his hair belied his cool facade. "I failed."

"You had me fooled."

"Maybe I should just get going," Tucker said, hooking his thumb over his shoulder to indicate the door behind him.

"And force me to eat my birthday dinner alone?"

"Are you teasing me or is it really your birthday?" Tucker asked suspiciously. Damn, the guy had a really low opinion of me. If I accomplished nothing else in my thirty-fourth year, I hoped to at least improve myself in his eyes. The first step was pulling out my wallet and showing him my driver's license.

"March 9, 1985," Tucker read out loud. "It really would suck for you to eat alone."

"Don't forget the part about me having to cook it for myself first."

"I haven't." Tucker gestured toward the back of the house where the delicious aromas were emanating from. "Lead the way."

Tucker followed me to the spacious, vintage kitchen with its original cabinetry and black-and-white checkered tile floors. "What would you like to drink? I have water, wine, beer, soda, and milk."

He looked hungrily at the Mexican dishes lining my counter-tops. "On a scale of mild to liquifying my insides, how hot is the food?"

"It's mild heat," I assured him.

"I'll still go with a glass of milk in case our ideas on heat vary greatly."

I was dying to toss out some innuendo, but I liked Tucker and wanted him to stay. "Milk, it is." I grabbed a bottle of beer for myself and poured Tucker a tall glass of milk. "These are my favorite dishes. Rosa used to make them for me every year when I was growing up. She gave me the recipes a few years ago."

"Rosa?" Tucker asked.

"She was our housekeeper and cook."

"Ah. Got it."

"It was as pretentious as it sounds," I said dryly.

Tucker slid his hands in his back pockets and rocked back on his heels. "I'm not here to insult your upbringing. I am curious why you've chosen to celebrate alone though. I'm sure your family would've loved to spend time with you, especially since you were gone for four months."

I tipped my head to acknowledge his comment. "It would come with a price I'm not prepared to pay today."

"Families are complicated sometimes, aren't they?" Tucker asked, letting me off the hook.

"They are."

"Well, I'm honored to help you celebrate."

I smiled wryly at him. "You haven't tasted my cooking yet."

"There's no way food that smells this good can taste bad. I'm great on a grill, but I could use some improvement during the other nine months of the year. Frozen meals and diner food get old after a while."

"The food at Edson and Emma's is wonderful, but nothing compares to a homecooked meal," I agreed.

"I get that at Grammie's every Sunday evening and munch on leftovers until Tuesday. The hours I work aren't always predictable, and I tend to sleep more than I should, which leaves less time for cooking."

I slipped on my oven mitts, carried the dishes over to the table, then sat across from him. I liked the dining room just fine, but I wanted the coziness the breakfast nook afforded us.

"I made white chicken enchiladas, cheesy Mexican rice, and cheesy corn fritters," I said proudly.

"You made enough to feed six people."

"I could've cut the ingredients in half to make smaller portions, but this meal is fabulous to heat up after a long day at work. If you like it, I'll send some leftovers home with you because I'll never eat it all."

"I couldn't."

"It's my birthday, so you have to do what I say."

Tucker shrugged. "If you want to send me home with leftovers, then who am I to turn them down?"

I noted the tightness in Tucker's shoulders and the hesitance in his eyes. Nervous energy radiated off him. An impulsive kiss like he gave me wouldn't dispel the awkwardness hovering in the room. This wasn't at all how I pictured our reunion. I shook my head.

"What?" he asked me.

I blew out a long breath. "I thought about this moment every day while I was away, and this stilted conversation isn't how I pictured our reunion. I don't want to blow this chance with you because I might not get another. I'm just going to be honest and real with you right now. No beating around the bush."

"Okay."

"Every night before I fell asleep, I promised myself that this would be the year I lived for myself, and I would make my happiness a top priority. You're a big part of that commitment, Tucker."

"Me?" he asked.

"Yes, you. I thought time and distance would diminish my feelings for you, but it didn't."

Tucker shook his head. "It didn't for me either."

"I want a redo on our date. You had a miserable experience last time, and I want another chance to prove I'm not a materialistic loser. I thought taking you to the restaurant would demonstrate how much our date meant to me, but I can see now it was a big mistake."

"Trent, I didn't have a miserable time, and I've never thought you were a loser." Tucker smiled wryly. "You're not the only one with regrets either."

"Really?" I asked hopefully.

"I let my insecurities ruin our date then acted like an immature asshole when you tried to talk to me about it afterward. I was fucking miserable when I thought you'd left town for good."

"Shit. I should've told you I was only leaving for a few months. I'm sorry."

"After the way I shut you down?" Tucker asked. "I can't blame you for giving up."

"I didn't give up; I regrouped. Let's prove we can both do better. Go out with me again, Tuck."

Tucker tilted his head and studied me through eyes that glittered with excitement and possibility. "Yes."

I took my first easy breath since returning to Blissville. "You won't regret it." I said confidently. As much as I wanted to shout for joy and devour his mouth instead of the food, I nodded toward the serving dishes and said, "It's time for me to wow you with my kitchen skills."

"Let's see what you got, Doc," Tucker said, serving food onto his plate. I had to bite my lip to keep from responding to his remark. He smirked because he knew where my mind had gone. "Ohmahgoditssogood," he said around his first bite. I imagined filling his mouth with my cock and eliciting the same response from him, but I bit my bottom lip until the urge to say so passed.

"What's that?" I asked, loving how he was so caught up in the taste he'd forgotten his manners.

Tucker just shook his head and moved on to the rice. "Mmmmm." *Yeah, baby.* His eyes rolled back in his head when he forked a piece of corn fritter in his mouth. "I've never tasted anything this good."

"Thank you." I loved that my cooking gave Tucker a foodgasm.

"You better dig in too."

During the rest of the meal, we kept our conversation light. Tucker caught me up on town gossip, and I told him about some of my adventures in South America. At one point, my foot bumped his beneath the table. Instead of retreating, I left my foot there because just that simple touch was more than I hoped to have on my first day back in town.

"I can't believe I ate that much," Tucker said after polishing off his second helping. "I'm slightly mortified."

"Don't be. I love feeding people."

"You're damn good at it," Tucker said, eyeing the pan of enchiladas.

"Would now be a good time to transition to making plans for our date?"

"Because it leads to mentioning the other things you're really good at?" Tucker teased.

I laughed but didn't dare touch that one. "How does next weekend sound?"

"I work every other weekend," Tucker said, and I was pleased to hear he sounded disappointed. "Are you available any night this week?" I was even more thrilled I wouldn't need to wait two weeks to take him out.

"Wednesday?" I proposed.

"It's a date." Tucker scooted back from the table. "Let me help you clean this up."

"No way," I said, shaking my head.

"Birthday boys don't do dishes. You just need to instruct me where things go, and I'll stick them there."

"Really?" I blurted. "I'm trying so hard to be good, but you just keep tormenting me."

"It's no accident," Tuck said with a flirty glance over his shoulder.

I rose from my chair and pulled down storage containers from the cabinet beside the refrigerator. "Here. Take half of everything."

Tucker looked like he was going to protest for all of two seconds before he put his leftovers together. I stored mine in the refrigerator and moved to the sink to help him.

"Huh-uh. I'm well acquainted with a dishwasher. Hang out with your feline friends." We looked over at the cats' corner of the kitchen. Boris and Natasha were curled up together and weren't remotely interested in hanging out with either of us.

"They look pretty content."

"You're a good fit for them."

"That might be the first time anyone has ever said that about me." I hadn't meant to say it out loud and regretted my impulsiveness. I wanted Tucker in my life because he wanted to be there, not because he pitied me.

"Seems to me you only know idiots."

"Not all of them are idiots. My best friend has recently moved back to Cincinnati. Ryder's a great guy, and I didn't realize how much I missed him until we reconnected before I left at the end of November."

"Is he one of the handsome guys in the photo from the gala at the Cincinnati Art Museum?" Tucker asked then stiffened. It seemed like I wasn't the only one letting things slip out I'd rather hold on to.

"Yeah, I believe so; although, I didn't read the article. Our families are old friends, and it was the first time we were all at the same event in several years."

"That sounds nice," Tucker said. He kept his eyes on his tasks of rinsing the dishes and stacking them in the dishwasher instead of looking at me.

"Some parts were nice but not all."

"It sounds like there's a story to tell."

"Yes, but best left for another day. It's my birthday after all."

"So you've said...a few times." Tucker turned and smiled at me before filling the sink with soapy water. I watched the play of muscles in his back and arms when he washed and rinsed the larger dishes that wouldn't fit in the machine. He set them in the rack to dry then laid the towel over them. "All done," he said, coming to stand in front of me.

"Thank you for having dinner with me," I said, unable to tear my eyes from his lips. If I could have one birthday wish, it would be to know what a real kiss from Tucker felt like.

"I'm the one who should be thanking you for sharing it with me."

"We're both lucky then," I suggested. "We're starting to sound a little awkward again."

Tucker laughed. "Maybe a little. Do you still have my phone number?"

"Of course."

"Let me know what time I need to be ready."

I finally tore my eyes away from his mouth to look into his dark eyes. "Okay."

"Doc, can I tell you what I regret most about the way our first date ended?" He'd lowered his voice an octave, and the husky timbre would've convinced me to agree to anything.

"Yes," I said breathlessly.

Tucker closed the short distance between us and cupped my neck. "I never got to kiss you goodnight. How do you feel about a birthday kiss instead?"

I closed my eyes and sighed. "Please." I melted into Tucker when he pressed his mouth softly against mine. The kiss was innocent at first with a few chaste pecks, then Tucker slipped his tongue inside my mouth when my lips parted on a delirious sigh.

Tucker tightened his grip on the back of my neck then placed his free hand on my hip, anchoring me in place. His tongue teased and licked against mine, turning me into a greedy, needy mess. When Tucker sucked my tongue into his mouth, I fisted his jacket with both hands to keep from sliding to the floor because my bones had turned to liquid.

He'd knocked me off-balance because I was used to being the one in control. I abandoned his jacket to slide both hands into his hair, holding his head in place so I could get in on some of the action. I turned the tables on him by sucking his tongue into my mouth, pulling a deep groan from his chest. I released his tongue then flitted the tip of mine against his as soft as a butterfly's wings. Tucker growled in frustration then thrust his tongue back into my mouth, seeking control once more. The dance of domination was sexy, thrilling, and made me maddeningly hard.

Tucker suddenly ripped his mouth from mine and took a step back, sucking air into his lungs. I reached my arm out and braced myself against the wall to steady myself while I caught my breath too.

"Jesus," he whispered. "I think I always knew kissing you would feel like getting caught up in a wildfire. Now I'm good and fucked."

"Well, not yet, but we can make it happen if you play your cards right," I quipped. Tucker narrowed his eyes suspiciously. "It's a figure of speech; I don't have any intention of making you jump through hoops before you end up in my bed."

"You know," he said, walking forward until I was sandwiched between the hard wall and his body, "I could get through my physical fitness obstacle courses faster if I knew the finish line ended with me leaping into your bed." We both smiled at the visual his remark conjured. "I think you know exactly what I meant when I said I was good and fucked."

"I did know what you meant, but not why you thought it." I covered his lip with my forefinger when he started to speak. "You don't need to explain; just give me a chance. That's my only birthday wish. Well, other than receiving the birthday kiss you just gave me."

"It was some kiss, huh?" Tucker asked once I removed my finger.

"A birthday kiss to rival all others." I rose on my toes and kissed him quickly. "You should probably leave before I forget I'm a gentleman."

"Is that right?" Tuck asked, lips curving into a wry smile. He was torn between leaving and pushing his luck to see how far I would take things. *To my bed, baby.* "I'm looking forward to Wednesday."

"Me too."

Tuck kissed me once more then stepped away. I remained leaning against the wall but turned my head to watch him walk to the door. "Happy birthday, Doctor Feelgood."

I stood there staring at the closed door until Boris meowed. He and Natasha stood in the archway watching me. Boris stood up and walked over to me while Natasha followed, leaping and swatting Boris's tail. I squatted down and scooped them both up and was rewarded by their affectionate purrs.

"Best birthday ever."

CHAPTER THREE

Signature: _____ Date: _____

Tucker

"**Y**O, TUCK," BRAXTON HILSOP CALLED OUT AS WE HEADED TO the Blissville Middle School locker room to regroup at halftime. "Wait up, man. You've been dragging during the first half of the game but suddenly find a burst of energy when I call out your name."

I stopped and waited for my best friend to catch up to me. "Sorry, Brax. I didn't get much sleep. I'll hydrate at halftime and dig deep. We're not losing to Blissville PD by much. We can make a strong comeback."

"You think that's what I'm worried about?" I looked into Brax's warm brown eyes and realized he didn't give a shit about the score. I was the knucklehead who hated to lose. Competitive didn't begin to describe my drive to be the very best at every damn thing I tried.

Outside of sports, I was pretty laid-back but my entire demeanor changed once I laced up my trainers or cleats. I lacked my usual enthusiasm to annihilate the competition, and my teammates had noticed, especially my best friend and father of my godchildren. Brax and Hailey were the couple I idolized and admired the most. They'd overcome major adversity on the way to their happily ever after, and I hoped to find love like theirs someday.

"Sorry," I said, looping my arm around Brax in a one-armed bro hug.

"Dude, not right now. Our difference in height puts my nose right in your sweaty pits." Braxton made gagging noises and pulled out of my embrace. "I love you as much as a man can love another he's not screwing, but I have limits."

I'd met Braxton on my first day of kindergarten, and we'd been inseparable friends ever since. He might've been a lot shorter than me, but his personality was that of a giant. He loved hard, worked hard, and was more loyal than anyone I'd ever known other than Grammie. We were opposites in every way, but we'd always clicked. Brax had never cared I was gay and was ready to challenge anyone who did have a problem with it. Hailey said he was like an ankle biter—a Chihuahua with the heart of a Rottweiler. What Brax did not have was little man syndrome. He was comfortable in his skin and didn't need to bristle, bark, and snarl to prove he was as manly as someone my size. He took the jabs and jokes with good humor and gave as good as he received.

"Everything is okay," I assured Brax. "I honestly didn't get much sleep last night, and I'm dragging a bit today."

"Drink some Gatorade," said Will Turner, our captain in the firehouse and on the basketball team.

If Brax took jabs about his height, then Will was hammered about having the same name as a pirate in the *Pirates of the Caribbean* movie franchise. To add more fuel to the fire, he'd married a woman named Elizabeth. Of course, they were married long before the world associated their names with the movies, but it never stopped anyone from quoting the movie or sending him pirate memes. I had to hand it to Cap; he took it in great stride.

"Have your legs turned to spaghetti or something?" asked Donovan Adamson, our second-in-command at the firehouse. "You know you're not supposed to let the air out of your muscles before a big game." Yeah, like those guys were turning their wives and girlfriends down for sex to save their legs for a recreational league basketball game.

"You have no room to tease anyone else, Van," Will said. "My five-year-old son could get up and down the court quicker than you, and you reeked of alcohol when you showed up. By the look and smell of it, Jilly had one hell of a birthday party last night."

"Come on, Cap. It's not every day a man's wife turns thirty. I had to take her out and celebrate her birthday properly."

"I can't argue there," Will agreed. "You just don't get to jeer at anyone else in your present condition."

"Fair enough," Van said.

"Drink up," Will said, passing out the bottles of Gatorade. "I say this in good jest because I respect and admire the work BPD does, but I'm not about to lose to those arrogant assholes. They came to play and brought out their big gun with Joey Simanski, so we need our big gun to step up his game." Will looked pointedly at me as if I didn't know who he meant.

"The guy is probably eight years younger than me," I told Will.

It was probably a huge exaggeration, but I was desperate for a little mercy. Van was right; I'd let the air out of my muscles three times while fantasizing about Trent. The first time was during a hot shower as soon as I got home, and the second was when I found myself having the hottest dream I'd ever had about the sexy doctor. I woke up fucking the mattress as hard as I fucked him in my sleep. I was too far gone to stop and rutted against my sheets until I shot my load. I was physically and mentally spent when I woke up a few hours before game time, not to mention crusty from inadvertently rolling back into the wet spot. I must've been too exhausted to notice until I had to pry the dried sheets from my body. If I were going to end up sleeping in a wet spot, I much preferred not to wake up alone. As soon as I hit the shower, I was thinking about Trent again and how right it felt to hold his hard body in my arms. God. I had it bad for the man.

"Bullshit," Braxton said, nudging me from my daydreams. "The guy is two or three years younger than you at best. He's strong and fast, but you're stronger and faster, Tuck. Your drive to win is unmatched by any other person I've ever known."

"Except for today, apparently," said Carl Michaels, who grinned when I gave him the middle finger. The very same one I dreamed of stretching Trent Love open with before I—*Nope. Not the time to spring wood.*

"Listen up," said Will firmly. "We're only down by eight points, and there's no way they can keep up the intensity during the second half. Here's what we're going to do; we're going full court press the entire second half. Hey—" he said when we all started to groan. "I'm not finished here. Keep it up, and you guys will each earn extra cleaning duties at the firehouse. You got me?"

"Yeah," we all mumbled in agreement.

"We need to start working on our perimeter shooting. We can't ask Tuck to carry us on his freakishly broad shoulders. Carl and Van"—Will pointed at each one—"you're both excellent outside shooters, and it's time we show them."

Will drew out some plays on the board in the locker room while we drank our Gatorade. I had to admit; the man was a born leader. Will didn't just bark orders at us while he planned to sit on the bench. He demonstrated in the field of work and play he was one of us. Will would never ask us to do something he wasn't willing to do himself. Each of us loved the man and never wanted to let him down. We listened, adapted our game plan, and returned to the court with renewed energy.

"Flame Fighters on three," Donovan said when we huddled

together seconds before the second half was due to start. "One...two...three—"

"Flame Fighters!"

"More like flamers," I heard someone sneer from the stands.

I didn't bother to look in their direction. It wasn't likely I would change the person's mind about homosexuality, and they sure as hell wouldn't change mine. It wasn't often I heard derogatory remarks like that in my hometown. Most of our community was very supportive, but the fringe dissentients were starting to get more vocal. A few months back, a zealot religious sect from a neighboring community started trouble here when they didn't agree with the subject matter in the high school play. According to them, love and acceptance wasn't a positive message for the kids and our community to learn. Their shenanigans failed, and their leader was on the run for violating non-profit tax laws, but it encouraged those who had agreed with them to speak louder. I was all for first amendment rights, but having the ability to say whatever you wanted didn't mean there wouldn't be consequences. I let it be the fuel I needed to power me through the second half.

We executed Will's game plan to perfection and turned an eight-point deficit at halftime to an eighteen-point victory when the game buzzer went off.

"What was that second-half performance all about?" Joey asked when we lined up to exchange high fives with BPD. "Did you lure us into a false sense of security, or did they switch you out for a body double at halftime?"

"A gentleman never tells," I tossed over my shoulder and kept walking toward the locker room.

Joey's chuckle was almost as warm as his brown eyes.

"He's a hot stud," Brax said, as he jogged up to me. "Thinking about asking him out?"

"Hot stud?" I asked. "How old are you?"

"Thirty-two."

"Then stop acting like a twelve-year-old."

"I'll take it under advisement," Brax quipped. "Well, are you going to ask him out?"

"No."

"Why not? Still hung up on the doctor?"

I could deny it, but why would I? I'd told Braxton about the chemistry that had flared between the good doc and me. Well, I'd told Hailey, and *she* told Brax. "Yeah."

"He's back in town."

"I know."

"How do you know? Did he call you?"

"Damn, Brax. You're starting to sound like Grammie. There can only be one Grammie."

"Bro, I just want you to be happy."

"I know," I said, reaching out for him, only for Brax to duck under my arm to avoid me. "Right. Armpits."

"Are you free for lunch? Hailey and I are taking Alex and John for pizza. They'd love to spend time with their godfather."

"Next week? I have a lot of stuff I need to do around the house before I head to Grammie's for dinner."

"I'm going to hold you to it, buddy."

I grabbed my gear then high-fived or bro-hugged the teammates who weren't concerned about my sweaty pits before heading out. I would've stopped by the diner to grab carryout if I didn't have delicious leftovers waiting for me in the refrigerator. Rather than shower as soon as I got home, I decided to clean and start laundry first. What was the point of getting clean only to get dirty again when I dusted, swept, and mopped?

Before starting my chores, I reheated the leftovers Trent had sent home with me. They were every bit as mouthwatering the second time around. I took advantage of eating alone and moaned my pleasure as I'd wanted to the previous evening. Damn, the man could cook. I scraped my plate clean then got to work cleaning my house.

Staying busy helped distract my mind from replaying all the reasons I could be making a mistake by going on a date with Trent. Sure, I saw a softer, more down-to-earth side to him the previous night, but the differences in our two worlds felt insurmountable to me. Still, I couldn't shake the feeling he could be truly special to me *if* I could get past my hang-ups. I wasn't the kind of dickhead who held someone's successes against them, was I? No. Trent's parents probably paid for his education, but he did all the work. He was the one who earned his degree then decided to do good things with it by volunteering with Doctors Without Borders. I'd looked up the organization after I'd heard the reason for his absence. I was impressed he'd sacrificed all his creature comforts to live in tents during extreme weather conditions in countries where their presence might not be appreciated by everyone. I needed to keep it in mind when my insecurities reared their ugly heads.

When I arrived at Grammie's a few hours later, I found her in the kitchen stirring a large pot of sauce on the stove. "Spaghetti and meatballs?" I asked.

Grammie looked over her shoulder and smiled, but her joy didn't quite reach her eyes. She was worried about something. "It's your favorite dinner." Grammie making my favorite meal was nothing out of the ordinary, but combined with the stunt she pulled the day before…

"Is someone feeling guilty for sending me to Dr. Love's house knowing he'd declined the coupons and certificates?"

Grammie turned her head back toward the stove and gave a subtle shrug. "Maybe a little."

I set down the tiramisu cake I had purchased on my way over then kissed her cheek. I breathed deeply, inhaling the smell of tomatoes and Italian herbs. "I'm not upset at you, Grammie. You were only looking out for me." Then I noticed the lovely purple orchid sitting in the window sill above the sink. "Where'd that come from?" I asked. The flower hadn't been there the previous week. "Do you have a suitor?"

"A suitor?" Grammie scoffed. "No one your age talks like that."

"I thought I'd speak the language you'd understand."

Grammie answered by jabbing her bony elbow in my gut. Luckily, I'd braced myself for impact. "Seriously, who gave you such a beautiful flower."

"You might not like my answer."

Why would I get upset over someone giving her a thoughtful gift? *Unless.* "Did Trent give you the flower?" Grammie stiffened beside me, giving herself away. "Was it before or after you sent me to his house?"

Grammie snorted. "After, knucklehead. He didn't bribe me to send you there. He thanked me for meddling."

"Trent said that? He thanked you for *meddling*?" I felt my eyebrows rising toward my hairline. I wouldn't appreciate Trent classifying her actions that way. It sounded shady and underhanded and… Fine. She had meddled but with the best of intentions.

"Whoa there," Grammie said, sensing my temper starting to rise. "I believe the phrase he used was gentle prodding or something equally innocuous."

"That's better."

Grammie removed her spoon from the pot and laid it on the spoon rest shaped like a rooster. She wiped her hands on her apron then turned to face me. "That young man is good for you, and I can't wait until you see it too."

"Grammie, don't get your hopes up. Trent Love is pretty far out of my league."

"Bullshit. He should be so lucky to earn the heart of a man as great as you." I scoffed like I always did when she implied I was something special. I viewed myself as an ordinary man. "You won't know unless you try, love. Do you really want to spend your life wondering what might've been?"

"Isn't it better to wonder than hold something wonderful in your hands only to have it yanked away?"

She offered me a loving smile then reached up and cupped my face. "Absolutely not, Tuck. Love and pain are normal experiences in life for everyone. I wouldn't trade the precious memories of your father, mother, and grandfather for a lifetime without pain. No one gets through life unscathed. We battle the demons the best we can. The lucky ones find ways to conquer the monsters and find happiness in spite of them."

"And the unlucky ones?" I asked.

"Allow fear to guide them into a life of loneliness. I don't want that for you. I need you to wake up someday soon and realize you are worthy of the love you admire in others."

"Okay, Grammie. I'll work on it." Part of me was saying it to pacify her, and the other part meant it. She must've realized I wasn't just trying to silence her because she gave me a genuine smile then rose on her tiptoes to kiss my cheek.

"I did say soon, Tuck. I'm not getting any younger. I need to bounce great-grandbabies on my knees while I'm still strong enough to hold them."

"Yes, Grammie." That time I agreed to hush her up and change the subject.

"Tell me about your dinner with Dr. Love."

"A gentleman doesn't tell."

"A gentleman doesn't *kiss* and tell. I'm glad to know you at least got the man in a lip lock. Do you need any pointers? I busted a kid watching gay porn at the library the other day. I must say, porn has come a long way over the decades."

"Grammie, please," I said, holding up my hands. "I'll tell you everything if you promise never to bring up porn in front of me again."

"That's my boy."

R̲x

PATIENT NAME: _____
_____
ADDRESS: _____
_____
_____

Prescription:

CHAPTER FOUR

Trent

D ON'T BE NERVOUS. DON'T BE NERVOUS. DON'T BE NERVOUS. "FUCK!" I exclaimed when I drove past Tuck's house. I looked in my rearview mirror and made sure no one was behind me before putting my car in reverse and backing up so I could pull into his driveway, hoping Tuck hadn't seen me flake out. At least I stopped a safe distance from his truck instead of ramming into the back of it. Calm the fuck down. How many chances do you think Tuck will give you, moron?

I looked at the potted orchid sitting on the passenger seat beside the bag with orchid food and the spray bottle of stuff the lady working at the florist counter recommended I buy. I'd purchased two of everything—one for Shirlene and one for Tucker. Doubt started to creep in, and I started second-guessing my decision to buy him an orchid. Some men liked flowers and others got insulted. I didn't want him to think I assumed he liked flowers just because he was gay. I just thought they were beautiful and exotic like the way I felt every time Tucker's eyes devoured me. No one had ever looked at me quite the way he did, and I craved it. Damn it. I was overthinking things again.

I took a calming breath and exited the car with the pot in one hand and the bag of supplies in the other. Tucker met me at the door before I had a chance to knock. A wry grin spread across his face. "Did you have trouble finding my house?" *Shit.*

"You don't get to tease me," I told him. "If you saw my stupid stunt, then you were watching out the window for me."

"I *was* watching for you," Tucker admitted shamelessly. "I've been looking forward to this since we made plans. I was hoping an emergency didn't pull you away."

I was stunned silent by his confession. What was I expecting from Tucker? Hesitance? Signs of him second-guessing himself? Doubt? The truth was I expected to see all those things warring for dominance in his dark eyes. His honesty startled me and bolstered my courage.

"I brought you an orchid."

"I see that," Tuck said, smiling warmly then stepping aside to allow me inside his house.

Tucker's living room was as clean as any operating room I'd been in, but it didn't look or feel sterile, even if the color palette was a tad on the safe side. A light-beige sectional sofa took up most of the space. The material looked soft and inviting, and I loved how one end was a chaise, allowing for someone as tall as Tucker to stretch out comfortably. If Tucker could stretch out, then I could straddle his lap and... I pushed my gutter thoughts aside to look around the rest of the room.

A large picture window let in plenty of natural light, and several black-and-white photos of Cincinnati hung on the ivory walls, creating a stunning backdrop. A beautiful area rug with a mix of earth tones and jewel-colored hues added warmth to the room, but my favorite part of the space was the wall of bookshelves bursting with books. I couldn't see an inch of space on any of the shelves.

"I have a problem," Tucker said.

I turned to face him with a puzzled expression on my face. Was he backing out of our date now? "Excuse me?"

"I have a book addiction," he said solemnly.

"I would expect the grandson of a librarian to appreciate books."

I was dying to walk across the room to see what kinds of books held his interest, but it would be rude. I should at least treat the man to dinner before I fingered his books. I choked on my saliva when I realized how dirty my thought sounded.

"Are you okay?" Tuck asked, sounding concerned. "Do you need a glass of water?"

"That would be nice," I croaked out.

"You can help me find a good place for the orchid before we leave on our date. I've heard they require a lot of light and care."

I was still dry hacking and couldn't answer, so I just followed him to the kitchen. Tucker grabbed a glass from the cabinet then filled it with ice and water from the refrigerator door while I set his gift on the counter. My fingers brushed against his when I accepted the glass from him. Delicious heat spread throughout my body, nearly making me forget I'd almost choked until I opened my mouth to say something and only a rusty squeak escaped. I lifted the glass to my mouth and gulped half of it before I came up for air.

"Better?"

"Much." I still sounded like a chain smoker, but at least I could form words. I drank the rest then set the glass down and cleared my throat. "Thank you." I was happy my voice sounded normal. I looked around the kitchen and was surprised to see how different this space was from his living room. Instead of muted colors, the kitchen was a mix of soft lemony yellow, white, and navy blue. It was like we'd stepped into someone else's kitchen.

"It's a bit much, isn't it?"

My eyes roamed over the yellow walls, the navy blue kitchen cabinets, and the white marble countertops. It seemed like an odd combination at first, but the sailboat wallpaper border with its various shades of blues and yellows outlining the perimeter of the room tied it all together nicely.

"I think it's a lovely space," I said. "It's full of warmth and cheer. I've never seen navy blue kitchen cabinets before, but I really like them."

"The kitchen was the only room I didn't alter when I moved in," Tucker said. "I'd purchased new paint for the cabinets but couldn't bring myself to paint them."

"I don't blame you. I think your orchid will add an extra touch of charm to the place. What do you think works best between the window sill above the sink or the kitchen table?"

Tucker looked at my suggested locations then decided to set his flower in the window sill. He turned to me and cupped my face in his supersized hands. "Thank you for the thoughtful flower. Grammie loves hers too." There was no censure or scorn in his tone, and the smile on his face indicated he was charmed. "How can I thank you for such a sweet gesture?"

"Kiss me," I whispered. "I haven't stopped thinking about your mouth since you left my house Saturday night."

Tucker moved closer, backing me up against the cabinet. "Is that all you've been thinking about, Doc?"

"Huh-uh."

"You've thought about my mouth on other parts of your body?"

"Fuck yeah."

"Is that why you got choked up?" Tucker asked me.

"Not this time. I was fantasizing about fingering your—"

Tucker struck fast, pressing his mouth against mine and urging my lips to part for his tongue. My heart beat erratically as my pulse soared. I clung to Tuck's broad shoulders and met him lick for lick and suck for suck. He broke the kiss after several minutes so we could inhale much-needed air into our lungs. Tuck's flushed face looked as red as mine felt. He dropped his hands from my face and gripped the countertop on either side of my hips.

"How sturdy do you think these cabinets are?" Tuck asked me.

Oh, God. I knew what the lust-dazed look in his eyes meant just as I knew I should discourage us from moving too fast. I opened my mouth with the notion I'd walk us back from the edge. Instead I said, "They look pretty damn sturdy to me."

"That's what I thought too." Tuck reached for the top button on my dress shirt. I expected his big hand to stumble with the tiny buttons, but he nimbly unbuttoned my shirt then pulled it free from the waist-band of my jeans. "Fuck me," Tucker whispered then proceeded to tenderly caress my chest like it was something precious and beautiful. His big thumbs ghosted over my nipples, making them achingly hard. My core muscles tightened and trembled with anticipation, catching his notice. "Damn, Doc, I had no idea you were so ripped beneath your clothes." While I wasn't genetically predisposed to amass bulk like Tucker, I made the best of what I had to work with by spending several hours a week in the gym keeping my body fit and tight.

I looked down and watched Tucker trail his middle finger down the line bisecting my cut abdomen. I captured his wrist, preventing his seeking finger from probing beneath my jeans. Tuck looked worried he'd moved too fast, so I quickly dispelled him of the notion by lifting his hand until his finger was inches away from my mouth. "Do you have other plans for this finger?"

Tucker grinned wickedly then pressed his finger inside my mouth. I moaned around the length of it, playing up the noises I would make when I finally sucked his cock between my eager lips. Tuck briefly closed his eyes and inhaled deeply before he started working his finger in and out of my mouth, getting it good and wet. With his free hand, he unbuckled my belt and unbuttoned my fly then I helped him shove my jeans and briefs to my knees. *Too soon,* my conscience said. *Don't blow this.*

"Jesus," Tucker groaned when he saw how hard I was for him. The tip of my dick glistened with precum. I continued to lave his finger the entire time while my pucker quivered with excitement. I was too far gone by this point to make smart decisions. As long as Tucker wanted me, he would have me. If he called a halt, then I'd just have to deal with my blue balls.

Tuck pulled his finger from my mouth then lowered it like he was going straight for the kingdom.

"Wait," I said suddenly. Tuck halted and looked curious. I was going to mention the unfairness of being the only one whose cock was dangling in the wind, but Tuck spoke before I could say anything else.

"You're right," he said, even though I hadn't said anything. "We need to do this right." Instead of reaching for his shirt or jeans, Tucker gripped my hip with a firm hand. "Turn around."

My knees grew weak, but Tuck's firm hand made sure I didn't melt to the floor when I turned and braced my forearms on the counter.

"Oh fuck," I moaned when I heard him drop to his knees behind me. Tuck's big hand massaged one taut ass cheek then the other.

"Damn, Doc, you must do hundreds of squats a week to achieve a round ass like this."

"Yes," I agreed breathless. "With weights." Why did I sound like I was giving out bodybuilding tips to a man who looked like he was carved from a mountain, especially when I could feel his hot breath ghosting across my pucker after he parted my cheeks for a better look?

"It's the finest ass I've ever seen." Was he still talking about my firm glutes or was he talking about my greedy hole begging for him to fill it? Tucker ran his hot tongue from my taint to the top of my ass crack with a long, wet pass then blew against my pucker, making me shiver. "I'm about to make it all mine."

CHAPTER FIVE

Tucker

"**P**LEASE," TRENT WHIMPERED.

I loved the way he shivered and moaned, so I blew across his hole again. "Like that?"

"Lick me."

I liked the needy, bossy way Trent commanded me to pleasure him, but it didn't mean I'd comply right away. I sank my teeth in his right ass cheek then licked the angry, marked flesh. "I had the sexiest dream about you the other night. I had you pinned beneath me in the center of my bed, and I was fucking you so hard the bedframe was knocking against the wall. I woke up fucking my mattress." Trent moaned and pushed his ass out more. "You were my first wet dream since I was a teenager. I haven't been able to get the memory out of my head. Will your pucker be as tight as I dreamed?"

"Probably tighter. It's been a really long time."

I didn't think it was possible for my dick to get harder, but I was wrong. "How long, Doc?" I wanted to know for more reasons than to simply stroke my ego; I didn't want to risk hurting him.

"How long since I've had sex with another person or since I bottomed?"

I wanted to say both, but only one was my business. "Since you last bottomed." I leaned forward and circled my tongue around his hole.

Trent moaned loudly. "Five years," he panted out as his pucker tensed and flexed. "I can't stop thinking about you pinning me down and taking me. There's something about the size of you that drives me wild. I've never wanted a guy to manhandle me before, but it's all I can think about right now."

"Okay, how long for the other one?" I couldn't resist asking, even if I feared the answer.

"The weekend before we met," Trent said, sounding embarrassed or uncertain.

I sat on my heels but kept his ass in a tight grip. "Not since July?" I asked.

"No," he whispered. "I thought about it, and even went clubbing a few times, but the idea of going home with a stranger made me feel hollow."

"We hadn't even kissed until this past weekend," I said, dropping my hands down to caress his muscular thighs, feeling his coarse hair rasping against my palms.

"It didn't matter. I could fantasize about the man I wanted while taking care of business myself, or I could attempt to find a poor substitute who would only leave me feeling unsatisfied and miserable."

"Wow," I whispered before I placed tender kisses against his taut ass cheeks. "I thought I was the only one."

"You haven't been with anyone else this entire time either?" Trent asked in surprise.

"No. I used my pent-up frustration as fuel in the weight room or doing physical things around my house or Grammie's. I think I cleaned the gutters on every house in this neighborhood in the fall."

"Speaking of gutters," Trent said humorously, "this is the weirdest dirty talk I've ever had during foreplay."

I removed my hands from his body and rose to my feet.

"No," he whined. "God, did I kill the mood?"

I gripped his hips and turned him around. I took his hand and placed it against my erection straining against my jeans. "Does this feel like you've killed the mood?" Trent's fingers tightened around my dick, and he began stroking me through the denim. "You've got me so fucking hard for you, but I want to do this right. I want to spread you out on my bed and kiss you everywhere before I live out the hottest dream I've ever had."

Trent cupped my neck with his free hand and pulled my head down closer to his. "I want it too. I want it so damn bad I'm quaking. Do you feel how much I want you?"

I pressed my lips against his as a hard shiver ran through him. I pulled back and cupped his face with my hands. "I do feel it, which is why we can't rush this thing. I have a big dick."

"I can feel that," Trent said, squeezing my cock harder. "And I want it buried inside me."

"Inside your tight, might-as-well-be-a-virgin hole," I reminded him.

"Muscle memory," Trent countered, nipping my bottom lip with his teeth before tugging it. He released my lip then ran his tongue over the sensitive flesh. "There's really no such thing as a born-again virgin, but if there were, I'd want to give my cherry to you."

I dropped to my knees in front of him and hurriedly stripped his jeans, underwear, socks, and shoes.

"While you're down there," Trent said, cupping the back of my head.

"Bossy much?" Gripping Trent's thighs, I leaned forward and

sucked his right nut into my mouth, tonguing it while applying the perfect amount of pressure on the taut globe.

"Jesus!" Trent shouted while fisting my hair.

I treated his left nut to the same attention then licked a path up his erection to gather the precum leaking from his slit, making him groan and quake. Then I stood up and hoisted Trent in the air so he could wrap his legs around my waist. Trent gripped my shoulders and devoured my lips while rutting against my abs. I held his ass in a bruising grip, teasing his hole with my middle finger.

It was a good thing I knew the layout of my house well because Trent wasn't about to release my lips for me to pay attention to where I was going. I turned into my bedroom but misjudged the distance. *Thump.* I ended up slamming Trent into the wall in the hallway beside my doorway instead.

He didn't seem to mind. I tore my mouth from his then kissed his neck until I reached the juncture where his shoulder met his neck. I sank my teeth in hard enough to make him cry out in pleasure but not hard enough to hurt him.

"I want to wear your marks all over my body," Trent said breathlessly. "Feel you for days, Tuck. Will you give me that?"

"I'll give you anything you want, Doc."

I stepped back from the wall then carried him into my bedroom. I placed him on the bed, but he didn't stay there.

"Let me," he said when I reached to remove my polo shirt.

Trent grabbed the bottom of my shirt and lifted it as I raised my arms to help him. "Look at you," Trent whispered in awe. He'd seen my bare chest at the pool party, but I hadn't been exaggerating when I said I'd worked out a lot since then. "Mmmm," he moaned, sliding his fingers through my chest hair. "I've never seen this before."

"I shaved it before the pool party," I admitted. "Not all guys like chest hair, and I wanted to impress you with my definition."

"Oh, baby, I was impressed, but please don't ever shave this again." Trent leaned forward and nuzzled his face against my short, dark chest hair. "My wet dreams would've been a whole lot wetter had I known the kind of fur you hid from me." He let out a playful growl then dropped to his knees. "The happiest of happy trails," he said moments before he licked a path from my belly button to my low-riding jeans. Trent pressed his nose against the wet spot on the denim, which grew bigger with every passing second, then inhaled. "I love how you smell, and I can't wait to taste you."

"This party will end much sooner than either of us want if you wrap those pouty lips around my dick." My voice was raw and rumbly with need. "I'm barely hanging on as it is."

"Glad to know I'm not the only one." Trent licked a path across my pelvis just above the waistband of my jeans. Then he eased the top button of my fly open and sucked the flesh he exposed while tracing my erection through the denim with his finger. Trent moved to the second button then hummed happily when he revealed another inch of bare flesh. "Commando."

"I hate underwear."

"I'm thankful you do."

Trent kept unbuttoning my fly until he reached the base of my cock where he ran his tongue through my trimmed curls while pulling my jeans down to my thighs. My dick sprung free, hitting him in the nose. Trent sat back on his heels and stroked my cock from root to tip.

"You're a whole lotta man."

"Having second thoughts?" I asked.

Trent's response was to lean forward and suck the head of my cock into his mouth. He pulled back and danced his tongue over my slit, capturing the bead of precum before licking a path from root to tip.

"Doc, you better pull back. You've got me on the edge."

Trent fisted the base of my cock with his right hand and fondled my balls with his left. He looked up at me with hungry, blue eyes. "I want to push you over the edge."

"Almost there."

"Let me take you the rest of the way there."

"But I want—"

I sucked in a sharp breath when Trent sucked my dick deep inside his mouth. He paused, breathed through his nose, and inched further down until he made a soft gagging sound. I tried to pull out of Trent's mouth, but he dug his fingernails into my ass cheeks, holding me there. His throat muscles worked the head when he swallowed around it, and I had to fight the urge to thrust my hips forward because I've never wanted to fuck anyone so bad. Trent's eyes watered and tears spilled down his face, but I didn't see panic or fear in their depths, only determination to unravel me. I brushed the tears from his eyes with my thumbs then gently eased my cock from his throat.

"Nice and easy," I said, slowly working my dick in and out of his mouth.

I saw impatience teeming in his eyes and knew I couldn't deny him for long. Then again, my balls drew up tight against my body and my spine tingled, signaling I wouldn't last long either.

"Gonna come," I warned in case he didn't want a mouthful.

Trent moaned then sucked my dick back deep into his throat before he swallowed around the head.

"Doc, I'm—"

Trent swallowed again, and I came hard. He continued swallowing, milking every drop until there was nothing left. Then he eased back until my wet dick slipped from his mouth to slap against my thigh. Saliva and spunk rimmed Trent's lips. I gathered it with my thumb and fed it to him before pulling him to his feet so I could taste myself on his lips as I walked him back to the bed. I didn't stop kissing Trent until I laid him down in the center of my bed and straddled his thighs just like I had in my dream.

"I once saw a porn video where a guy straddled his lover's face and fucked his mouth. He was so deep inside the guy you could see his dick moving in his throat. I've always wanted to try it but never found a man big enough to pull it off." Trent reached between us and fisted my softening dick. "Until now."

"Another time," I said, dropping a quick kiss on his lips. "Now it's time for me to take care of you." Trent rolled over onto his stomach, presenting me with the sweetest ass I'd ever seen or tasted. It was time to live out some of my fantasies. "I once saw a porn video where a guy made his lover come with just his tongue in his ass."

"Fuck me," Trent moaned.

"All in due time, Dr. Love."

Rx

PATIENT NAME: _____

ADDRESS: _____
_____
_____

Prescription:

CHAPTER SIX

_____

Signature: _____ Date: _____

Trent

I FELT TUCK'S HUNGRY GAZE ON MY ASS. I WANTED TO SPREAD MY LEGS and expose my hole to him, but I couldn't with his strong thighs bracketing the outside of mine. Anticipation hummed through me as I waited for him to make his next move. Rather than grip my ass as I expected, Tuck placed his big hands on my shoulder blades and dug his thumbs into my rhomboid muscles.

"You're so tense," said Tucker in a gravelly voice.

"It's from excitement."

"You're not a little worried about my big dick stretching open your tight ass?" Tuck dug his digits into the ever-present knots of tension. "These feel like stress knots to me."

"I have plenty of stress in my life, but doubting my ability to take your dick isn't a contributing factor." I wanted Tucker's hands to move lower at the same time I wanted them to stay put. I moaned when he pressed deeper and began working the knots earnestly. "That feels so damn good."

"It's only the beginning, Doc."

Famous. Last. Words.

I heard my cell phone ringing in the kitchen. I wanted to kick my feet and howl like the girl at the animal shelter when I recognized the ringtone I set for my on-call service, but instead, I said, "No. No. No." Tucker rolled to the side, and I quickly got up from his bed and hustled to the kitchen where I fished my phone out of my jeans pocket seconds before the call went to voicemail. "This is Dr. Love," I said into the phone.

"This is Brittany with Goodville General, Dr. Love." She quickly added, "I know you're not on call tonight, but we have a situation requiring your attention."

My greedy hole needed attention too, but I knew Brittany wouldn't be calling me without a legitimate reason. "Go on."

"It's Casey Abernathy," Brittany said.

"Casey is sick?" I asked.

"Not just him," Brittany replied. "All four Abernathy kids are sick, and Tricia is beside herself. She called the after-hours service line, and I referred her to Dr. Hinman who was on call. Dr. Hinman instructed Tricia to bring the kids to the ER because of their symptoms. She's worried they might all have influenza A since it's spreading like wildfire around here. Tricia brought the kids in like instructed, and it all went to hell from there."

"Did Casey react badly to one of the nurses or doctors?"

"Yes," Brittany said with a sigh. "Dr. Steller was the one who attempted to treat him, but we all know the old bastard has the bedside manner of a raging bull."

My blood began to boil because I could only imagine just how badly the doctor reacted to the autistic child. "What did he do?" I demanded to know.

"He told Tricia if she couldn't get her child under control, then he couldn't help her."

"Give me Tricia's number," I gritted out. "I'll call her and let her know I'll meet her at the ER."

"You're a gem, Dr. Love," Brittany said.

"I'm a human being with compassion for other human beings," I countered.

"Regardless, your patients are lucky to have you."

I set my phone on the counter after disconnecting the call then slid my underwear and jeans back on. Calling my patients' mother while naked just felt wrong. Tricia answered on the second ring. "Ms. Abernathy, it's Dr. Love."

"Oh, Dr. Love, I'm so glad it's you. Casey is so sick. I took him to the ER as Dr. Hinman instructed, but..." Her voice trailed off. Was she worried I might not help her if she insulted one of my colleagues? I wanted to tell her I knew the man was a raging dickhead, but it wouldn't be professional and wouldn't make Casey feel any better.

"I can be at Goodville General in twenty minutes. Can you meet me there?"

"Thank you so much," she said then began to cry.

"Hey now," I said gently. "It's going to be okay."

Tricia sniffed as she tried to stop crying. "I'll see you soon."

"Yes, you will."

I disconnected the call and turned to face Tucker who leaned in the doorway between the living room and kitchen. "I'm so sorry."

Tuck straightened to his full height and walked toward me. "Don't you dare apologize for putting your patients first. It's a beautiful trait in a man."

"You say that now, but..." Firm, gentle lips cut off what I was about to say. Our mouths lingered for several seconds, but neither of us attempted to deepen the kiss.

Tucker pulled back and rested his hands on my neck. The heavy pressure felt reassuring instead of threatening. "There will be plenty of times when I'm the one who gets called away, so I have no right to be upset."

"I like that you're looking ahead to future dates with me, even if some of them will get ruined by emergencies," I said. "But maybe this interruption was a good thing."

My remark earned a doubtful arched brow from the larger-than-life man who captured my attention from the word go. "How is developing a case of blue balls a good thing for you?"

I worried my bottom lip between my teeth. "I don't want to sound cheesy."

"I doubt you could," Tuck said tenderly.

"I don't want to cheapen the way you make me feel. I don't want you to think I'm only interested in sex. I don't have a fireman kink or anything."

"It never crossed my mind that you did," Tucker said, shaking his head. "We're grown-ass men, and we don't have to adhere to the three-date rule."

"I'd settle for one date at this point," I told him. "I'm serious, Tuck. Our first attempt was terrible. Our redo was interrupted. Maybe the third time will be the charm."

"I feel pretty charmed right now," he said huskily.

I recalled the grunts and groans he made when he came down my throat. "I need to go," I said, stepping from his embrace.

"You can always stop by later, and we can pick up where we left off," Tuck suggested.

"No," I said, shaking my head. "You're not a damn booty call. What are you doing tomorrow night?"

"I'm working."

"Damn. Friday?" I asked, unwilling to get discouraged.

"Working."

"Double damn," I groused.

"I work second shift this weekend. I could do brunch on Saturday morning."

"I know a great place," I said, giving Tuck a quick peck on the lips before I finished getting dressed. "Can I call you later if I get home at a decent time?" I asked when he walked me to the front door.

"That sounds perfect. Drive carefully."

"Will do."

Tuck grimaced. "Sorry. Saying that has become a habit for me."

I was curious to know why but didn't have the time to ask. "I like that you care," I said instead. I couldn't recall a time when someone told me to drive carefully, not even my parents after I obtained my driver's license. I quickly kissed Tuck again before trotting down the steps. "I like it a lot," I called over my shoulder, in case there was any lingering doubt.

Tricia Abernathy looked more exhausted than any human being I'd ever seen. She practically sagged with relief outside the ER when she saw me coming. Casey stood beside her wearing his sunglasses and noise-canceling headphones. I could see he was still agitated, but he appeared to be winding down. I knew better than to reach out and touch him yet. I knelt a safe distance from him, putting myself at his eye level.

"Hey there, Casey," I said gently. "I hear you're not feeling well. I want to make you feel better."

Casey stiffened but didn't jerk away, cry, or scream because I made no advances toward him.

"Casey," Tricia said pleadingly, "Dr. Love is here to help you. Okay?"

Casey looked at his mother then back at me. "Okay."

Tricia extended a hand toward him and waited for Casey to make a move. The young boy adored the very air his mother breathed, but when he was having an episode, he couldn't stand for even her to touch him because it hurt him so much. It was heartbreaking to witness. A parent's instinct is to gather their child close to comfort them, but it was the opposite of what Casey needed.

The family followed me back inside the ER. I stopped by the registration desk and was happy to see Ava working. She was kind and patient and looked at Tricia with empathy in her eyes, not pity.

"I'm so sorry, Ms. Abernathy."

"It's not your fault," Tricia told her. "I want to be angry at the other doctor, but right now, I only care about making Casey feel better. I'm positive the other three"—she gestured to Casey's younger sisters—"are coming down with whatever he has."

"I'm going to see if there's a room free for us, and we'll take a look at all four kids," I said to Tricia, knowing I was leaving her in good hands for a few minutes. "I'll be right back, Casey. I promise." To Ava, I said, "Please make sure you enter Mary, Amanda, and Tracy into the system and get them ID bracelets too." I didn't want Dr. Steller lodging a complaint I was circumventing procedures. He was already going to be pissed when I stomped all over his fucking toes.

I found the old bastard when he stepped out of one of the rooms looking like he'd just sucked on a lemon. "What are you doing here?" he asked. "You're not on call tonight."

"I'm the Abernathy kids' pediatrician, and I need a room to examine them."

"Did *that woman* call you?"

"Are you referring to Ms. Abernathy as *that woman*?" Steller jerked to a stop when he heard my angry tone. I didn't stop though; I kept walking until I was practically in his face. "Watch it, or I'll report you to the hospital administration myself."

"Ohhh, I'm scared," he said with a mock tremble in his voice. "The sissy boy is going to tattle on me." He had to be pushing seventy, yet he honestly thought he could beat me in a fist fight. It was hard not to laugh in his face.

"You're not going to goad me into violence, Steller. Following protocol doesn't make me a sissy. Grown men don't take it out to the parking lot and duke it out. Step aside and allow me to do my work, or I'll call security."

He scowled for a few more heartbeats then turned and strode off angrily. I heard slow clapping from behind me and turned around to see who had witnessed the exchange. There were several nurses, technicians, and the physician's assistant standing behind me. Andy Vale, the PA, was the one clapping. He looked me up and down appreciatively, but I ignored the heat in his eyes. Even if Tuck weren't in the picture, I wouldn't date anyone I worked with. I'd told Andy this on more than one occasion and would continue to do so until he understood I wasn't going to change my mind.

"You are magnificent," Julie said. She was my favorite nurse, and I was happy to see she was working.

"Glad you think so, Julie. You can assist me with the Abernathy kids."

"I'll happily assist you, Doctor *Love*." I should've either legally changed my name or chosen a different profession. She spun on her clogs and headed toward the ER waiting room to get my patients.

"I can assist you too," Andy said.

"I'll let you know if Julie and I need another set of hands, but let's see how it goes. I don't want to trigger Casey again."

"Fair enough." Aside from his shameless flirting, Andy Vale was a wonderful PA.

I entered the room and waited for Julie and the Abernathy family. I could hear them coming long before I could see them. Two of the little girls were coughing, and the third was crying. I picked up little Tracy when they entered the room, and she rested her head on my shoulder. I could feel her body heat radiating through her clothes and knew she was running a fever.

"Poor baby," I whispered to Tracy, rubbing her back. Julie helped Mary and Amanda onto the bed while Casey climbed up on his own and sat beside his sisters. I felt his eyes on me even if I couldn't see them through the dark sunglasses. I was happy to see he'd removed his headphones, which I thought was a good step.

I guided Tricia to the chair with my free hand. "Sit in the chair before you fall. Are you coming down with this too?"

"Possibly," she said pitifully. "I've had a horrible headache for a few days."

"Is there anyone you can call on to give you some help?"

"My mom is on her way from Kentucky now. She's going to stay with me for a week or so until I get everyone nursed back to health." I was relieved to hear it.

"Well, let's see what's going on here."

With Julie's help, we checked their ears, lungs, and throats before we swabbed their noses for the flu. I made Julie do the last part because I hated making kids cry. I let her demonstrate on me first so the kids could see it wouldn't hurt them. Casey was having no part of Julie coming at him with the swab, but he allowed me to do it. Casey's throat was fire-engine red and his tonsils looked inflamed, so we also did strep tests on each of the kids. I also ordered chest X-rays for anyone whose lungs didn't sound clear.

When the results were all in, Mary had bronchitis and influenza A, Tracy had pneumonia and strep, Amanda had a double ear infection and bronchitis, and Casey had influenza A, strep, and an upper respiratory infection. Tricia burst into tears.

"I'm a horrible mother," she said between sobs.

"Oh, honey," Julie said, rushing to her side. "You aren't responsible for viruses."

"Julie's right," I said, kneeling in front of her. "This is a terrible year for illness. There are outbreaks everywhere. Let's focus on getting all of you better." She nodded and wiped her nose with the tissue Julie handed her. "I think we need to check you out too." I turned to the kids on the bed. "What do you think? Should we check Mommy?"

"Yes," they all said.

"Okay, but can Julie demonstrate the flu swab on you again? I wasn't sure I caught it the first time."

"Ha ha ha."

Tricia giggled. "Sorry, Dr. Love. Laughter is the best medicine, right?"

"In this case, you're all going to require some strong meds in addition to the laughter before you feel better."

Tricia had a sinus infection, a double ear infection, and bronchitis. "I can't remember the last time I've felt this bad," she said.

"I'll send your prescriptions to your pharmacy. You should all be feeling better in a few days. If not, you know what to do. I want to follow up with the kids in ten days."

"I'll call and make appointments in the morning. Thank you."

"I hope you all feel better soon," I said, giving high fives to the kids as they followed Julie out of the room. "Take care, Tricia."

She flung her arms around me suddenly, catching me by surprise. "You're the best, Dr. Love. Don't say you're just doing your job either. You went above and beyond, and we both know it. Thank you."

I patted the exhausted woman's back. "You're welcome. Get some rest, okay?"

She nodded. "I will."

I sent their prescription orders to their pharmacy then entered my notes into the system. Luckily, Dr. Steller was on a break when I finished, so I could leave without another confrontation. I was tempted to drive straight back to Tucker's house, but we'd end up having sex, and I'd meant what I said. I wanted to do things right with Tuck.

I settled for calling him once I showered, put on a pair of comfy sleep pants, and settled into bed with my frisky felines snuggled up next to me. "Hey, Sparky," I said when he answered the phone.

"Sparky?" he asked.

"You light a fire in me."

"Sparky," Tuck said again like he was testing the way it sounded. "I guess it's better than Smokey. Tell me about your night."

Tucker knew I wouldn't be able to say much because of privacy laws, but he listened and commented on what I could share with him. I'd never had anyone ask about my day, and it was...nice. Better than nice. It was as amazing as the man on the other end of our connection.

"What are you doing tomorrow morning?" I asked suddenly.

"Sleeping."

"Could I entice you to work out with me?"

"And keep my hands to myself?" Tuck asked. "Am I being punished for something?"

I laughed. "Come on. What do you say?"

"What time?"

"Six thirty."

"In the morning? Gross," Tuck said. "I guess I can get up at an ungodly hour to see you glistening with sweat."

"I'll treat you to breakfast afterward," I cajoled.

"Deal. Do you want me to pick you up, or do you want to meet at the gym?"

Driving separately made the most sense, but we lived in a small town and could quickly get from point A to point B. Besides, I wanted the extra time with him.

"Pick me up," I told him.

"Okay."

"Sweet dreams, Sparky." Tucker groaned on the other end, and I knew he recalled the dirty fantasies and dreams we'd shared during the heat of the moment.

"Sweet dreams, Doc."

R_X

PATIENT NAME: _____

_____

ADDRESS: _____

_____

_____

Prescription:

CHAPTER SEVEN

Signature: _____ Date: _____

Tucker

G RAMMIE ALWAYS SAID ARRIVING ON TIME MEANT SHOWING UP
fifteen minutes early, and it was a concept I often struggled
with. I always meant to arrive early but usually decided to do
a last-minute thing before leaving my house. My impromptu projects
often took longer than predicted, which was why I was perpetually
late to everywhere except for two places: my shift or a meal. At least
those were the only two places until a sexy doctor invited me to work
out with him. I pulled into Trent's driveway at six fifteen on the dot.
There wasn't a light on in the house, so I looked around to make sure
I'd pulled into the right driveway. I rechecked the time on the radio
and my watch to make sure I hadn't screwed up. Then I sat frozen in
my truck debating if I should ring his doorbell or drive back home.
Trent might not be happy with my interruption if he'd decided to

sleep in, but on the other hand, he might've forgotten to set his alarm clock. Waking him up might prevent him from being late to work.

A light came on in a second-story window, which must've been Trent's bedroom. I hadn't made it past the first floor of his house, but I had big plans to explore more of it and its owner soon. Seconds later, the curtain parted slightly, giving me a view of a sleep-rumpled Dr. Love that made my dick start to swell. *Damn, I want to wake up to that view and maybe muss him up some more before taking on the world.* Trent smiled broadly and held up a finger to let me know he was coming, then he dropped the curtain closed and disappeared inside the room. Seven minutes later, my jaw dropped when he stepped onto his porch looking like an immaculate, blond Ken doll, wearing track pants with a matching windbreaker and carrying a gym bag.

I hit the unlock button for him to climb into the cab then fought the urge to pull him over the console so he could straddle my lap. "Damn, you look better than anyone has a right to after seven minutes of grooming." I sniffed the air appreciatively. "You smell ridiculously good, and it's making it hard for me to concentrate."

"Good."

"Good?" I repeated.

"I like that you find me attractive and think I smell nice. I want you to think about it a lot when we're not together."

"Behave, Doc."

"Too early for serious flirting?" he asked me.

"Too early and not enough caffeine."

Trent smiled sheepishly. "Sorry?"

"Don't be. I'm glad to spend time with you, even if it's at the ass crack of dawn."

Trent laughed hard. "Why do I think you learned that phrase from your grandmother?"

"Because we both know it's true. I'm not nearly as colorful as Grammie is—in style or personality."

"I like you just the way you are."

I should've put the truck in reverse, back down his driveway, and head toward the gym, but I couldn't look away from his penetrative blue eyes. Who was this guy who proudly spoke his thoughts out loud without shying away from them? Was he as sincere as he seemed?

"What?" Trent asked.

"Are you for real?"

"How do you mean?" He looked genuinely confused.

"Are you always so open about what you're thinking and feeling?"

"I am *now*," Trent replied. "Does it bother you?"

Did it? I was much more reserved in my actions, both verbal and physical, but it was refreshing not having to guess what Trent was thinking or feeling. "Not at all," I finally said. "I'm just not used to it with the guys I've dated."

"Are we officially dating?" Trent asked, wearing a sly smile on his face and sporting a hopeful expression in his eyes.

"Let's see if we can survive the grueling workout I have planned for you."

"Yeah?" Trent asked, biting his lip in anticipation. "Sounds a lot like foreplay to me."

"I guess it could be if we skipped breakfast at the diner and—"

"Nope," Trent said adamantly. "I'm going to be honest with you, Tuck. I can't stop thinking about your monster cock in my ass, and I want it really bad."

"But?" I asked.

Trent's lips quirked up like he wanted to crack a joke but knew it wasn't the right time. "I'm a little worried I'll get addicted to your cock, then you'll freak out again and run. That's just cruel."

My heart galloped like a runaway racehorse. "So this is a test?"

"No, Tuck," Trent said, reaching over to stroke my jaw. "I'm not testing you, and I'm not pressuring you either."

"Then what do you call it?"

"Dating. We see if we're compatible and have similar goals for the future."

"Then what?" I asked.

"Then we unleash this fire raging between us and hope it doesn't consume us."

"I'm kind of worried about Blissville," I told Trent, turning my face so I could kiss his palm.

"You worried about what the people in our town will think of us as a couple?" he asked, pulling his hand away.

"No, I'm worried we'll blaze hot enough to burn the town to the ground."

"Oh God," Trent said, his voice cracking.

I chuckled at the desperation in his voice then put the truck in reverse and backed down the driveway.

Fit-N-Feisty opened at six thirty, so we were the first members through the door. Even though I normally worked out at the gym in the firehouse, I had a membership because the owners were two of my dearest friends.

"How goes it, Tuck?" Mitch Daniels asked. "Long time no see, brother." He and his wife, Sandy, were high school sweethearts, prom king and queen, and the valedictorian and salutatorian. Mitch never failed to brag about marrying the smartest person in our senior class.

"Hey, Mitch," I said, accepting his bro hug. "It's good to see you. How are the kids?"

"They're healthy as can be according to Dr. Love," Mitch said, patting Trent on the back. "Ornery as hell, but you wouldn't expect anything less from my kids."

"You're finally convinced the kids are yours, huh?" Sandy asked, entering the gym from her office.

"What are you talking about?" Mitch asked her, sounding genuinely puzzled.

"You're always saying to me 'your kids did this' and 'your kids did that,' so I assumed you doubted their paternity."

We all laughed because their daughters looked just like Mitch.

"Don't let us keep you," Sandy said. "I'm sure you're here early because you have places you need to be soon. We'll be in the office doing last-minute tax prep."

Mitch shuddered. "Let the crying begin."

"Good thing we keep plenty of tissues on hand," Sandy added.

"We have to stock up because both the ladies and fellas get upset when Dr. Love fails to notice their attempts to gain his attention," Mitch said.

"Oh really?" I asked, quirking a brow at Trent who just shook his head.

"False." Trent looked at Sandy and Mitch. "Thanks a lot."

"That's our cue to leave, honey," Sandy said to her husband. "Must you always cause trouble?"

"Yes," Mitch said as they walked toward the office. "You act as if you don't know me."

I would've told them goodbye, but the two of them were too busy giving each other a hard time. It would be rude to interrupt them. I turned to face Trent once we were alone. "Where do you want to start?"

"I need to get this outer layer of clothes off, then I want to warm up on the treadmill."

"Right. The locker room," I replied then had to swallow hard. The two of us alone in the locker room was a temptation I wasn't sure I could resist. Who was I kidding? If it was left solely up to me, I'd drop to my knees on the tile floor and warm him up in the best possible way, but Trent wanted to prove something to me, and I would let him.

I followed Trent to the locker room and set my gym bag down on the low wooden bench running the length of the metal lockers. "Hmmm." I bent over and tested the sturdiness of the bench. Trent snickered, causing me to glance up. He wore a knowing smirk, and his eyes seemed to glow with wickedness. "What?" I asked nonchalantly. "I'm just testing out the quality of construction. I'm a big guy, and I'd hate to break my friends' bench."

"You're testing the sturdiness to determine if you could live out your locker room porn fantasies on my ass." *Busted.*

"Mmm-hmm. Like you don't have any?"

"Of course I do, but I'd prefer to live out all my fantasies with you in private."

I nodded. The idea of someone walking in on us while we were having sex didn't appeal to me either.

Trent unzipped his windbreaker and I followed suit, stripping down to our tank tops. I raked my eyes over his strong shoulders and biceps. His tank top clung to his torso, affording me a glimpse of his perfectly developed pecs and ripped abdomen. Trent couldn't tear his eyes off the bit of chest hair showing above my tank top. He bit his bottom lip while clenching and unclenching his fists, making the sexy veins in his forearms flex. I loved the visual signs of Trent's arousal and wondered if his heart was racing as fast as mine. I could press my fingers to his neck to feel his pulse, but I wouldn't be pacified by a simple touch. My hands would drift lower and—I jerked my gaze away from his body and propped a leg on the bench so I could unzip the bottom of my track pants. Trent chuckled and did the same.

I was glad to see his shorts fell to mid-thigh, but my relief died a quick death when I followed him out of the locker room and saw how the material clung to his ass.

"You're evil," I hissed. "You wore those shorts to drive me insane, didn't you?"

"Me?" he asked, spinning around to face me. "You know how your chest hair makes me purr like a frisky kitten. I just want to rub my face against it." Trent lifted his hand and traced the neckline of my tank top. I felt his touch everywhere on my body.

"Keep it up, and we're going to experience an entirely different form of cardio than Mitch and Sandy intended for their members," I said in a low, rumbling voice teeming with desire.

"Let's hit the treadmills."

Thankfully, the televisions hanging on the wall were playing episodes of a home improvement show instead of the world news. Nothing sucked the life out of a person more than starting their day off with violent crimes, politics, and civil discord around the world. Trent and I warmed up by walking for two minutes before we started to jog. We fell into perfect cadence beside each other, and it made me think of all the other ways we could find harmonious rhythms together. I turned my head slightly to check him out and saw he was doing the same. We exchanged easy smiles then turned our attention back to the televisions. Our leisurely jog turned into a full-out run for twenty-five minutes before we reversed the process and ended with a cool-down walk.

"That felt good," Trent said, sounding barely winded. He noted my same condition. "I wouldn't think a big guy like you did a lot of running."

"I've always played sports that required a lot of conditioning. Plus, I've found running, when paired with lifting weights, is an effective way to maintain the amount of muscle mass I want. I started lifting weights in high school, and it was the one place I could tune out everything bothering me and just focus on my breathing and improving my technique. I bulked up pretty quickly, and coach recommended I add cardio into my routine so my muscle mass didn't impact my agility."

"It must be the perfect combination because you have the most amazing body I've ever had the privilege to touch or taste."

"Trent," I said in a warning tone.

"Yeah, okay," he said, wiping the sweat from his face with one of the gym towels. "Upper body, legs, or full body?" Trent ran his eyes over the length of my body on the last part.

"There's no way I can watch you squat in those shorts and not get a hard-on." Trent had been nothing but honest with me, so I gave it right back to him. "We'll work on our upper body today."

Even with Trent looking deliciously sweaty, I was able to find my zone and work my shoulders, arms, back, and core abdominal muscles. Lifting weights was my version of yoga. I found my Zen and the endorphins pumping through my body would improve my mood and motivate me to keep moving throughout the day. Only when we returned to the locker room did I realize those mood-lifting hormones also amped up my libido.

"Did you want to shower here before we go to breakfast or wait until I drop you off at home?"

Trent looked over his shoulder at the shower room, which had both an open shower area and private stalls for those preferring privacy. We could so easily fit inside one of those stalls and—

"We better wait," he said, wiping his body down to remove the sweat glistening on his skin. Damn, I wanted to lick him. A little bit of sweat didn't turn me off at all, but he might think it was gross.

"Yeah, I want to lick you all over too," Trent said, correctly reading the expression on my face. "And I will…someday."

"Tease," I groused.

We made quick work of toweling off and putting our jackets and pants back on. Ohio weather in March was fickle at best and psychotic at worst. It could be a warm sixty-five degrees one day and a freezing twenty-two the next. It was no wonder everyone was sick. Luckily, the weather was on the mild side when we walked outside the gym, so we decided to walk the block and a half to Edson and Emma's diner.

It was still early enough that the diner was mostly empty except for the local farmers who met daily to eat breakfast and discuss how they'd solve the world's problems by noon if they were in charge. Planting season would start at the end of the month or the first of next, so they'd be taking a few weeks away from their morning meetings until they tilled their fields and planted their soy beans and corn. The topics would shift from politics and world issues to weather as they waited to see what kind of spring Mother Nature would unleash on them. Would it rain too much and flood the fields, flushing the newly planted seeds from the ground, or would it be too dry? Only time would tell, but it didn't prevent them from hashing and rehashing the topic to death in advance.

Trent and I chose a quiet corner booth on the opposite side of the diner so we could talk privately, not that Earl, Bob, Stan, or Jeff would pay much attention to us.

"Morning, fellas," our waiter, DJ, said when he approached our table. I saw the curiosity in his gaze when he looked between Trent and me. "Need a menu, or do you know what you're having?"

"I'll take crispy bacon, two eggs over easy, hash browns, and wheat toast," Trent said. "Oh, and a cup of coffee."

"Cream and sugar?" DJ asked him.

"Hazelnut creamer but no sugar, please."

"Got it," DJ said. "What about you, Tuck?"

Trent raised his brow over the younger guy's familiarity with me. "I'll have my usual."

"Turkey sausage and a Spanish egg white omelet?"

"Yep."

"No toast or hash browns, right?"

"You got it. I'll take a tall glass of orange juice on ice instead of coffee, please."

"I'll have your food out to you in a few minutes, fellas."

DJ strode away, and I noticed he added an extra sway to his hips. Was he hoping to draw Trent's attention? I glanced to see if my breakfast date was watching him, but he was looking at me through narrowed eyes instead.

"What?" I asked, wondering what I'd done wrong.

"Did you date that kid?" he asked.

"Date? No."

Trent blanched. "Fuck?" he asked in a stunned whisper.

"No," I said, grimacing. "DJ's not a kid, but he's much too young for me."

"He wanted to climb you like a jungle gym though, didn't he?"

I shrugged. "He might've hinted he was open to the idea."

Trent scowled and rubbed the back of his neck. "But you've never been tempted?"

"Tempted? Yes, I was. I knew nothing would come of it other than regret when my actions put a strain on my relationship with Emma, who is one of Grammie's dearest friends."

"Is he related to the owners?"

"DJ is their grandson," I explained.

"Oh man. You'd have to stop coming here or risk having them spit in your food."

"I doubt Edson or Emma would react so extremely, but it would get back to my grammie, and she'd be disappointed in me."

"I love the relationship you have with her," Trent said, abruptly changing the subject.

"She's all the family I have," I told him. "What about you? Are you close to your family?"

"I have a wonderful relationship with my sister and adore my nieces and my brother-in-law. My parents, on the other hand, don't even know I'm back in town unless Mercedes told them."

"Oh, wow." His confession took me by surprise. "I'm sorry."

"What are you sorry for?" Trent asked me. "It's not your fault I have a strained relationship with my parents."

"I know it's not my fault, but I'm still sorry the tension exists."

"I would prefer it wasn't there either, but I don't regret standing my ground, even if it took me far longer than it should to find my footing."

There was a big story there, but DJ arrived with our plates before Trent could say more—*if* he were going to say more. It felt like an awfully heavy topic for the time of day and stage of our relationship. I saw the sad questions in Trent's eyes when I mentioned Grammie was my only family, but I'd turned the focus on him before he could ask them.

Our conversation turned to much lighter subjects while we ate, and the tension that had appeared when I brought up his family faded from Trent's body. His lips softened into sweet smiles, and his eyes were bright with humor as we recounted some funny stories from our misspent youth.

"Of course, getting away with things in Blissville was nearly impossible," I told him. "I'm pretty sure it was the sight of the first neighborhood watch."

"They say it takes a village," Trent quipped.

"I'm not sure about that, but it doesn't hurt to have so many people looking out for you."

The bells above the door chimed as our police captain, Gabe Roman-Wyatt, walked inside the diner. He took one look at Trent and his expression changed from jovial to menacing in a heartbeat as he approached the counter to place a to-go order.

"That guy really has it in for you," I teased. "Surely he knows his husband is crazy about him, right?"

During the pool party at the Roman-Wyatts' house, I'd noted Gabe's frosty demeanor toward the good doctor. When I asked Trent about it, he confessed he and Josh used to date back in college. He'd told me it had ended badly, but Josh had forgiven him for his bone-headed behavior.

"He's not worried I will take Josh away from him. He hates me because of the way I hurt Josh."

"You said Josh accepted your apology," I pointed out to him.

"Gabe isn't willing to forgive me, which is okay."

"I guess I don't understand why he's mad if Josh isn't."

"I don't either, but then again, I don't think I've ever loved anyone as deeply as Gabe loves Josh." Trent tilted his head and studied me. "I'm guessing you haven't either."

"Not like that, no. I was in love with a guy who didn't return my affection because he was still hung up on his ex. He wanted to love me but couldn't. We broke up after a few years, but we've remained friends. Grammie told me what I felt was more infatuation than love, but it sure felt like my heart broke when our relationship ended."

"Is he anyone I know?" Trent asked curiously.

"Yes," I replied.

"That's it? Just yes?"

"For now," I teased. "You have a date with a shower so you can get to work on time. You don't want to keep your patients waiting."

I signaled DJ for the check and snatched it up before Trent could.

"Hey," he said. "I invited you to breakfast, so I should pay."

"You can pay next time." Trent smiled at hearing there would be a next time.

Once we exited the diner, I reached for his hand like it was as natural as breathing. Excitement sparked from the point where our hands touched and spread throughout my body while contentment settled in my heart. *I could really get used to this.*

R̲X̲ PATIENT NAME: _____
        _____
     ADDRESS: _____
        _____
        _____

Prescription:

CHAPTER EIGHT

_____
_____

Signature: _____ Date: _____

Trent

"**A**RE YOU GOING TO WALK ME TO THE DOOR LIKE A GENTLEMAN?" I asked when Tucker pulled into my driveway and parked behind my car.

"I'm not feeling all that gentlemanly right now." Tucker's guard was completely down when he turned and looked at me. I saw his naked need and desire. "I will walk you through your door and press you against the foyer wall and—"

"Okay," I said, releasing my seatbelt and opening the passenger door without waiting for a response. I didn't wait for him to escort me to the door, but I'd only taken a few steps before I heard Tuck's door open and shut. His footfalls were steady as he followed me, but I was willing to bet his heart was racing as quickly as mine.

My hands shook when I tried to unlock the door, and I dropped my keychain on the porch. I bent at the waist to pick it up just as Trent placed his big hands on my hips and pressed his groin to my ass. A pitiful whimper escaped through my parted lips.

"I warned you I wasn't feeling gentlemanly," Tuck said darkly.

I scooped my keys off the porch and straightened before my neighbors witnessed our bump and grind, but I pushed my groin tighter against the growing bulge in Tuck's pants instead of putting space between us.

"Unlock the door, Doc."

I fumbled with the lock but managed to get the door open. Tuck pushed me through it like he said he would then kicked it closed behind us. He spun me around and backed me up against the foyer wall.

"What are you going to do to me, Sparky?"

Rather than answering me verbally, Tuck showed me with his hands and mouth what he planned to do to me. Tuck placed a warm hand at my nape and pulled me to him for a scorching kiss while his other hand slipped beneath my track pants, shorts, and briefs to grip my stiffening dick.

I moaned into Tucker's mouth when he slowly stroked upward with the perfect amount of pressure. He twisted his wrist when he reached the crown then slid his hand back down my length. I was fully erect by the second pass.

I tore my mouth away from his and let my head fall back against the wall. "I won't last long. Get your cock out and jack us off together with your big hand."

Tucker chuckled then pressed his mouth to my exposed throat. "So." *Nibble.* "Bossy." *Kiss.* He worked his mouth up and down my throat as he continued stroking my dick until my legs shook. Tucker licked and sucked my Adam's apple before he stepped back and looked into my eyes. "I like it."

Instead of pulling out his dick, he dropped to his knees in front of me. "No, Tuck," I weakly said when he moved to pull my clothes down to my thighs. "I'm all sweaty. I must stink."

Tuck answered by pressing his nose against the fabric of my pants then inhaled deeply. "You smell like a man, and I want your dick in my mouth." He looked up at me from his knees, and I couldn't resist his pleading, dark eyes, especially when I wanted my dick in his mouth just as much.

I hastily shoved my pants, shorts, and underwear to mid-thigh. Gripping the base of my dick with one hand and cupping Tucker's neck with the other, I slowly pushed my erection between his eager lips.

"So hot," I said, watching my dick sink inch-by-inch inside his mouth. I wasn't as thick or as long as Tucker, but I had a mouthful and then some. "You been thinking about my cock? Wondering what I taste like?" Tucker moaned around my shaft, sending vibrations straight to my taut balls. I kept slowly feeding him my dick until the head nudged the back of his throat. I started to pull back, but Tucker dug his thick, strong fingers in my ass and sucked me down until his tongue teased the base of my dick and the top of my sac.

"Fuck!" I roared loud enough to wake the neighbors. Tucker glanced up at me through impossibly long eyelashes then swallowed around my cock. "Oh fuck!"

Tucker took his sweet old time pulling back until only the head of my dick remained in his mouth. My hips thrust forward of their own accord, acting independently from the rest of my body. Shallow thrusts at first, creating the perfect amount of friction on the sensitive spot just beneath the crown until I couldn't take it any longer. I snapped my hips forward, fucking his mouth hard enough for my balls to slap his chin. Tucker's eyes glowed with approval as he sucked eagerly and noisily. Seeing this big strong man on his knees pleasuring me was too much and not enough at the same time. I couldn't get enough, but the tingling in my spine said I wouldn't hold out much longer.

"My balls. Massage my balls."

Tucker did as I asked, milking them with just the right amount of pressure. My head fell back, and my eyes rolled back in my head. "Gonna come," I warned. "Gonna... Unh," I grunted when the first spurt jettisoned inside his hot mouth. I continued fucking his face with short jerky thrusts until there was nothing left to give, then I eased my dick from Tucker's swollen lips.

It was a good thing I was leaning against the wall for support because my legs shook as hard as they did on leg day at the gym. Tucker continued to lick my dick, gathering every bit of cum that had escaped his mouth and dribbled down my shaft.

"What about you?" I asked shakily. "I need to—"

Tucker rose swiftly to his feet and kissed my lips. Tasting myself on his tongue was a huge turn-on. Tucker pulled back to catch his breath. "It's my turn for blue balls." He pointed to my softening dick. "Need help tucking it away?"

"Huh-uh."

"Have a good day, Doc. Call me later if you get a chance." Tucker turned to leave then stopped when he noticed the multitiered cat jungle I'd purchased and installed since the last time he was at my house. Natasha poked her tiny head over the edge of the lowest carpet-covered platform while Boris stared down at us from the highest one. "Too spoiled to climb down and see your old pal, huh?" Boris yawned and Natasha dove back down out of sight.

"Aren't you going to lecture me about installing a safety net in case they fall?" I asked him as I pulled up my clothes. I would just be taking them off again as soon as I went upstairs to shower, but my legs were too weak to duck waddle my ass up those steps without falling and breaking something.

Tucker rolled his eyes and chuckled. "You really are cruising for a swift swat on the ass."

"Don't you promise me a good time then walk out of here."

"You're the one who needs to be at work in an hour," Tucker reminded me.

"You saw how quickly I can get ready when I need to." I could tell by his expression he was wrestling with temptation. Should I stay, or should I go?

"I'm going to need a lot longer than forty-five minutes for the things I want to do to your body."

I hummed happily. "Have a good day, Sparky."

Tucker started to leave but spun around and pulled me to him for one last kiss. "So addictive," he whispered against my lips. That too was another first. No one had ever made me feel irresistible before, and I was finding it just as addictive as he found my mouth. One more quick peck and he was gone, and I felt like someone had zapped me with an electrical wire. Energy pulsed throughout my body, restoring my batteries.

Meow.

I looked over my shoulder from the bottom of the steps. Boris appeared to be scrutinizing me. Was he judging my worthiness of a man like Tucker Garrison? "Don't be silly," I said out loud. "He's just a cat."

Meow. How could one feline put so much scorn in a simple meow?

"Good morning, Dr. Love."

"Good morning, Becky," I said. "How's the day looking?"

"I'm the only medical assistant today since Michelle is sick with the flu. Suzy and John are the only nurses who reported for duty, and we only have Nikki and Karen handling the phones and checking patients in."

"This flu epidemic is wreaking havoc on our small town," I told her.

Blissville Family Medicine consisted of two pediatricians, two family practitioners, and two internal medicine specialists. The six doctors shared two medical assistants, three nurses, three ladies who handled scheduling appointments and checking patients in and out, one overworked person in charge of billing and insurance, and one office manager. We didn't have enough staff to keep things running smoothly on a good day at our thriving practice, so missing several key staff members would hit us hard.

"We'll just do the best we can," I told Becky. The smile I aimed at her was meant to instill positivity, but judging by the look on her face, I missed my mark.

"Unless we're on the set of a toothpaste commercial, you might want to dial down your smile a bit."

"I shouldn't be in a good mood? I shouldn't try to project happiness wherever I go?"

"I will stab you in the throat with my spoon," John said from behind me. "Ain't no one got the time or the patience for your Mary Poppins bullshit with the flu epidemic sweeping through our town, mowing us off one by one."

"Mowing us off? Do you mean mowing us down?" I asked, trying hard not to laugh at the irritated expression on John's face.

"Don't do that either," he said, waving his empty spoon in the air before plopping it down into his cup of low-fat, sugar-free, triple-thick, bad-tasting Greek yogurt. John narrowed his eyes and studied me from head to toe. "New tie?"

I looked down at my bluish-gray tie. "Nope. I wear it at least once a week." It paired nicely with my white, gray, blue, and even black dress shirts.

"Your pants and shirt aren't new," he remarked. A wide grin spread across his face. "I spy with my little eye something different about the dashing doctor."

"Dr. Love has asked you to keep your 'little eye' tucked away during office hours," Becky said.

"Hag, don't even try me today," John fired back. "Oh my God. I know what it is. You got l—"

"Don't finish that sentence, John," I said firmly. "We might have an informal, laid-back environment here, but there are still lines we don't cross."

"Not in his world," Suzy said, joining us.

John ignored Suzy. "Since when?" he asked me.

Good point. "Starting today."

John just smirked. "I wasn't going where you think, Dr. Dirty Mind."

"Oh, really?" Becky asked, crossing her arms over her chest. "You weren't about to accuse Dr. Love of getting laid."

John gasped and briefly covered his mouth. "Becky! I would never say something so vulgar to Dr. Love."

It was my turn to ask, "Since when?"

"Starting today," John said haughtily. "I think you should report Becky to the office manager for her inappropriate behavior."

"Mike has better things to do with his time," I told John. "Okay, now that we've all had a good laugh this morning, we need to get our game faces on to tackle the rest of the day. It's going to be a long one. Let's meet back here for lunch so we can all take a guess at which true crime show John watched last night."

"Go on and laugh it up, bitches," he said, pointing to Becky and Suzy, who happened to be his sister and his cousin, "but I bet I could commit the perfect crime and get away with it."

"Glad to see you're spending your free time wisely," I quipped. "Who's up first?" I asked Becky, steering the conversation to work.

"The Hempstead twins," she said. "They're in exam room four. Jennifer suspects the flu."

"Okay," I said then looked at John. "It's your turn to make the kids cry."

It didn't take long for our good moods to sour. One patient after the next came in with various stages of flu, pneumonia, bronchitis, strep throat, and ear infections. Crying kids, scared parents, and overworked staff made for a stressful day.

"Dr. Love," Becky said, poking her head into my office where I'd retreated to eat a protein bar and sip coffee since I worked through my lunch break. "I hate to bother you, but do you think you can squeeze one last family in this afternoon before we close for the day? Dr. Hinman has a family commitment and has to leave on time. John and I will stick around, and Karen at the front desk said she was willing to stay also."

"Sure thing," I said without asking who the patient was.

Two and a half hours later, I discovered my emergency patients were two of Gabe and Josh's five kids. The couple had adopted infant twins not long after they'd married then had taken in three siblings as foster children, who they were now in the process of adopting. Gabe looked disappointed when I walked through the door.

"Dr. Hinman has a family engagement she couldn't miss, so you're stuck with me."

The scowl on his face softened slightly, and he said, "I'd embrace the devil right now if he made my girls feel better."

"I'm not quite as bad as the devil, but I'm positive I can help your girls."

The ladies in question rested on both of his knees and leaned their heads against their father's chest. I squatted down so I was at eye level with the girls, ages two and five. "Hello, sweet ladies. I'm going to help you feel better soon."

Destiny, the two-year-old, was sucking her thumb, and she waved her remaining four fingers at me. Rochelle offered me a half smile but clung tighter to Gabe. I rose to my feet and pulled some stickers from my lab coat pocket. Destiny grabbed the Minnie Mouse, and Rochelle chose a unicorn. I put the rest of the stickers back in my pocket and made a mental note to replenish my supply.

I dropped onto the stool and looked at the laptop where John had made notes about the girls' symptoms. "Sounds like they might have the respiratory stuff that's going around. Mind placing them on the exam table so I can listen to their lungs?"

"Sure," Gabe said.

"Big breath," I said to Rochelle and demonstrated pulling air deep into my lungs. She shook her head no. "Maybe I should try this on Daddy first?" Rochelle seemed to like this idea even if Gabe's scowl said he didn't.

"I'll be gentle," I said to Gabe who glared at me before giving in to his girls.

Gabe was standing behind his daughters to act as a barrier so neither fell off the back while I examined them. He remained there but turned to the side so the girls could see me walk up behind him. They turned their little heads and raptly watched me press the stethoscope to Gabe's back.

"Big breath," I told him. Gabe inhaled and puffed up like a blow-fish, making Destiny and Rochelle giggle.

"That's good," I said after listening to his lungs. I moved the stethoscope over to the left and said, "One more." Gabe inhaled sharply then coughed. "That's what I thought. The girls aren't the only ones who will be leaving here with a prescription." Gabe turned to face me with a raised brow. "You have bronchitis."

"What? I only have a dry cough, and it's not too bad."

"You have bronchitis, and it could get much worse if left un-treated. You're welcome to obtain a second opinion."

"I guess you know what you're doing," Gabe said begrudgingly.

"I honestly do."

John knocked on the door and helped me examine Destiny and Rochelle who also had bronchitis and double ear infections.

"I should check your ears too," I said to Gabe who only gave in because his daughters insisted. "Ears look a little red, but there's no fluid behind your eardrums. The antibiotic I'm giving you for bron-chitis will knock out an ear infection if it develops. Call us if the boys start showing similar symptoms, and we'll squeeze them in like we did for your girls. I'm sending your prescriptions to your pharmacy, but I'd call ahead before driving to pick them up. I would imagine they're swamped right now."

Gabe tilted his head to the side and studied me for a few seconds. "I guess you're okay," he finally said before he scooped up his daughters and left the room.

"We should totally use his ringing endorsement on our next marketing campaign. *Dr. Love is okay.* Oh, I know: *Dr. Love is okay enough for our police captain, so he'd be okay enough for you too.*"

"Smart-ass," I said before heading to my office.

I hung up my lab coat and slipped my suit jacket on. My phone vibrated in my pocket with an incoming call. "No," I groaned when I saw who it was. I was barely clinging to my good mood from the morning. Picture a man dangling over the edge of a cliff and the only thing preventing him from plummeting to his death was a thin tree root. In my case, the thin root was my hard-fought independence from my family. Knowing I couldn't avoid her forever, I accepted the call and said, "Mother."

"Son," she said with equal dryness. "Imagine my surprise when I picked up Madison from preschool, and she told me her uncle Tee Tee was home and had two new kitties." *Snap.* The imaginary root ripped apart, and I could feel myself tumbling into the abyss of misery.

"Imagine my surprise at learning you picked up Madison from preschool."

"That's not the point, Trent."

"What is the point, Mother?"

"When did you arrive home from South America?"

"Friday evening," I admitted.

"You've been home for almost a week and haven't called me?" She sounded angrier than I expected. "You know how I worry when you're in *those* countries."

My work with Doctors Without Borders was often grueling and didn't afford comfortable sleeping accommodations, but I wouldn't change the experience for the world. The patients I saw always offered so much gratitude, and they radiated joy over the smallest acts of kindness. If given a choice between living in a hut in South America or moving back in with my parents, I'd choose the hut.

"If anyone realized your value, they'd kidnap you for ransom." Please. It wasn't like my father had made a Forbes list.

"The only thing the people cared about was my ability to make their kids feel better, Mother. You can't put a price on that kind of peace of mind."

"I didn't call to argue, and I won't even bother trying to make you feel guilty for inviting Mercedes, Benjamin, and the girls over to your house this weekend without calling your father and me."

"Mom, do you know what Saturday was?" I asked. Silence.

"It was your birthday. I didn't bother trying to call you because I didn't think you were home."

"You could've tried," I said. "A happy birthday message from you would've been a nice surprise if I were thousands of miles from home. Finding a birthday card in the mail when I got home would've been even nicer."

"Who sends cards anymore?" she asked.

She completely missed the point, which wasn't a surprise to me at all. I wasn't going to waste my breath trying to explain it to her. "If you didn't call to wish me a happy birthday or berate me for not calling when I got home, then why are you calling me?"

"To tell you about this wonderful man I met at a benefit over the weekend. He's educated, handsome, and has a great sense of humor."

"I hope you'll be very happy together," I said dryly.

"Not for me, silly. I want to introduce him to you. I've heard he's bisexual, but that's not a deal breaker for you, right?"

"It wouldn't be a deal breaker *if* I were in the market for a boy-friend." Why would I care if a guy was also interested in women? Then again, in my mother's world, attraction equaled sex.

"Are you seeing someone?" Mother asked hopefully.

"I am." I had no idea if things would work out with Tucker, but I had no intention of lining up a guy to fall back on if it didn't.

"Is he anyone I know?"

"Absolutely not, Mother. You have horrible taste in men."

"How can you say that? I picked your father."

Elon was a disgusting excuse for a husband and father, but Mother had always turned a blind eye and pretended not to notice. I wasn't touching that one with a ten-foot pole.

"I've introduced you to some lovely men, Trent."

"They are lovely for someone other than me," I pointed out. "You don't have to worry about me anymore."

"It's serious then?"

"I didn't mean to imply my relationship with Tucker was headed to the altar; I simply meant I'm not spending my nights lonely and miserable."

"Tucker? What an unusual name. Does he live in Blisstown with you?"

"*Blissville*, Mother, and yes, he lives here too. That's all I'm going to say. Things are new between us, and I don't want to jinx it by getting ahead of myself." More like I didn't want her showing up on Tuck's doorstep and scaring him off.

"Okay," she said calmly. "I'm just glad to hear you're home safe and you're dating. I'm not sure what to think about your cats. I'd never guess you were a cat person."

"I wasn't exactly sure what kind of pet I was going to adopt until I saw Boris and Natasha at the shelter. They were meant to be mine." I looked forward to seeing them when I got home each night.

"Keep in touch. It's embarrassing when my granddaughters know more about you than I do."

"Take care, Mother. We'll talk soon."

Natasha and Boris were waiting for me by the door when I let myself in. I wanted to think they were thrilled to see me, but they'd quickly learned it was dinnertime when I walked through the door.

I mixed their fancy wet food with the dry and set it down for them to chow on. My phone buzzed with an incoming text. I hoped it was Tucker; although, I had no reason to expect a message from him since he was working. I chuckled when I saw it was from Mercedes.

Why didn't you tell me you were seeing someone?

I typed back a quick response. *It was too new. I wasn't sure it was going anywhere.* I still wasn't sure, but I was going to give it my all.

I want to meet him.

You sort of already did. I laughed, waiting for her reply.

???

Mr. March. Mercedes had practically drooled over Tucker's calendar photo, and I worried she was going to steal it from me when I wasn't looking.

Lucky bastard.

She wasn't wrong.

R̷x

PATIENT NAME: _____

ADDRESS: _____

Prescription:

CHAPTER NINE

Signature: _____ Date: _____

T HE MOOD IN THE FIREHOUSE ON SATURDAY NIGHT WAS SOMBER because of the three-car accident scene we were called out on earlier in the day. A pickup truck ran a stop sign and plowed into the side of a sports car, causing it to spin out of control and directly into the path of an oncoming SUV. We'd had to use the Jaws of Life to free the driver in the sports car, but there was nothing medically we could've done to save him. He'd died on impact and was pronounced dead at the scene. Those images would be burned in my mind forever.

As it always did with fatal accidents, my thoughts turned to the crash that claimed my parents' lives. Had they known they were going to die, or did it happen so fast they didn't know what hit them? The details of the accident were public record, but I'd never looked up the crash report or searched for details in the newspaper archives from Delaware, Ohio, where we lived at the time. I worried knowing the truth would be so much worse than guessing about their accident, but not knowing caused my mind to spin with so many scenarios—each one more heartbreaking than the one before.

On days like this, I replaced the bloody body in the car with a version of the smiling woman and man in the photographs hanging on Grammie's wall or the photo albums she cherished. I couldn't remember anything about them because I was only nine months old when they died. I didn't know if my mother's hair was as soft as it looked or what kind of laugh my father had. Was it loud and robust or calm and deep? What did my mother's voice sound like when she sung lullabies to me? How many nights had I fallen asleep to my father reading books to me? Those were stories I'd heard from Grammie but couldn't recall for myself. Reading about their deaths in a coldly worded police report wouldn't suddenly allow me to remember those precious moments, so what purpose would it serve?

"Tuck," Braxton said, pulling me out of my sullen thoughts. "You have a visitor."

I sat up on the bed where I'd been resting. "Okay."

"I'll just send him back."

Him? I expected Grammie had heard about the fatal car crash and decided to check on me, but Trent was the one who walked into the sleeping quarters carrying takeout bags.

"Hey there," Trent said, looking unsure about his decision to pop in, and I couldn't allow that.

I rose from the bed, took the bags of food from his hands and set them on the table, then pulled Trent into my arms. I probably held him tighter than I should, but I couldn't seem to help myself. We'd talked every day on the phone, sometimes more than once, but it was the first time I'd seen Trent since I left him standing in his foyer on Thursday morning.

"It's damn good to see you, Doc."

"It's good to see you too, Sparky."

I chuckled and relaxed my arms but didn't release him completely. "Don't let the guys hear you calling me Sparky, okay? I'll never live it down."

"You got it," Trent said. He tilted his head back and looked into my eyes. "I heard you've had a rough day today."

"The worst," I admitted. "I chose this job to help people during their time of need, and it hurts when I fail them."

"From what I've heard, there was nothing you or anyone else could've done to save the man." I heard what Trent said and knew he was right, but it still hurt. "I know how it feels, though," he told me. "Working on the oncology floor at Children's Hospital during my rotations nearly killed me, Tuck. I'm not ashamed to admit I cried my eyes out every night when I went home."

I stroked his cheek with the back of my hand. My reticence about our relationship faded in tiny increments every moment I spent in Trent's presence or talked to him on the phone. I loved learning all the facets of his personality and hearing him speak so passionately about his work. "You're exactly what the doctor ordered for me right now," I whispered before I dropped a lingering kiss on his lips. I wanted to deepen the kiss, but it wasn't the most private location for a make-out session.

"What doctor? Should I be jealous?"

"I only have eyes for you, Doc."

"You say the sweetest things and hold on to me like you never want to let go, but then you call a halt when I try to take things farther with you."

"You're the one who thinks he has something to prove to me," I reminded him.

"Oh, that's right," Trent said, placing sweet kisses on my neck from my collarbone up to my ear. He nipped my earlobe then sucked it between his lips. "I forgot what I was worried about," he said. "Do you remember?"

"I can't even remember my name when all my blood is rushing down to my dick."

"Come over to my house when you get off your shift, and we can discuss it privately."

"Okay, but I have a basketball game in the morning, so I probably shouldn't do anything that will make my legs weak two Sundays in a row."

"How many times did you come while fantasizing about me last weekend?"

"Three."

"Did you win on Sunday?"

"Yes," I admitted.

"Then I don't see what the problem is," Trent said, pulling back to look into my eyes. "You're obviously conditioned to *perform* well and require very little recovery time."

"Doc, I'm a little concerned about what will happen once I finally—"

"Mmmmm, what smells good?"

Trent and I jerked apart and whirled to face my grandmother. She grinned mischievously while assessing the situation.

"I clearly came at a bad time," she said.

"There's no such thing when it comes to you, Grammie."

"I was worried about you when I got back from playing bridge with the ladies and heard about the fatal accident. Are you doing okay?"

"I'm hanging in there. Trent brought me dinner."

"He's a good man," Grammie said, smiling approvingly at Trent.

"There's more than enough for you too, Shirlene."

"I wouldn't dream of interrupting your time together," she said. "I would love it if you could join Tucker and me for dinner tomorrow night."

Trent looked at me to gauge my reaction to the invitation before he responded. "I'd like it too," I told him.

Trent smiled at Grammie and said, "Thank you, Shirlene. I'd be honored to dine with you."

"I'll be on my way then and let you guys spend some time together. I'll see you both tomorrow night at five thirty."

"She means five fifteen," I mock-whispered to Trent.

"Five o'clock it is then," he said with an easy smile. "Unless I see you sooner at Tucker's basketball game, Shirlene." *Wait. He was coming to my game?*

"Grammie doesn't—"

"Even better," Grammie said, cutting me off. "It won't hurt to miss one garden club meeting." She blew me a kiss then winked. "See you boys tomorrow. Try hard to misbehave. Life's too short."

Trent laughed as we watched her dart through the door, then he turned to me when we were alone again. "Are you okay with me coming to your basketball game tomorrow? I probably should've asked first."

I let my warm kiss answer for me. Thinking about Trent watching me in the stands did funny things to my insides. I had to bring my A game.

"Are you hungry?" Trent asked when our kiss ended.

"Starved." For so much more than food, but I was mindful there were at least ten guys milling around outside the doors. I chose to acknowledge the hunger in my stomach. "It's Braxton's turn to cook dinner tonight, which means he'll be making his famous five-alarm chili. It's delicious, but that stuff has to be eating away at our stomach lining."

"That hot?" Trent asked with a raised brow. His tone of voice said he might want to give it a try.

"Think about the activities we want to explore tonight and tell me if you really want to give his chili a try."

Trent tipped his head to the side, acknowledging my point. "We'll go with the selection I brought then." I followed him to the table and watched as he unpacked the carryout containers from the bags. "I wasn't sure what you were in the mood for, so I picked a variety of things. I brought pulled pork, smoked turkey, and beef brisket sandwiches to choose from along with baked beans, coleslaw, German potato salad, and baked macaroni and cheese. I hope that—"

I cut him off with a scorching kiss. His thoughtfulness touched me deeply, and I showed him the only way I knew how. We were both breathing hard when we finally broke apart.

"The food isn't the only thing I bought," Trent whispered against my lips. "I made an extra stop in case you agreed to come over tonight after your shift." I quirked a brow in question. Magnum condoms? Extra lube? A paddle for me to swat his pert ass? I was quickly forgetting all about the delicious food he brought and shifting my mind to the sexy ass I wanted to eat. "Um…" He sounded nervous, and I didn't like that he felt unsure around me.

"Show me."

Trent reached back inside the paper bag and pulled out a small plastic one. I recognized the logo of the store: Kinky Kim's.

"Oh boy," I said gleefully, mentally rubbing my hands together. The bag was too small to hide a big surprise, but amazing things came in small packages. "I hope it's a cock ring so I don't make a big fool of myself."

"No, but I wish I'd thought of it. I'd love to see your balls all trussed up and eager to unload."

"Fuck!" I whispered. "Show me what you bought so I can think about it until my shift ends."

"I'm hoping to use it now rather than wait until your shift ends. Do you have a private bathroom?"

I grabbed Trent's hand and led him inside our bathroom. There were four stalls, but none of them were occupied. I locked the door and turned to face him. Trent smiled when he saw the desperation clawing at my guts was also mirrored on my face. "Show me," I growled.

Rather than teasing me any longer, Trent opened the plastic bag for me to see the butt plug and bottle of lube inside it. "Want to help me?"

I pushed Trent against the door and ravaged his mouth. Trent met me with equal desperation, digging his fingers into my ass and pulling me tighter against his body like he wished he could crawl inside me. I was hours away from being inside him, and it was the realization I needed to pull back and suck much-needed air into my lungs.

"Brace yourself on the sink." My voice was so rough and raw I didn't recognize it.

Trent handed the bag to me then hustled over and got in to position. Our eyes met and held in the mirror when I walked over and stood behind him. I set the goodies on the counter then reached around to unbuckle Trent's belt and open his pants. He whimpered when I reached inside the gap to stroke his erection through his underwear. With my eyes still locked on his, I released his cock so I could shove his underwear and jeans to his knees.

"Push your ass out a bit more so I can see your pretty pucker."

Trent moaned and did what I requested. I wanted to drop to my knees behind him but knew I'd lose whatever grip I had on my control. As much as I wanted to tongue-fuck his ass, I wouldn't do it in a firehouse full of men. I wanted to take my time and draw out his pleasure and mine. Our eye contact broke when Trent's head fell forward like it was too heavy for his shoulders to support. I spread his ass apart with one hand and drizzled lube onto his pucker with the other. I circled his hole with my thumb, spreading the lubricant and stimulating the nerve endings to excite him.

"I might come just from this," Trent whispered. "I want you so fucking bad."

No games. No pretense. It was almost as big of a turn-on as the way Trent pushed his ass against my thumb, seeking penetration. I released his ass and poured lube over the two fingers I wanted his hole to meet.

"Hurry," Trent pleaded. "I need to—Ohhhh," he moaned when

I slid my middle finger past the first ring of muscles. I teased him by working the digit in and out of his tight clench before adding a second one. "Oh my God," he cried out. "I need more."

I rotated my wrist to corkscrew my fingers inside his greedy hole. "Like this, Doc?"

He raised his head once more, and I looked away from the prettiest ass I'd ever seen to meet his gaze. "More."

I couldn't wait for the freedom to finger-fuck him without the possibility of embarrassing interruptions. I knew time was of the essence and gently removed my fingers so I could prep the butt plug.

"I need you." Trent's moan was so needy I nearly dropped the plug on the floor.

"And you'll have me," I promised him. "Until then, this will have to do."

The plug he bought wasn't the largest one I'd ever seen, but it definitely wasn't a beginner's plug either. I made sure it was good and slick before pressing the narrow tip against Trent's flexing pucker.

I leaned over Trent's back and placed my left arm next to his on the counter while pushing the plug ever so slightly inside his tight clench. "You're so fucking sexy to me. I love the way you own your need for me to fill your tight, cherry-ish hole." Trent's lips tilted up at the corner to acknowledge my jest, then his mouth fell open and his eyes squeezed shut as I pushed the plug a little deeper inside him.

Unable to resist watching him take the plug, I straightened back up and gripped his hip with my left hand. "Ready for more?"

Trent nodded his head but didn't open his eyes or speak. The look of complete bliss on his face was nearly my undoing. Rather than push the plug the rest of the way, I pulled it back until only the tip remained inside him, earning a desperate whimper from Trent. I circled the toy around in the tight ring of muscles then pushed it back in, deeper than I had before.

"Oh fuck!" Trent's eyes opened and locked on mine. "Do it again."

"Huh-uh," I replied, shaking my head. "Only my dick or tongue gets to fuck this pretty pucker. This," I said, pushing the plug fully inside his ass until the base nestled against his hole, "is only allowed to stretch you open for me."

"I need to—"

"Oh, you will," I promised. "Stand up."

Trent rose to his full height, and I could see his flushed, leaking cock in the mirror. I reached around and gathered his precum from the slit and smeared it over his lips then licked them clean. Trent turned around and kissed me with every ounce of passion raging through his body, but I somehow found the strength to tuck his overstimulated dick back inside his underwear and refasten his pants and belt.

"How do you feel?" I asked after a long, hot kiss.

"Full."

"You haven't felt anything yet," I teased him, "but it's a good start. Eat dinner with me?"

"How can you even think about eating dinner at a time like this?"

"I'm more interested in observing the way you react to the plug in your ass."

"You want to watch me squirm?"

"Yes," I admitted. "The plug is pressing against your prostate, so sudden moves and wiggling might be enough to push you over the edge."

"You'd take pleasure in seeing me come in my pants?" he asked.

"Knowing I was the reason? Yes."

"I don't want to come in my pants; I want to come when your dick is stretching me open instead of this plug."

"Then you better not make any sudden moves."

Someone knocked on the door. "Um, Moose," Braxton said, "I hate to interrupt whatever you're doing in there, but I thought I should warn you the guys are circling your dinner. I won't be able to hold them off much longer."

"Be right there," I said.

"Moose?" Trent asked. "Is it because of your size?" I grinned wickedly at him, and he laughed when he realized he stepped into that one. "I meant your height and freakishly broad shoulders."

"Yeah," I said, rolling my eyes. "I earned the nickname in high school and haven't shaken it yet. It's why I don't want the guys hearing the new nickname you've given me."

"You got it." Trent lifted his hand and pretended to zip his mouth shut. He started to throw away the imaginary key until I gently grabbed his wrist.

"I have big plans for your mouth later, so I don't want you to lose the key."

I pressed a quick kiss against his lips then checked to see if our shirts hid our erections. I put the butt plug packaging back inside the plastic bag and shoved it deep inside the trash can. I slipped the small bottle of lube inside my pocket and looked around to make sure I didn't miss anything. Once I was certain we didn't look too guilty, and I'd buried all evidence of the butt plug, I opened the door. Just as Braxton had said, the guys were hovering over our food.

"Back off, vultures. My guy brought dinner for me, not you." Trent's hand stiffened in mine, and I realized what I'd said. Then he squeezed my fingers, letting me know he liked it. I didn't dare take my eyes off the hungry beasts eyeing my dinner.

"Told you, Moose."

"I'm sure Braxton is going to make you something delicious to eat."

"There's more food here than one guy can eat," Will pointed out.

"Because it's dinner for two, Cap," Braxton told our captain.

"Come on, guys," Van said. "Our ladies have brought us dinner before, and Moose didn't ruin it by interrupting us or trying to steal our food."

"Always the sensible one," Carl groused.

"It's usually Moose, but he's preoccupied right now," Van

countered, giving me a playful wink. "Come on. Let's help Brax cook dinner. Maybe we can distract him from putting too many spices in the chili this time."

"Good luck with that, fellas," Brax said, helping Van steer the guys out of the room.

"You work with a fun group of guys," Trent said when we were alone again.

"They're my brothers," I told him. "There's no one I would trust my life to more than those men."

"That gives me a lot of comfort," Trent told me. "Your guy, huh?"

"Moving too fast?"

"Not at all," Trent said. He started to rise on his toes to kiss me but stopped and gasped. "Oh."

All I could do was grin wickedly while imagining what was happening inside his body. His ass was tightening around the base of the plug, and the tip of it was nudging his prostate when he rose up.

"Oh, indeed. Do you want the pork, turkey, or beef brisket?"

"I think you know what I want," Trent countered.

"All in good time," I promised him.

"I'll take the turkey."

I gestured for Trent to sit down then smiled when he wiggled and fidgeted in his chair while sweat beaded on his forehead and upper lip. "Too much?"

"Not enough," he whispered hoarsely. "What time are you getting off?"

"About two strokes after you do."

Trent snorted. "I'm serious here."

"So am I." I took pity on him and said, "My shift ends at eleven, but I don't plan on getting off until a few strokes after midnight."

"I'll die."

"I'll revive you." I waggled my brows.

We dropped the innuendo long enough to eat our food. My

cease-fire ended when I walked Trent to his car and pinned him to the driver side door before devouring his mouth. Trent fisted one hand in my hair and the other in the back of my uniform shirt.

"Don't come," I whispered when we broke apart. Knowing Trent's car shielded us from prying eyes, I reached around and gave the base of the plug a little nudge. "Wait for me."

I released him and started walking backward. "Drive carefully, Doc."

"See you soon, Sparky."

As luck would have it, Trent said it just as Will walked out a door on the side of the building.

"Sparky?" Will asked. He turned around and headed right back inside the firehouse. "You guys, Tucker has a brand-new nickname."

"You did that on purpose, didn't you?"

"No, but it seems like an adequate payback after the mean stunt you just pulled. Are you going to retaliate?" He looked hopeful.

"I guess you'll just have to wait and see."

CHAPTER TEN

Trent

I WAS AS NERVOUS AS A VIRGIN AND AS NEEDY AS A COCK ADDICT. TIME seemed to crawl by as I waited for Tucker's shift to end. I groomed myself and showered with the gel Tucker loved so much, but it didn't distract me from the ache of my arousal. I eventually adapted to the plug's presence and wasn't on the verge of orgasm every two seconds when I moved, but I craved more.

At ten forty-five, I sent Tuck a text. *I left a key for you in the mailbox by the door. You'll find me waiting for you upstairs in the second room on the right. Don't be late.*

His reply came quickly. *Damn, you make my dick hard.*

I set the scene in my room by dimming the lights then stacked two pillows in the center of the bed and set a strip of magnum-sized condoms and a bottle of lube beside them. I pulled a pale blue jock strap in place then crawled onto the bed and lay across the pillows so my ass was in the air and hopefully the first thing Tucker noticed when he walked through my bedroom door. I should've felt silly literally showing my ass, but I knew how obsessed he was with it.

My front door opened two minutes after eleven. I heard Tuck speaking softly to the cats before his heavy footfalls sounded on the steps. My heart raced with anticipation of his reaction. Would he think I was too forward? Would he—

The bedroom door softly creaked when Tucker opened it, cutting off my inner ramblings. He growled hungrily then closed the door behind him. I heard him removing his shoes, their thud against the floor sending shivers down my spine. I wanted to look over my shoulder to see the expression on Tucker's face as he finished undressing, but I remained where I was, excitement humming through my body, making my muscles quiver beneath my skin. I wanted to wriggle, fidget, and rut against the pillow when Tuck's sure, purposeful strides echoed in the room, yet I remained still.

The bed dipped beneath his weight as Tucker climbed onto it. The only sound he made was a raspy moan when he placed his hands on the back of my thighs. Tucker slid his hands up impossibly slow until he reached the elastic straps of my jock. He slid a finger beneath the band on both legs then let them snap back against my skin.

"Unh," I groaned.

Tucker's hands spread my legs apart wider so he could fit his thick thighs between mine, then he moved his hands to grip my ass.

"Please," I begged, rutting my hips against the pillow.

Instead of pulling the plug out and making me his, Tuck slid his strong hands over my hips and waist and inched them up until he reached my shoulders. Then he leaned over me, pressing his hard dick against my spread cheeks and resting his lips against my ear. "I'm going to wreck you in all the best possible ways."

I pushed my ass back against him, which shoved the plug against my prostate. "Tucker, please."

"Not yet, Doc. I have so many things I'm going to do to you before I let you come."

"I need you."

"You'll have me."

He moved his mouth to the base of my neck and bit down gently. I squirmed beneath Tucker's weight but settled when he began licking a path down my spine as he lowered himself until my thighs bracketed his shoulders and my ass was right in his face.

"Fuck me. You smell out of this world."

He licked along the crack of my ass until he reached the base of the plug. He circled his tongue around my stretched opening, soothing and igniting nerves at the same time. Above him, I grunted and rutted against the pillows, seeking friction against my dick.

Tuck reached between my spread thighs and released my cock and balls from their confines. I moaned loudly, and he chuckled against my ass cheek before he bit it.

"Stroke me. Please."

"I like letting you think you're in charge," Tucker whispered against my ass as he trailed kisses all over both cheeks.

He stroked my cock a few times, and I felt precum trickling from my slit, coating his fingers. Trent repositioned my dick so it was aiming down and no longer pinned between my stomach and the pillows. My cock pulsed in his palm as he teased the sensitive frenulum with the tip of his tongue before licking up the length of my cock until he reached my taut sac.

"Suck my balls. I need your mouth on me," I pleaded.

Tuck sucked one firm nut in his mouth then the other before he introduced his tongue to my taint. I bucked against his face, trying to get his mouth where I wanted him the most. The problem was I didn't know where that was—on my cock, balls, or his tongue teasing my ass? As if Tucker knew it, he started all over again with my cock, ignoring the pulsing hole which made the plug jiggle and dance for him.

"Tuck!" I roared after he'd licked my cock, sucked my balls, and teased my taint a dozen times. I reached back and fisted Tucker's hair to show him I meant business. "Take the plug out and either eat my ass or fuck it."

"I love how you flip from a needy, greedy cock slut to one who demands I pleasure him." Tuck gripped the base of the plug, but instead of pulling it out, he twisted and pushed it to press against my prostate.

"I'm going to come," I said. "I swear to God I will."

Tuck gently pulled the plug out as I whimpered. "Your pucker is nice and stretched, but it won't be enough to take my dick yet." He ran his thumb around my crinkled entrance, dipped it inside, and then replaced his thumb with his tongue.

"Fuck! Oh fuck!"

Tuck worked his tongue in and out of me until I was a quivering mess then reached for the lube I'd laid on the bed. I turned and watched over my shoulder as he oiled up three fingers. I whimpered with lust, pulling Tucker's eyes up to meet mine. Our gazes remained locked when he gently pushed them inside my hole, stretching me even farther. Tucker rested his free hand on my lower back, and the weight of it comforted me.

"Still with me, baby, or is it too much?"

"Don't you dare stop until your monster cock is buried inside me. Do you hear me?"

"Yes, sir."

In. Out. In. Twist. Repeat.

"Fuck me now, Tuck. Don't make me wait any more."

He slowly removed his fingers from my ass and rolled the condom down his dick until it was snugly secured around the base.

"I'm wet enough," I protested when Tucker reached for the bottle of lube.

"Not nearly enough," Tuck countered, unwilling to skip this step. "You might think you want me rutting inside you like a beast, but you would regret it later. I refuse to hurt you. Let me do this right."

"Okay," I said. Tucker laughed at the sulkiness in my voice.

"Tantrums earn spankings in my world."

"In that case." I bucked against the pillow a bit. "I want your cock, and I want it now." *Smack.* Tucker's hand came down firmly on my right ass cheek. "Gah." It stung for a few seconds then a delicious heat spread from where his palm landed. "I regret not buying those cute little paddles Kim has by the register. They have fun little messages cut in the leather like 'naughty' and 'bad boy' to leave an imprint on your ass. There was even one with a row of hearts," I said over my shoulder. "You could mark me."

"I could also sink my teeth in your ass. It would last longer."

"Do it." I had no idea what it was about Tucker that made me cast aside all inhibitions, but I liked it. I could tell he did too.

The mattress shifted as Tucker lowered himself on the bed, then I felt his hot breath against my left ass cheek. "I spanked the right, so I'll bite the left." Tucker sank his teeth into my flesh. I gasped and moaned, bucking beneath him. He released my flesh then studied his handiwork. "So sexy."

I looked over my shoulder again, wishing I could see the red mark he'd left behind. Thank God for whoever invented mirrors. "Fuck me now." I didn't beg; I demanded.

Rising up between my legs, Tuck grabbed the base of his dick and lined the broad head up against my hole. His free hand returned to the small of my back to hold me down, comfort me, or maybe both. Whatever the reason, I loved having his hand there.

"Relax for me," Tuck whispered when he pushed the crown inside me.

"Oh God," I moaned, turning my head back around to rest it on my forearm. I'd never been stretched so far. "Damn, baby, you do have a moose-sized dick." I'd had his monster cock in my mouth and throat and knew it only got thicker toward the base.

Tuck stilled his hips. "Do you want me to stop?"

"Fuck no," I growled. "Just go slow. Okay?" I could feel my erection softening as the pressure and burn took the edge off my arousal. "I want you bad."

"If it gets to be too much, all you have to do is tell me to stop, and I will. I won't betray your trust." The strain in his voice was a testament to how much it cost him to hold back. I felt his dick eagerly pulsing inside me.

"I trust you. Give me a little more."

Tucker eased in another inch or two then stopped again for a few seconds before pulling back until only his head remained inside me. He slowly pushed forward again, eliciting a moan when his fat head nudged my prostate.

"I just saw stars behind my eyelids. Give me more."

Tucker slowly rocked in and out, pushing farther inside me with each inward stroke until his groin pressed firmly against my ass. By then, my dick was fully hard again and leaking from excitement. "Ready?"

I answered by pushing my ass against him. "I was made for your cock. Don't hold back."

Tucker didn't fuck me mercilessly into the pillow as I'd encouraged. He took his time shuttling in and out, drawing out my pleasure until I was nearly in tears.

"Please. Touch my cock. Peg my prostate. Do both. I need to come."

"All in good time, Doc," Tucker teased.

"Pin me down with your big body and fuck me." I wasn't willing to concede control. "I want to feel you for days."

"Doc," he said in a warning tone, but he laid his bulk over my back. He reached beneath me and shifted my cock so it was once again pinned between the pillow and my abdomen. Then he took my hands and wrapped them around the wooden slats in my headboard and threaded his fingers through mine. My heart thundered in my chest as he slowly pulled his dick out of me. My body trembled as I waited for him to slam back home. Tucker snapped his hips forward, filling me up and making me scream out in pleasure. "Your neighbors are going to hear you," Tuck whispered in my ear.

"I don't care. Do it again. Fuck me hard." Tucker repeated his slow retreat and fast re-entry. "Faster. Harder."

Tucker gave me what I demanded, fucking me hard and fast. The slapping of our flesh echoed around my room along with my shouts of pleasure and encouragement. *Jesus!* I'd never been manhandled and mastered like this, and I couldn't get enough. The friction of my cock against the pillow just elevated my pleasure until my eyes rolled back in my head and I became incapable of forming coherent words.

"I love making you grunt for my big cock," Tucker said, his voice raw and rough. "Come for me, baby. Let your sweet ass milk my orgasm from me."

"I-I-I'm g-g-gonna…come."

"Hell yes, you are." Tuck shifted on his knees and aimed his cock directly at my prostate where before he'd only grazed it with each forward and backward stroke. "Give it to me."

"Tuck!" I shouted as the most powerful orgasm I'd ever experienced ravaged my body. My vision grew dark, and my cock kept spurting my release onto the pillow as Tucker chased his orgasm.

"Fuck yes," he roared, punching his hips forward in short, jerky movements. "Take all of me. Your ass is squeezing me so tight." Tucker grunted when he came deep inside me. I'd never once resented the barrier a condom created until then. "Is my weight too much?"

Even with his oxygen levels depleted, Tucker's first concern was my comfort. He was such a gentle giant, and it only made me want him more.

"You're perfect," I said drowsily. "Absolutely perfect."

I started to drift to sleep until Tucker rose and eased out of my body. He gently massaged my pucker, and the stimulation soothed me and encouraged the muscles to contract, closing my hole. "If you roll over, I'll help clean you up."

"Don't you dare think about sneaking off once I fall asleep, Tucker Garrison."

"You want me to stay?"

I rolled off the pillow onto my back so I could see his face. "Hell yes."

A gentle smile slowly spread across his face. "Okay." The conversation was in direct contrast to the heated dirty talk we exchanged during sex. I liked the dichotomy.

Tucker eased off the bed and walked into my bathroom to presumably remove the condom and clean up. I wasn't at all surprised when he returned to my room with a warm washcloth, but he did catch me off guard when he rejected my attempt to take it from him. I lay there watching his handsome face with his flushed cheeks, swollen mouth, and glittery, intense eyes while he tenderly washed my cum away. It was the nicest thing any lover had ever done for me, and coming from Tucker, it meant more to me than maybe it should. The part of me that was afraid to hope warned this was the same man who turned cold after our first date, but the rational part of me knew we'd moved past his initial fears.

"Just set it on the nightstand," I said when he finished. "I'm about to crash, and I want to do it in your arms."

Tucker tossed the cloth onto the table then removed the extra pillows from the bed too. At least they were spares I kept in the linen closet in case I ever had guests, so neither Tuck nor I had to worry about sleeping on the cum-soaked pillow. I'd already stripped the duvet and top sheet before Tucker arrived, so I only had to roll over to my usual spot to make room for him beside me.

Once he was settled on his back, I scooted over next to him and rested my head on his chest. I loved feeling Tuck's chest hair against my cheek and smelling his masculine scent. "Is this okay?" I asked.

"No," Tucker replied. I started to pull away, but his hand on my waist kept me tight against him. He reached across his body to grip the back of my thigh then pulled my leg up and over his pelvis. "Much better," he whispered, content and sated, before drifting to sleep.

I kissed his chest and allowed the steady rhythm of his heartbeat to pull me into sleep after him.

Tucker

AWARENESS CAME TO ME SLOWLY RATHER THAN A BIG TAH-DAH! FIRST, I noticed the pillow beneath my head wasn't as firm as mine; then, I noticed the sheets were a whole lot softer than the ones on my bed, and they smelled like Trent. A smile stretched across my face before I even opened my eyes as I recalled the things we got up to in those sheets. *Damn, the man will be the death of me.* The next thing I became aware of was a soft weight on my chest that purred.

I cracked open one eye and found Boris curled up sleeping on my chest. Gone was the rusty, unused purr from adoption day, and in its place was the melodic sounds of a well-loved feline. Softer sounds of contentment came from my left ear, so I turned my head and found Natasha curled up on my pillow. Beyond her, Trent's side of the bed was empty, and it dimmed my happiness until I smelled bacon.

I gently maneuvered Boris off my chest and padded across the floor to Trent's bathroom to relieve myself so I could follow the aroma of sizzling meat to find my sizzling man.

"Tone it down," I whispered to myself. "Don't be too kitschy or you'll run him off."

Once I finished, I noticed a brand-new toothbrush still in its package with a note beside it on the counter.

There was a buy-one-get-one-free sale at the store. I don't stock up for potential overnight guests, and I didn't make assumptions that you'd stay over. I hoped but... Fuck! I'm rambling. Who rambles in a note then leaves it for someone to find instead of tearing it up and starting over? I guess I want you to see the real me. Yeah, I'm nervous you might be regretting last night. I hope not, but I promise not to make things difficult for you if you do.

I chuckled the entire time I brushed my teeth. Trent might think his rambling was embarrassing, but I found it endearing. Trent seemed so poised, polished, and calm all the time, so I loved seeing these other sides of him. In bed... Oh my God. The man was hot enough to warrant a combustion warning label.

Boris and Natasha were waiting for me on the bed when I exited the bathroom. I scratched under their chins and behind their ears to great them with a proper good morning. Boris jumped down and I picked up Natasha to carry her down the stairs to find her human. I set her down once we reached the first floor, and she scampered off toward her kitty cat jungle while I hurried toward the kitchen, eager to claim proper good morning of my own. I froze in the doorway, mesmerized by the sexy view.

Trent's sweats hung low on his hips, allowing me to see the tops of the dimples dotting both ass cheeks. I wanted to drag him back to his bedroom and spend a lot of time with my tongue inside those divots. He was shirtless but wore an apron around his neck and tied at his lower back. I'd never found feet sexy before I met him. I'd noticed them at the pool party and imagined holding them in my hands and massaging the arch, making him moan with pleasure.

A voice inside the kitchen yanked me out of my lustful daze. "And what about the guy out in California," a man said.

"Which one?" a female asked. Then she started singing the chorus of "It's Raining Men."

I looked around the kitchen and didn't see a television or radio, which meant he was playing something on his phone: a video, show, or podcast. Trent laughed when the guy joined the lady in singing the song.

"Jill, we're a little fucked in the head," the man said once they stopped laughing.

"You're just now figuring that out, Jack?"

Jack and Jill. How cute. Who the hell were they, and why was Trent so obviously enthralled with them? He set the spatula down and shifted a pan of something off the burner.

"We're discussing gruesome true crime stories one minute and busting out into song the next," the guy named Jack said. "Do you think we could get a discount if we both started seeing a therapist?"

"Like a buy-one-get-one-free deal?" Jill asked him.

"They could at least knock off twenty-five percent. We're fucked up, and they're set to make a ton of money from it."

"My family said there's no help for me," Jill told Jack. "I've accepted and embraced my weirdness."

"That's the spirit," Jack said jovially. "I'll try to do the same as I pivot from our depravity to that of another."

"Oh, the guy in California you mentioned."

"Yes, him," Jack said. "They call him Mr. Perfect because everything about him is…"

"Perfect?" Jill asked.

"Yes. You're smart *and* deviant. No wonder you're obsessed with serial killers."

"Jack, dear, sip this coffee I made for you," Jill said in a saccharine-sweet voice. "I'm trying out a new creamer, so just ignore the suspicious aftertaste." I could imagine the woman was waggling her brows as she laughed wickedly.

"Very funny," Jack said then noisily slurped his coffee. "Mr. Perfect is believed to have killed two women and three men so far."

"Ah, an equal opportunity serial killer. Do these victims have anything in common?"

Trent was completely fascinated by the conversation as he placed four pieces of bread in the toaster and pushed the lever to begin toasting them. I found their chatter interesting also, but I was more intrigued by the doc's interest. I leaned against the arched doorway and settled in to observe him for as long as I could.

"They're all brunettes, and they all use the same dating website," Jack told Jill.

"Is it a dating or hookup site?" she countered. "There is a difference."

"The articles I read referred to it as a dating site, but it might be more out of respect to the victims' families. The site isn't one I've ever heard of before, so I imagine the police are looking hard at the developer since none of the victims were matched to the same person."

"Unless the killer deleted his profile from their history somehow. Maybe he deleted the notifications and any private chats between him and the victims on their phones."

"Damn, girl. You are devious."

Jill laughed. "I'm just thinking beyond the obvious. Still, the company would most likely have a record of any matches on their end, even if the notifications were somehow deleted from their accounts. I'm sure the cops are obtaining the appropriate warrants to get their hands on those details. So, what does Mr. Perfect do with his victims?"

"Well, he gets his victims to trust him enough to invite him into their homes for dinner. It would appear he drugs them, sexually assaults them, and then strangles them with an item of their clothing."

"Sick bastard," Trent said vehemently. Of course, Jack and Jill couldn't hear his remarks since he was listening to a recorded broadcast. It reminded me of the numerous times Grammie gave me the evil eye for yelling at a referee while watching a game on TV. They couldn't hear me, but I sure felt better. "Not very original either," Trent added, earning a raised brow from me. Maybe I should've been hightailing it out of there, but I was rooted to the spot. I'd take my chances that Trent Love wasn't a serial killer in the making.

"Yikes," Jill said, all traces of humor fading from her voice. "He must be a really smooth talker to earn their trust. Who invites a virtual stranger into their home these days? I assume we're using masculine pronouns because he leaves behind semen or something."

"Actually, he leaves behind no trace evidence at all. We call him Mr. Perfect because it's what he calls himself."

"Calls himself that how?" Jill asked. *Yeah, how?*

"There's always a flower bouquet found in the center of the table with a card addressed to the victim and signed by Mr. Perfect."

"Interesting," Jill and Trent said at the same time.

"They need to track down the florist," Trent said. Jill echoed his thoughts a heartbeat later. I bit my lip to keep from laughing.

"Is there anything else consistent at each crime scene besides the flowers and method of killing?" Jill asked.

Trent walked closer to where his phone lay on the kitchen counter. "Oh, that's an excellent point. I wonder how he's drugging them. Wine!" Trent blurted loudly. "I bet he brings them flowers and a bottle of wine. He probably injects the drug into the wine by sticking a syringe through the cork. It's tainted when he arrives. He just doesn't drink the wine."

"Authorities have found a bottle of merlot at each scene, but it's not the same brand or vintage," Jack told Jill.

"Aha! I knew it."

"That means he's probably not using the same florist either," Jill said absently. "Hmm. What about the meals? Are the victims serving the same meal?"

"That could be a clue right there, if so," Trent said, nodding.

The toaster popped the slices of toast up, and Trent gasped and covered his chest.

"Did you think Mr. Perfect had you?" I asked from the doorway.

"Oh fuck! How long have you been standing there?" Trent asked, whirling around to face me. A pink flush bloomed across his chest and spread up his neck toward his face.

"Long enough to know you're fucking adorable," I said, straightening to my full height and crossing the room. "Every time I think I have you figured out…"

"I manage to surprise you again?" he asked hopefully.

"Absolutely."

"Is that a good thing?"

"So far," I said, "it's a wonderful thing."

"You don't think my addiction to true crime podcasts makes me weird?" Trent asked then worried his bottom lip between his teeth.

I gripped his chin, and he released his lip. Leaning forward, I licked the pouty flesh then captured his mouth in a molten kiss hot enough to make him melt against me. "I think your passion for true crime is another way you'll bond with my grandmother. She hasn't discovered podcasts yet, but she worships the ID channel like it's her religion."

"I'd love to introduce her to some of my favorite podcasts if you think she'd be open to it," Trent said.

"I think it's a great idea. Can I request one thing?"

"Sure," Trent said, nodding.

"No discussing grisly crimes during mealtime."

"I promise." Trent rose on his tiptoes and kissed me quickly before pulling out of my arms. "Are you hungry? I woke up full of energy this morning and cooking and baking is my outlet if I'm not working out."

"Baking?"

Trent nodded. "Are you a fan of baked goods?"

"Does my cock fit your ass perfectly?"

"Yes," he said breathlessly. Trent's eyes began to glaze over as his mind ventured away from food and back to his bedroom where we shared the most explosive sex I'd ever had. The reality of Trent Love far surpassed the fantasy of him. "If memory serves me correctly, you had three orgasms last week and managed to win. So far, I've only given you one."

"One orgasm with you is more powerful than ten solo ones."

"*Just* ten?"

"Possibly a dozen," I amended.

"I didn't do any baking this morning, but I made bacon, scrambled eggs, hash browns, and toast. All of which is getting cold because I got sucked into the podcast, and then you kissed my face off."

"I'd rather share a cold breakfast with you than a hot one with anyone else."

"Aww. You're so sweet," Trent said. "Will there be time to fool around before we need to leave for your basketball game?"

"I bet we could manage."

We managed to shovel our food in like we hadn't eaten in days before hustling upstairs to his bathroom. Podcasts, Mr. Perfect, and every other thought faded away when we took turns sucking each other off. Trent wanted my dick inside him again, but I knew he'd regret it once he had to sit on those hard bleachers when my game started. He settled for my middle finger and shouted when he came down my throat. Then we swapped positions, and Trent made my legs go weak from the eager blow job he gave me. I couldn't care less about my performance on the court right then.

"I want to bottom for you," I said afterward.

"Now you tell me," Trent teased. "I would love to take your ass for a drive."

I quirked a brow. "I think I tried to use that as a pickup line once."

Trent laughed and rested his forehead against my shoulder. "It was a bad line, wasn't it?"

"It's slightly better than 'Honey, your ass is prettier than a new set of snow tires,' but not by much."

"Now you're just being mean," Trent said, tightening his arms around my waist. The humor in his voice let me know he wasn't remotely upset. "I'm extra sorry I didn't buy the 'naughty boy' paddle."

"The day is still young."

"I don't know, Sparky. There's something wrong about shopping for sex toys before going to your grandmother's house for dinner."

"You shouldn't feel that way," I told him. "Grammie has a Kinky Kim's rewards card."

"Seriously?"

"Grammie is adamant that age is only a number and a person is never too old to enjoy great sex."

"I meant the part about the rewards card. Why wasn't I offered one?" Trent asked.

"You're supposed to be shocked that my grandmother shops at an adult toy store."

"Why in the world would I be shocked by that? What about your grandmother screams she's a conventional woman?"

I narrowed my eyes because he was accepting the news too easily. Not a hard shiver or a stunned gasp anywhere in sight. "You've run into her there, haven't you?"

"Once or twice," Trent admitted.

After our shower, we cuddled on his sofa with the cats and finished listening to the Jack and Jill podcast I interrupted.

"Do they have several episodes?" I asked.

"This is their third season, so there are dozens of episodes for you to listen to." Trent nestled tighter against me. "They're interesting, aren't they?"

"They really are," I admitted. I'd never been intrigued by the inner workings of a serial killer's mind, but Jack and Jill, or maybe it was the sexy man in my arms, had me viewing things differently. "I like the contrast between the serious subjects they discuss and the humor they inject. It sounds inappropriate for there to be humor included in their episodes, but it works."

"It's because they're not aiming the humor at the victims or investigators and they're not mocking the killers. Their humor is directed at themselves and their fascination with the macabre."

"I'm a person who can appreciate contrast," I said. "Take you for instance."

"What about me?" Trent asked, propping himself on his elbow so he could look into my eyes.

"You're full of contradictions."

"Name one," he challenged.

"We'll start with your home."

"What's wrong with my home?" Trent asked, sounding affronted.

I rolled my eyes. "Lower your fur, hellcat. I'm not insulting you." I nuzzled my nose against his neck until he relaxed. "Your home is a beautiful mix of old and new and bold and subtle. You pair traditional stained hardwood floor with modern furniture. The wall colors are either bold with classic art hanging on them or subtle paint colors with bold abstract art."

"I'm eclectic," Trent said.

"And I like it. I love that you have an antique grandfather clock that looks about one hundred years old in one corner of the living room and a metal butterfly and flower sculpture hanging on a wall near it. My home is boring in comparison."

"Your home is warm and inviting just like you. There's something I've been dying to do since the first time I was there," Trent said huskily.

"Oh yeah?" I asked.

"Tuck, how many dates do we have to go on before you let me finger your...books."

"What?"

"I've wanted to trail my fingers over their spines and spend hours perusing them. I have a feeling I'll get to know a lot about you by looking at the books you've chosen to read."

"Doc, I'll let you finger anything you want."

"We need to change the subject before I get turned on again," Trent whispered.

"We definitely won't have time for round three before we need to leave."

"Is that a challenge?" Trent asked, repositioning his body so he could lie on top of me. "I see I'm not the only one with *big* ideas. How long has it been since you bottomed?" Trent asked me.

I only blinked at him, stunned by the sudden change of topic.

"Oh, wow," he said, correctly guessing the truth. "Not even a toy?"

I shook my head.

"Is it because you've never wanted to bottom before?"

"No," I said. "I've always had the urge, but I guess, based on my size, people always assumed I wanted to top."

"So, unlike my cherry-ish hole, yours is truly a virgin hole."

"Yes."

Trent released a half-moan-half-whimper sound. "Are you sure the team needs you at the basketball game?"

"It's not likely they will win without me," I said, realizing I sounded like an arrogant jock.

"Winning is that big of a deal to them?"

I nodded.

"On a scale of one to ten, with one being mildly annoyed and ten meaning they'd tie a knot in your oxygen hose, how mad will they be if you skip the game?"

"Twelve."

"We can't have that," Trent said, shifting his body back to lie beside mine. "Besides, I'll want a lot of time to make your first time special. Want to listen to another podcast to take our mind off our libidos?"

"It should do the trick."

"I'll take you back to the very first one where they discuss Jack the Ripper."

"Yep. All thoughts of sex have fled my mind," I said, but it was more than okay with me.

Trent wasn't a hookup or a means to get off. I wanted to learn everything about him and open myself up to him in ways I never had with anyone else, and I didn't just mean my cherry hole. I didn't want to spend all my time holding him at arm's length while worrying how it would feel if he decided to walk away; I wanted to hold him in my arms and focus on the joy he'd brought into my life.

Whoa.

"What?" Trent asked, lifting his head to look at me. I hadn't realized I vocalized my surprise from my revelation. "Is everything okay?"

"Better than okay, Doc."

Trent studied me for a few seconds while waiting for me to say more but returned his head to my chest when I just continued smiling like a giant dork.

So much better than okay.

CHAPTER TWELVE

Trent

"**W**HY DO YOU LOOK NERVOUS?" TUCKER ASKED WHEN HE turned off his truck.

"I look nervous because I *am* nervous."

Tuck looked surprised. "Why? Are you seriously worried my friends won't like you?"

"Why wouldn't I be worried?"

"What's not to like about you? You're kind, funny, and smart."

It wasn't like me to feel so insecure about my position in a man's life, but then again, I hadn't cared enough in the past to worry about it. With Tuck, I cared. I cared a whole fucking lot. "You didn't say anything about my looks," I teased, trying to lighten the mood.

"Your looks won't matter to them," Tucker told me. "Besides, Grammie loves you. They'll see it and trust her instincts."

"Okay."

"You don't sound sure."

"These people aren't just your friends," I told him. "You referred to them as your brothers, so their wives or significant others are your family too."

"Trent, would it change how you feel about me if your family didn't like me?"

"Of course not." The probability of my parents liking Tucker was slim. Mercedes would love him once she saw his inner beauty was even more impressive than his looks and hot body, and that was all that mattered to me. Even if Mercedes didn't approve, it wouldn't change how I felt about Tucker.

"I feel the same way, but I also know it's nothing you have to worry about. They're going to love you."

I nodded, feeling better. "Let's do this."

I squared my shoulders and held my head high when we entered the gymnasium. I was proud to be on this man's arm. Well, he had his hand at the small of my back, but it was the same principle. He'd marked me as his with the placement of his hand there because it was as intimate as holding hands in my book.

Many of the guys I'd seen at the firehouse were already there wearing their uniform. We swung by Tuck's place for him to change and grab his gym bag. His brothers smiled when they saw the two of us together, and a group of women, who I assumed were their wives or girlfriends, advanced on us.

"Brace yourself," Tucker whispered dramatically.

"Well, looks like someone has been holding out on us," a tall brunette said.

"Trent, this is Elizabeth Turner. She's married to our captain, Will."

I just blinked. Will and Elizabeth Turner. *It's too soon to joke. It's too soon to joke.*

"It's okay," she said with a knowing smile as she shook my hand.

"I'm used to the jokes that come from having the same names as two of the main characters in the *Pirates of the Caribbean* movies."

"I don't know what you're talking about," I said innocently.

"Keep him," Elizabeth mock-whispered to Tucker.

"It's nice to see you when I don't have crying, sick kids, Dr. Love," Hailey said. "I don't believe you've met Braxton yet."

"I actually met him last night when I brought dinner to the firehouse," I told her.

"How interesting," Hailey said, shifting her attention to center court where the guys were watching our introductions. "He didn't mention it to me." Braxton casually shrugged when Hailey looked at him with a quirked brow. "I guess he figured it wasn't his story to tell."

"That's never stopped them before," a stunning, curvy redhead said. "My name is Jillian, but my friends and family call me Jilly. Donovan and I don't have any children yet, which is probably why we haven't met. We're still newlyweds."

"Newlyweds?" a petite blonde asked. "You've been married for two years."

"I'll consider us newlyweds until we reach our fifth anniversary, or so I'm telling our parents who ask us weekly when we're going to get pregnant. 'We're' is the key word here." She used air quotes for emphasis.

"Like Van will experience half of the morning sickness, swollen feet, and stretch marks," Elizabeth joked.

"He would if he could," Jillian said wistfully, smiling at her husband. "Maybe I'm selfish to wait." Then she turned to look at me and said, "What do you think? Am I selfish?"

Um… Here was my chance to either impress them or blow it. "If you're not ready to become a mother, then I don't think you're being selfish."

"Really?" Jilly asked hopefully.

"You'll know when you're ready. And Elizabeth is right; Van can want to share the side effects of pregnancy with you, but he can't. Is Van upset you're not pregnant yet?"

"No," she said, shaking her head. "We're enjoying our vacations and making memories as a couple before we expand our family."

"It doesn't matter what anyone else thinks."

Jilly's eyes watered, and she seemed to be too choked up to speak. Elizabeth hooked her arm around Jilly's shoulders and kissed her temple before smiling at me.

"We like you," Elizabeth proclaimed like she was speaking for the group. The rest of the ladies nodded in agreement.

"Yo, Moose! Are you going to get changed and warm up or are you going to gossip with our wives all day long?" Braxton hollered from the court.

I was relieved he hadn't called him Sparky, but I thought he was probably biding his time for the right moment.

"I'm coming," Tucker yelled back. Then he kissed me full on the lips with everyone watching. "Ladies, be good to my guy." Tucker winked at me then jogged toward the locker room. I noticed Braxton broke away from the group and followed him, wearing a huge grin on his face.

"Oh, wow," Elizabeth said. "It's about damn time." I looked at her curiously. "Surely you see the way he looks at you. He's crazy about you. It's so damn adorable."

"I…"

"Leave him alone," Jilly chided Elizabeth. "It's amazing he hasn't run for the door after I put him on the spot after just meeting me. I'm so sorry," she said. "I don't know what's come over me. My hormones are all over the place lately, and I'm so tired all the time."

"Let's have a seat, shall we?" I asked, gesturing toward the bleachers.

Jilly and I followed Elizabeth and Hailey to the bleachers. We made it to the fourth step before Jilly started to sway a bit. I gently grabbed her in case she started to fall.

"Whoa," Jilly whispered. "That's the second dizzy spell I've had today. I must have an inner ear thing going on."

Hearing Jilly's soft gasp, Elizabeth and Hailey turned around on the steps and rejoined us.

"Are you okay?" Elizabeth asked.

"Did you nearly pass out on the steps?" Hailey questioned.

"No," Jilly said, shaking her head. "I just got a little dizzy." She looked at me and added, "Thanks for supporting me in case I did fall."

"No problem." Based on the two symptoms she mentioned and the one I witnessed firsthand, I was pretty certain of her diagnosis.

"Let's sit down here," I said, gesturing to the empty bench. "You don't need to be climbing steps with dizzy spells."

"Spells?" Elizabeth asked

"As in more than one?" Hailey followed.

Elizabeth and Hailey looked at each other and grinned.

"Raging hormones," Elizabeth said.

"Exhaustion and dizziness," Hailey added.

"Any nausea?" I asked.

"A little," Jilly answered. A slow smile spread across her face. "Are you thinking what I'm thinking?" she asked the group.

"We think you're pregnant," Elizabeth told her.

Jilly looked at me and asked, "You do?"

"Based on these symptoms, it would be my educated guess. There's one way to take the guesswork out of it."

"I'll take a test when I get back home," Jilly whispered, looking and sounding dazed.

"You have tests already at home?" Elizabeth asked. "I didn't think you guys wanted to have kids for a few more years. Surely those tests have a shelf life."

"Um," Jilly said, voice breaking. "I haven't been completely honest with you. Van and I have been trying to get pregnant for the past ten months, but nothing was happening. We've been telling people we weren't ready because we didn't want to talk about our failed attempts. If we didn't discuss it, then it wouldn't be real. Van and I told ourselves not to worry about it and said we'd enjoy our freedom until it did happen, but we haven't taken measures to prevent a pregnancy. I honestly accepted it wouldn't happen without help from a specialist. I'm so afraid to hope right now."

"Oh, sweetie," Elizabeth said, wrapping Jilly in a gentle hug, allowing her friend to cry quietly against her shoulder. I scooted over so Hailey could join in and make it a group hug amongst the three friends.

Donovan glanced up from stretching his hamstrings just then, and a look of worry crossed his face when he saw them huddled around his wife. He straightened up and jogged up into the bleachers.

"Babe, what's wrong?" he asked nervously.

Elizabeth and Hailey lowered their arms from around Jilly and moved over to sit beside me, allowing Donovan to crouch down in front of his wife.

"I have some big news, but I'm not sure this is the place to tell you," Jilly told him. The smile she aimed at her husband smoothed out his furrowed brow.

By the look on his face, he knew what the news was. "Are you sure?" Donovan asked, beaming at his wife.

"Not until I confirm it with a test, but…"

"Come on," he said, standing up. "Let's go home."

"What? No. We can't leave now. You have a game to play," Jilly told him.

"You're more important to me."

"I know, babe, but this isn't an emergency. Nothing will change in the next two hours. Go play with the boys, then we'll go home and take the test."

"I don't know, babe. I think you should go home and prop up your feet or something."

Elizabeth snorted, and Hailey giggled.

"We'll take good care of her," I assured him. If I had to sacrifice sexy time with Tucker, then Donovan could wait a few hours too.

"If you're sure…"

"Van," Tucker yelled from the court. "Are you going to gossip with the ladies and Trent, or are you going to play ball?"

"Go," Jilly said, shooing her husband away. "Everyone is staring at us."

"Are you sure?"

"Damn, Van, this will be the longest forty weeks of your life if you don't start listening to her," Elizabeth said dryly. "We got your girl. Go play ball."

Donovan leaned forward and kissed Jilly on the forehead then whispered something in her ear that made her laugh then cry. He wiped away her tears and kissed her once more before rejoining the guys. They gathered around him to make sure everything was okay, and he assured them everything was fine with fist bumps and bro hugs.

I was so caught up with Donovan and Jilly I hadn't noticed Tucker coming out of the locker room. *Damn, baby.* His basketball jersey showed off his big guns to perfection. I knew firsthand how strong his biceps and triceps were, but looking at them under the bright, fluorescent lighting, it was nearly impossible for me to think about anything else other than me wrapping my legs around his waist while his strong arms supported me against a wall so he could fuck me long and hard. I'd seen wall-fucking in porn but never experienced it for myself. Tucker's eyes met mine, and I started to fidget on the hard bench. *Oh.* The minor discomfort was a delicious reminder of having him inside me. *I can still feel you.*

Tuck's wicked grin broadcasted to me, and probably everyone else in the gym who happened to be looking at us, that he knew exactly what I was thinking. I had to fight the urge to wiggle more.

Luckily for me, a lavender-haired lady walked into the gym and pulled my attention away from deviant thoughts. Shirlene searched the bleachers for me then smiled and waved when she spotted me with the ladies. I rose to my feet when she reached us and accepted the hug she offered me.

"I'm so happy I skipped my garden club meeting to spend time with you and watch Tucker play basketball. Hello, girls," she said to the women. "It's so good to see you again." She hugged each of the women before taking a seat on my other side. "I should've asked if you have any food allergies when I invited you over for dinner."

"None that I'm aware of, and I've eaten some weird things during my travels overseas."

"I bet," Shirlene said. "Do you like Italian food? It's Tucker's favorite."

"Is it?" I asked, filing the information away for future use. Shirlene nodded. "I happen to love it too."

"Great. I was thinking about herb-crusted chicken cutlets and eggplant parmigiana. How does that sound?"

"Amazing. Would it be okay if I brought dessert? I have an amazing recipe for mini cheesecakes I can quickly whip up after the game."

"Cheesecake is Tucker's favorite dessert," Shirlene said with a smile. "It's not likely they will make it past your kitchen. Maybe if you cuff him to your bed."

"Shirlene," Elizabeth gasped. "I freaking love you."

Hailey and Jillian giggled and echoed Elizabeth's sentiment. "I love you girls too. I couldn't have chosen better wives for my boys. Now that Tucker is finally settled, I can turn my attention to Carl. He needs to meet a nice guy or gal." I loved how Shirlene thought Tucker and I were a foregone conclusion.

"Guy?" Hailey asked.

"Do you know something we don't?" Jillian asked.

"I don't think Shirlene is implying Carl is gay, pan, or bi," Elizabeth said. "She's just not making assumptions."

"That's right," Shirlene said. "Assumptions are hurtful, and they make a person look foolish."

One of the referees blew the whistle, signaling the game was about to start. Tucker and the guys huddled up around Will, whose expression was as serious as if they were about to battle a fire. I recalled my conversation with Tucker this morning and realized he wasn't exaggerating about their intensity. I looked at the expression on my guy's face, and it was every bit as intense as Will's. Gone was the affable, gentle giant, and in his place was a fierce competitor.

"Did Tucker warn you about his competitive streak?" Shirlene asked.

"No," I admitted.

She patted my knee. "You're in for a real treat then."

"We're playing the Goodville Grave Diggers today," Elizabeth said. "They're good, but we're better."

"Grave Diggers? As in they work at a cemetery?" I asked.

"As in they will 'bury their competition.' We'll just see about that," Hailey said.

"I recognize the look in Tucker's eyes," Shirlene said. "Those Grave Diggers will be limping out of here with their tails between their legs."

I had to bite my lip because I knew all about limping away from Tucker, but for a very different reason. Regardless of Shirlene's open mind, I planned to keep the little tidbit private.

Shirlene hadn't been joking. Tucker's fierceness when he lined up across from the other team's center for the jump ball stole my breath, or so I thought. I realized a small whimper must've escaped me when Shirlene snorted and patted my knee again.

The referee tossed the ball in the air, and Tucker convincingly batted it to Braxton, who was their point guard. The Flame Fighters dominated the Grave Diggers from the first whistle blow to the very last, easily beating them by double digits. Other than during sex, I'd never seen Tucker looking so sexy. His dark, wet hair was plastered to his head, highlighting his chiseled cheekbones, sweat glistened on his bulging muscles, and his eyes glittered with elation from conquering his opponent. And his cocky swagger... *Oh. My. God.* I found this side of Tucker was equally as delicious as his tender, nurturing side.

"Our Tucker put on quite a show for you today, Trent," Elizabeth said smugly.

"Oh, I doubt that." I wouldn't pretend it didn't thrill me deep inside to entertain the notion.

"Believe it," Shirlene said. "I haven't seen him play this well since high school."

"I agree," Hailey said.

"I think you should join us every weekend," Jilly added. "We often gather at one another's houses to eat and celebrate afterward. Tucker's not much for cooking, but he slays on the grill or smoker."

"He's not much for cooking yet," I corrected. "I suspect he has more hidden talents than any of us know." The ladies waggled their brows, deliberately misreading my remark.

After the teams exchanged high fives, the Flame Fighters huddled around each other again where they seemed to jab good-naturedly at one another. Tuck took most of the accolades and the teasing, but I could tell by the big grin on his face he was having a good time. Then he looked up and caught me watching them. Somehow, his smile got bigger and brighter.

"Whoa," Elizabeth said. "Colgate should feature him in their next campaign. All they need to do is hide you behind the camera where Tuck can see you."

"It's so sweet," Hailey said. "We've waited a long time for this."

"We sure have," Jillian added. "Let's go get our victory kisses."

We rose to our feet and headed down the steps. I wasn't sure if Tucker was going to plant a big kiss on my face in front of the opposing team and their fans. Some couples, regardless of their orientation or gender, just weren't into PDA. I held Jilly's hand to keep her steady because she was lightheaded when she stood up too quickly.

Donovan met us at the bottom of the steps and scooped his wife into his arms. "See you guys later," he called over his shoulder as he carried her toward the exit.

"I'm not sure whether to envy or pity the lavish treatment Jilly is about to receive," Elizabeth told Hailey.

"It could be adorable or suffocating," Hailey replied.

"She'll just need to speak her mind if it starts to feel overbearing," Shirlene added. "Van adores her, and he'll listen."

I didn't know the couple's dynamics enough to comment one way or the other, so I hugged all three ladies. "Shirlene, I will see you in a few hours. It was lovely getting to know you," I said to Hailey and Elizabeth. "I'll see you next weekend."

"You'll see me sooner than that because I'm bringing Tucker's godchildren in to see you for their annual checkups."

I didn't know Tucker was the godfather to Braxton and Hailey's sons. *Was it too soon to quote lines from the movies?* "I look forward to it," I told her.

Tucker broke away from the conversation he was having with players from both teams when he saw me walk away from the ladies. "How'd it go?" he asked.

"I had a great time. The ladies are wonderful and watching you play basketball is making me think naughty things. You were amazing out there, Sparky."

Tuck started to lean forward then must've changed his mind because he straightened up suddenly. "I'm gross and sweaty."

I leaned into him, and he lowered his head when I crooked my finger for him to come closer. "You're sexy, and I can't wait to get you back home. I thought of another fantasy I wanted to live out with you."

Tuck's eyebrow lifted. "Yeah?"

"I want a wall-banging good time."

"Jesus," Tucker whispered.

"Did you save any energy for me?"

Tucker growled softly in my ear. "Just let me towel off and change out of this uniform."

I wanted to protest, but Tucker stepped away and headed toward the locker room before I had a chance. I started to rejoin the ladies but stopped when my phone rang. I grimaced when I saw my mother was calling but knew ignoring her would only make things worse. I ducked out of the gym and answered once I was in the hallway.

"Hello, Mother."

"How are you, Trent?"

"I'm doing great. I'm going to have dinner with Tucker and his family in a little while." I'd exchanged warmer conversation with total strangers at a basketball game than I did with my own mother. I was beyond feeling sadness over it though.

"How quaint and ironic since I was calling to invite you and your *Tucker* to dinner at the country club Saturday evening." I hated the way she said Tucker's name, and I regretted even mentioning him to her.

"Tucker works a lot of weekends, so I can't make any promises."

"Hmm," Mother hummed. "Is that the truth, or are you only delaying the inevitable?"

"I'm telling the truth. I have no reason to lie."

"I hear the hesitation in your voice. Is there another reason why you don't want to introduce us to him? Are you ashamed of him? Or perhaps he's just a fling and doesn't warrant an introduction to your family."

Fury raced through my blood. "Listen to me well, Mother. I'm not ashamed of Tucker, and he's not just a fling. I'm actually ashamed of you and Father."

"What?" she asked. Her shock was the first real emotion she'd shown me in years. "How could you say something like that about us?"

"You're arrogant, elitist assholes sometimes, Mother. I refuse to subject Tucker to an evening where you and Father make him feel like he's not worthy of my affection with your passive-aggressive bullshit."

"Trenton David Love, like it or not, I am still your mother. You will speak to me with respect. Forgive me for being direct, but you've never treated me in such a disdainful manner. I don't know what in the world has come over you. Does your new attitude have something to do with your new boyfriend? Is this a result of your *roughing it?*"

I hung up on her before I lost my cool then slipped my phone back in my pocket.

"There you are," Tucker said from behind me. I turned to face him, and my expression must've given away the rage I felt. "What's wrong, Doc?"

"My mother called, and it didn't go well."

"I'm sorry," he said, pulling me into a hug.

"Thank you. I've never hung up on her before, but she was so hateful."

"About?" Tucker inquired.

"Us. She invited us to dinner at their country club next weekend and got angry and downright nasty when I didn't jump on the chance right away."

Tucker's brow furrowed. "Why didn't you? Don't you want me to meet your parents?"

"No."

Tucker's eyes widened, and he took a step back. "I see."

"No, you don't, Sparky." He relaxed when I used his nickname. I closed the gap between us and reached for his hands. "You're too good for them, and I won't have my parents treating you with disrespect and making you feel unworthy."

"And you think they would treat me so callously?"

"I know they will. They're not good people, Tuck. My sister is an amazing woman, and I'm dying to introduce you to Mercedes, Benji, and the girls. I could go the rest of my life without introducing you to my parents though."

"That's not a very pragmatic approach though, is it?"

"I guess not," I admitted.

"Trent, I want you—all of you. I'll take the good and the bad.

There's nothing your parents can say or do that will make me care about you less. I need you to trust me."

Tucker looked so sincere, and he gazed at me with so much adoration. I wanted to believe he could withstand my parents' onslaught of arrogance and entitlement, but I'd seen what happened when Mercedes brought guys home to meet the family. None of them stood a chance until Benji came along. He was respectful toward my parents, but he stood his ground. Looking at Tuck, I realized he would be the same.

"If you're sure…"

"I am," Tucker said confidently.

"Okay. I'll wait until Mother and I have both had enough time to cool off, then I'll call her back and accept her invitation." I was desperate to recapture the playful, sexy mood from earlier, so I fisted Tucker's shirt and pulled him down until his lips were nearly touching mine. "About my fantasy…"

CHAPTER THIRTEEN

Tucker

T RENT'S SWIFT TOPIC CHANGE CAUGHT ME OFF GUARD, BUT I understood his need to put the upsetting conversation behind him. If a little kernel of doubt remained in the back of my mind, it was all on me. Trent had said exactly what I needed to hear, and I knew he wasn't just placating me either. I could dwell on my fear that I wasn't good enough for Trent, or I could take him home, put him up against the wall, and help him live out his fantasy.

Unfortunately, his sister called him as soon as we crossed his threshold. I only heard Trent's side of the conversation, but I could pick out enough to know his mother was outraged and Mercedes was on the receiving end of her fury. I wasn't sure how long their conversation would take, so I stretched out on the couch with Natasha and Boris, aka Pinky and The Brain. Of course, it was obvious Boris had no desire to escape his new home, so I could stop referring to him as The Brain.

"Sis, I'm sorry," Trent said contritely after listening to her speak for several minutes. I glanced over and saw a pained expression marring his handsome face. I hated how his blue eyes had lost their sparkle and vowed to remedy it by any means necessary. "I never meant for you to get caught up in any of this. I should've called our parents when I returned home instead of having your family over for a clandestine lunch. I'm not sorry for standing up for myself and Tucker today. I—" Mercedes must've cut him off. "Yes, I did tell her I thought she and Father were elitist assholes. I—" Mercedes' loud laughter came through Trent's phone. "I'm glad you find it funny." More laughter. Trent's lips twitched as he struggled not to smile. "I wanted to get together with you, Benji, and the girls next weekend, but now I'm rethinking my decision. I'm not sure I want to introduce Tucker to my stark-raving-mad sister." It was Trent's turn to laugh at whatever Mercedes' response was. "Okay, fine, but you need to remember to keep your hands off Mr. March." I groaned, and Trent blew me a kiss.

Boris nudged his head against my chin, and Natasha batted my ear. I couldn't remember a time when I felt as content and relaxed as I did right then. Boris purred louder and settled beneath my chin while Natasha gave up attacking my ear and curled up beside my head on the armrest of the sofa. My eyes got heavier and heavier. *I'll just close them for a few minutes while Trent talks to his sister.*

"Bang!" said a loud voice from the kitchen. My eyes popped open, and I jackknifed up into a sitting position, dislodging Boris from my chest. The first thing I noticed was the room was darker than when I'd lain down, and Trent had covered me with the throw blanket he kept on the back of his sofa. I rubbed the sleep from my eyes and willed my foggy brain to catch up. *How long was I out?* It was still daylight, but the sun had shifted more to the west, casting this side of the house in shade.

"Jack, you scared the hell out of me," Jill said. "Why didn't you just say the killer shot the victim in the head instead of demonstrating your gun noise?"

"For effect, of course. It worked. You should've seen the way you jumped."

"I nearly pissed my pants."

"Even better," Jack said.

"Idiot." I imagined Jill had rolled her eyes when she said it. "What about this case stuck out to you?"

Once my heart stopped racing, I realized Trent was in the kitchen listening to another podcast.

Hurried footsteps bounced off the floor and grew louder as they got closer. "Damn it. I didn't mean to wake you up."

I glanced over toward the doorway where Trent stood wearing a worried expression and his adorable apron. My eyes raked over him from his blond hair to his bare feet. One of these days, I was going to ask him to wear nothing but his apron. "C'mere."

"Um," he said, looking over his shoulder into the kitchen. "I really want to, but I don't want to mess up the berry compote and whipped cream I'm making to go with dessert."

"Dessert?" I asked. My sweet tooth ranked second to my libido in priorities.

"I made mini cheesecakes to take to Shirlene's for dinner."

I moaned happily. "Cheesecake is my favorite."

"Stop making those sexy noises, or we'll be late," Trent told me. "Why don't you go upstairs and shower to wake yourself up while I finish down here. Your hair is a mess, and you have dried saliva on your face from drooling."

I wiped my mouth and was horrified to discover Trent wasn't teasing me. What did I expect after a night of great sex and an afternoon of kicking ass on the basketball court? "Is this really saliva?" I asked with a quirked brow.

Trent crossed his arms over his chest. He tried his best to look insulted by my suggestion, but his trembling lips gave him away. "Is that something that appeals to you?"

"I don't think so."

"You don't think so?" Trent repeated. "The jury is still out?"

I tipped my head to the side like I was giving it serious consideration. "I'd much rather be an active participant and be awake when you splatter my face with cum. Why don't you join me in the shower, and we can give it a test run? I can help you finish making dessert afterward."

"Huh-uh. Shirlene warned me about you. She suggested I cuff you to my bed so you couldn't eat all the cheesecakes before we left the house."

"I'm equally appalled and turned on right now."

"Turned on by the thought of being cuffed to my bed?" Trent asked.

"Yes, but appalled Grammie was the one who suggested it. I'm not sure we can ever go through with it now. It would be like she is standing at the foot of the bed offering advice. *Tighten down those cuffs, Trent. You don't want him to be able to get away,*" I said in my best Grammie voice. *"You should've purchased the fur-lined ones to prevent chafing."*

"Trust me," Trent said, delicious wickedness dripping off his tongue, "your grammie will be the furthest thing from your mind once I have you cuffed to my bed." Trent sniffed the air then said, "Fuck! I don't want my berries to burn."

I chuckled when he ran into the kitchen. I glanced at the time on his grandfather clock and noticed it was already after four. I couldn't believe I crashed hard enough to sleep for three hours, missing out on wall sex and my opportunity to swipe a mini cheesecake.

The shower felt great and revived me—*all* of me—but I ignored my nagging dick other than to give it a good wash in case he was called off the bench to get some play time later. I put on the extra clothes I'd grabbed from my house then headed back downstairs. Trent was engrossed in his podcast again as he scraped whipped cream from a silver bowl into a glass one then covered it with a blue plastic lid.

"In the refrigerator you go," he said cheerfully.

"I bet that's what one of your serial killers says when he puts severed heads or limbs in his refrigerator."

"Damn it, Tuck!" Trent said, whirling around to face me. "Must you sneak up on me all the time?"

"It's not my fault you get so wrapped up in whatever you're doing that a large, six-foot-five man sneaks up on you without trying. A person would expect you to be a little bit more observant after listening to hours of how serial killers stalk and kill their prey."

"One would, wouldn't they?" he said, looking me up and down. "Why do you look so damn delicious in dark jeans and a pale-gray Henley?"

I looked down at my simple clothes. "I'm sure many people would find my ensemble boring."

"I think it allows a person to focus on your best assets." I craned my neck to look over my shoulder like I was checking out my ass. "I'm not talking about those kinds of assets, but I must say I like what I see." Trent waggled his brows. "I meant the pale color complements your tan skin. Your clothes don't distract me from noticing your pretty smile and dark, wicked eyes."

"Dark and wicked, huh?" I crossed the room until I was standing in front of him. I took the spatula from his hand and slowly licked the cream from it. "I think you bring it out in me."

"It's been there all along," Trent countered. "You were simply saving it for the right guy." He leaned forward and licked the other side of the spatula. "That's me, in case I wasn't clear."

"Crystal clear." I took the bowl from his arm, dropped the spatula inside, and set it on the counter. I leaned down to kiss him, and he stood on his tiptoes to meet me halfway. His homemade whipped cream tasted that much sweeter on his lips and tongue. God, I wanted to devour him until he physically became a part of me.

"I don't think I've ever had homemade whipped cream before," I told him as I kissed a path down his neck. "You've ruined me for the store-bought stuff now."

"I'm glad you like it because I made a double batch for us."

I raised my head and looked into his lust-filled eyes. "Why, Doc, just what do you intend to do with the extra whipped cream?"

"Put it on the extra batch of mini cheesecakes I made just for you."

"Just for me?"

"I'm hoping you'll share them with me too," Trent confided.

"I'm going to balance one on each of your glorious ass cheeks then lick the whipped cream off your pucker."

"Now?" Trent asked breathlessly.

I glanced at the clock on his stove. "You told Grammie we'd be there at five and it's already four thirty. Twenty-five minutes isn't enough time, but maybe we can make our excuses to leave early."

Trent smiled. "We won't fool her for a second."

"Nor will she care."

"All right, then. Let's get this packed up and head over to her house before we find ourselves in a little trouble." I took his hand and placed it against my erection. "Big trouble," Trent amended.

CHAPTER FOURTEEN

Trent

S HIRLENE'S HOME WAS AS COLORFUL AND ECCENTRIC AS THE LADY WHO lived there. Vivid wall colors, oversized furniture with bold fabrics, and knickknacks and photographs decorating every available surface. My eyes didn't know where to look first. For as cluttered as the place would feel to some, I found it to be a comfortable and curious place. I wanted to know the stories behind the pieces she had sitting around. Were they handed down from generation to generation or had she purchased them from a yard sale or an estate auction? This cozy home was so far away from the McMansion I grew up in it might as well be on another planet. I couldn't help but smile when I imagined the disdainful look on my mother's face if she were here.

I'd told Tuck I would make peace with my mother and accept her invitation to dinner, and I meant it, but I needed time. Her words still stung. I was in no hurry to subject him to my parents' horrid treatment either. Mercedes told me our mother was convinced Tucker was a member of some cult and had brainwashed me because she couldn't see any other reason for my behavior. Mercedes and I got a good laugh out of that one, but my sister's parting words before we hung up ruined any humor I'd found in the situation.

"They're thinking about hiring a private investigator to look into Tucker's background, Trent. I'm not assuming or implying they'll find anything troublesome, but maybe you stop this before things get out of control and irreparable harm happens to someone."

I knew Mercedes was right; I needed to get a handle on the situation before it spun out of control, but I wasn't sure the best way to go about it. I refused to bow to Mother's demands because I'd worked too long and hard to distance myself from their toxic influence. Placating Mother so she wouldn't hire a PI felt an awful lot like taking a dozen steps backward. I had to stand my ground and not give in, or she wouldn't just take an inch; she'd destroy the hard-fought peaceful life I'd made for myself.

"You're looking pensively at my birdhouse collection," Shirlene said, coming up to stand beside me. "You're not planning on stealing one, are you? I've been working on the collection for forty years."

I shook myself from my maudlin thoughts and turned to face my host. Her hair was pulled back and clipped behind her right ear while her lavender curls softly framed the left side of her face. White feathers hung from leather cords secured to the end of her barrette. The cords were various lengths, giving the feathers a waterfall effect. The bottom feather brushed against the collar of her polka dot dress. Shirlene looked serene, peaceful, and happy. Without answering her question, I gathered her in my arms and hugged her tight.

"I can't say I'm disappointed, but what did I do to deserve such a warm hug from you?" She rubbed circles between my shoulder blades then pulled back enough to look into my face without breaking our connection.

"I'm so glad Tucker grew up with you in his corner, Shirlene."

Her eyes searched mine, but she didn't ask any questions. "I've loved Tucker from his first breath, and I'll love him beyond my last."

"Grammie, are you trying to steal my guy?" Tucker asked when he re-entered the living room after storing the dessert in the refrigerator. "I'll fight you to the finish, old woman, and I'm not even playing."

Shirlene tilted her head back and laughed. "See what I mean?" she asked me. "How could I not love him?"

"What did I miss?" Tucker asked, looking bemused and a little confused too.

"I accused him of plotting to steal my birdhouses, and he asked me to run away with him."

"Is that so?" Tucker questioned.

"Ignore me," I said. "I got a little emotional thinking about my phone conversation from this afternoon, and I was expressing my joy that you have someone like Shirlene in your life."

Tucker crossed the room and kissed me. "And now you do too."

"We're a package deal," Shirlene agreed.

"Sold," I declared.

Tears stung the back of my eyes when Tucker looked at me with adoration. Needing to find sturdier footing, I said, "Shirlene, Tucker tells me you're a fan of true crime."

"Oh, yes. I read books and watch the ID channel way more than I should. Every time I hear a twig break outside my window, I'm convinced my time is up."

Tucker and I laughed. "I love true crime too, and I started listening to a podcast you might like."

"Listen?" Tucker asked with a raised brow. He turned to Shirlene and smiled. "This one talks to the podcast hosts like they can hear him."

"Like you yell at the referees on television?" she asked.

"Just like that," Tucker said, nodding his head. Tucker started to tell Shirlene about me listening to the Jack and Jill podcast while preparing breakfast, but she cut him off.

"Breakfast?" she asked with a knowing smirk.

"Come on, Grammie. You sent me over to his house last weekend to jump his bones, and you know it."

"Tucker Garrison," she said, clutching invisible pearls. "I only wanted the nice doctor to receive the coupons and certificates that came with his adorable cats. I cannot help it if you mistook my intentions."

"Uh-huh." Tucker didn't sound at all convinced, and I was too busy laughing to remind her I'd declined the coupons.

"Do continue with your story," Shirlene told him. I saw interest spark in her eyes when Tucker told her about the first podcast we listened to and the one about Jack the Ripper. "That sounds really good. How can I find these podcasts?"

"They're free in the iTunes store and on Spotify," I told her. "They're great to listen to while driving, cooking, or cleaning."

"I'm not sure anyone wants me listening to the podcasts while I drive," she said sheepishly. "I already have a lead foot. I can see myself getting so caught up in the podcasts that I stop paying attention to my speedometer."

"Okay, maybe you stick to listening while cooking and cleaning," I suggested.

"And gardening," Shirlene said.

"I'll help you download some to get you started," I offered.

"Sounds great but not until after dinner. They sound addictive."

"Let me help you, Shirlene."

"No way," she said, waving me off. "I dug out some of my favorite photo albums of Tucker for you to look through."

"Grammie," Tucker moaned.

"They're not naked bathtub pictures, Tuck," she said. "Besides, he's already seen you naked."

Tucker's head fell forward as he accepted defeat. I kissed his cheek, and he wrapped his arm around me.

"Come pour the man a tall glass of my sweet tea, then you can sit next to him and absorb his adoration when he sees how incredibly beautiful you were."

"Still are," I whispered against his lips.

"That too," Shirlene said.

"She has ears a bat would envy," Tucker mock-whispered.

"Did you just call me an old bat?" Shirlene asked.

Tucker grinned. "Not this time, but the night is still young."

I sat on the cream, canary yellow, and lime green plaid sofa, which somehow looked good up against the eggplant-purple wall. I picked up a large, leather-bound photo album off the coffee table and set it on my lap. My breath caught in my throat when I opened it and saw the first photo inside.

A blonde woman with long curly hair piled on top of her head cradled a baby in her arms. The woman wore a hospital gown, and the baby was swaddled tightly in a hospital blanket and a tiny, blue, knitted hat adorned the top of his head. Tendrils of wet hair clung to the mother's forehead and tears of joy ran down her face. The infant's face was red with anger from being booted from his warm cocoon, and his tiny mouth was open to broadcast his displeasure. I realized I was looking at Tucker's very first minutes of life. I studied his mother's face, looking for any resemblance to the man I knew but couldn't find any. I did see the adoration on the young woman's face as she stared down at her son and touched his tiny fists sticking out of the top of the blanket. I turned the page, and my jaw dropped when I saw a similar picture, but this time, Tucker was cradled in the arms of his father, who wore the sappiest smile I'd ever seen. Tucker looked so much like his father it was eerie. The term carbon copy came to mind.

The photo on the next page showed Tucker resting in the arms of his mother while she sat in a wheelchair in front of a hospital. His father stood proudly behind her with his hands resting on her shoulders. The happy couple looked excited to take their son home. I knew Shirlene raised Tucker, but I didn't know how old he was when his parents died.

I glanced up when I heard Tucker re-enter the living room. The smile on his face died when he saw my somber expression. He set both of our glasses on the table then sat beside me. Tucker brushed his hand over my cheek, and I was surprised when it came away wet. I wasn't aware I'd been crying.

"I'm sorry," I said. "I feel like I'm intruding on something very personal by looking at these photos."

Tucker put his arm around my shoulders, and I leaned into him. "Those are my parents, Jack and Melanie Tucker. They were beautiful, weren't they?"

"Stunning."

"They looked so happy and full of life in this moment," Tucker added. "They had no idea they'd die in a car accident nine months later."

"I'm very sorry," I said, unsure of how I should respond. To say nothing felt wrong, but saying I was sorry felt like empty words.

"Thank you." He squeezed me a little tighter.

"That's why Grammie came to see you when she found out about the fatal accident. She knew it would remind you of losing your parents."

Tucker nodded. "They're the reason I decided to become a fireman and paramedic. I hoped to spare other families from the heartbreak mine suffered."

"You're a very noble man, Tuck."

"I don't know about noble, but I'm very passionate about my work. I do take it to heart when our attempts to save lives fail."

"You're quite possibly the best man I've ever met. I'm having a hard time believing you'd choose me to share this sofa with."

"I'm constructed of flesh, bones, fears, and flaws just like everyone else." Tucker gently traced his finger over my lips. "I think you're truly special too."

I've always thought falling in love would be like getting hit in the head with a baseball. One minute you were fine, and the next...

WHAM! It hit you. I realized it could gently wash over you and settle into your heart and soul when you're sitting on a wildly colored sofa and staring into your lover's eyes while holding pieces of his greatest heartache in your hands. It wasn't as scary as I imagined it would be; it felt pretty fucking awesome.

It was too early to express those feelings yet, so I leaned forward and kissed Tucker instead.

CHAPTER FIFTEEN

Tucker

SEEING TRENT CRY AS HE LOOKED AT THE PHOTOS OF MY PARENTS touched a part of my heart no one else had been able to reach, not even Grammie. I never took her love and adoration for granted, but it was expected. She was my family, the person who raised me, so of course, she looked at me like I hung the moon. I'd been on the receiving end of someone's crush, infatuation, and even lust, but no man had ever looked at me the way Trent did. He thought I was noble and special, and the soft kiss he pressed against my lips made me feel those things.

It was during our slow, lingering kiss when an epiphany struck me as suddenly and as solidly as if someone hit me over the head with a blunt object. *I love him.* It was too soon and too new, but there was still no denying what I felt for the man in my arms was a million times stronger than anything I'd ever felt before, including my first crush. I wanted to take on his pain as my own and find ways to ease the hurt just like he wanted to do for me. *I love him.*

I pulled back from our kiss and stared into his eyes. Trent blinked a few times like he was trying to clear his head, but the adoration remained in his gaze. *Did he feel this too?*

"What's wrong?"

"Wrong?" I asked. "Nothing is wrong."

"You look a little dazed."

"So do you," I said, running the back of my hand over his cheek.

"I'm always that way when I'm around you."

"Charmer."

"Are you boys ready to eat?" Grammie asked from the kitchen.

"Always," I replied.

"Don't I know it?" she quipped.

Trent gently closed the photo album and carefully set it on the coffee table like he recognized how precious it was to Grammie and me. My heart swelled with more love, and a little bit of smugness too, and I silently congratulated the organ for a job well done. *You chose well, pal.*

I rose to my feet and held out my hand for Trent, who not only accepted it but kissed my palm before linking our fingers and standing up beside me. *Where he belonged.* Rather than head straight to the kitchen, I couldn't resist one more kiss.

"The breading on the eggplant parmigiana will get soggy if it sits too long," Grammie warned.

"She's all for us playing kissy face unless it impacts the integrity of the breading," I whispered against Trent's lips.

"We can't have soggy eggplant," Trent agreed.

"Not after she went to so much trouble for us."

Trent and I joined Grammie in the kitchen. The second thing I noticed after the delicious aroma was how well her purple orchid was flourishing. My orchid looked good, but Grammie's practically radiated joy from its place of honor in the window sill above the sink.

"Why does your orchid look better than mine?" I asked, ignoring the dishes of food lining the counter.

"Don't just stand there," Grammie told me, nudging me with her elbow as she walked by. "Slip on some oven mitts and start carrying dishes before Trent does."

"I'm more than happy to help," he protested.

"You're my guest," Grammie said gently. "You don't set the table or clean up afterward. Tucker can do those things."

"Seriously," I said, studying the orchid closer. "Owen is receiving the same amount of sunlight as your orchid, and I'm using the food and spray mist Trent bought me. What are you doing differently?"

"I play classical music for Olivia in the evenings while I clean the kitchen and get ready for the next day."

"Classical music," I repeated, wondering if Owen would like classic rock.

"I'm sure it doesn't have to be classical music," Grammie said. "Owen might like rock or even country."

"Nah," I said shaking my head. "Country music might make him sad. He'll think his wife, kids, and dog left him. He'll wither away and die."

"I wouldn't play heavy metal," Grammie cautioned. "I've seen what it does to rats. Makes them violent and turn on each other."

"I bet Owen would like oldies. Who doesn't like Elvis?" I asked her.

"Owen and Olivia?" Trent asked suddenly. Grammie and I turned to face him. "You named your orchids?"

"Of course," Grammie and I said at the same time.

"Deal breaker?" I asked him.

Trent smiled then laughed. "Hell no. Plenty of people name the things they care about, but I'm used to it being their cars, electronics, or even their appliances. I don't think I know anyone who's named their plants."

"Plants are living, breathing things that enhance our lives and make oxygen. They deserve names more than cars and appliances," Grammie told Trent.

"I agree," Trent said.

"You've never met anyone like us," Grammie assured him. "I'm sure we're not as exotic as we seem because most people keep their eccentricities hidden. We—mostly I—wave them around like a flag."

"I can tell you one thing Owen won't be listening to," I said, looking at Trent. "No way he's listening to your podcasts. I don't want to sleep with one eye open."

Grammie and Trent laughed especially hard at my joke, and we joked about the concept being an excellent idea for a sci-fi book while we finished setting the table. Grammie tried to bully Trent into sitting down and letting us do the work, but he wouldn't have it.

"I will be helping with the dishes afterward," he informed her. "I'll get you started on a podcast, and you'll forget we're even here." Trent looked at me. "She can use headphones or keep the volume low so Olivia doesn't start getting ideas."

"He's one of us now," Grammie said with an eerie voice and mischievous gleam in her eyes.

"I figure if we don't scare him off after this, nothing will," I told Grammie.

"Please," Trent snorted. "I could share many hilarious tales about my time overseas."

"We'd love to hear them," Grammie said. "My only significant traveling comes from reading books."

Trent tipped his head and pondered her remark for a second. "I've never really looked at books as a gateway to adventure and travel. For so long, the only books I read were mandatory reading assignments in high school or textbooks I needed for college. I can't remember the last time I sat down and read a book for pleasure."

"Pleasure reading can be about so much more than entertainment," Grammie said, her eyes glowing with merriment. "They're magical portals that can take you anywhere you want to go. One of my patrons at the library has a tattoo on her forearm that I absolutely love. It's a stack of her favorite books. The top one is open to let the magic escape, and there's a message at the bottom that says: I've lived a thousand lives. It's true. I've been a queen and a servant. I've been a vampire, a werewolf, and a shifter. I've fallen in love with hardheaded heroes and feisty females. I've traveled the world through the eyes of the characters, and I've learned who I want to be as a person. Reading has opened my mind and heart to the struggles other people face and has made me a kinder, more compassionate woman. Some say you get lost in books, but I say you find yourself there."

"And I've done both," I said, smiling at her across the table. "I am grateful every day to Grammie for passing her love of reading on to me. She never once bought into the notion that reading was only for girls. She introduced me to adventure books at an early age, and it fueled my love of reading. As I got older, my interests expanded to mysteries and thrillers, romantic suspense, and the biographies of people who interested me. I also love a good romance, and I don't care who has a problem with it."

"They're not dumb enough to say it to your face," Grammie said.

"True."

Grammie passed the platter of perfectly breaded chicken cutlets to me. I speared one and placed it on my plate then passed the chicken to Trent. Since the eggplant parmigiana casserole dish was too hot to pass around, I handed my plate to Grammie who gave me two large pieces of golden, cheesy eggplant.

"I'm not a growing boy anymore," I teased.

"Hush, you need your stamina," she chided. Trent nearly dropped the platter of chicken before handing it back to Grammie. "Sorry. I'm just so happy he's finally—"

"Grammie," I said in a warning tone.

"—found someone special."

"Uh-huh," I said. She was probably going to say she was happy I was finally getting laid.

"So, Trent," Grammie said, scooping two portions of eggplant onto his plate also, "tell us one of your travel stories so Tuck and I will feel less weird."

"There's nothing weird about either of you," he said, smiling at her while squeezing my knee beneath the table. "I think the most interesting part of traveling is learning the various lore from all around the world. Whether they're true or not, I love the tradition of passing stories from generation to generation. The first one that comes to mind is the chupacabra. One night, we gathered around a campfire listening to the locals tell gruesome accounts of the legendary creature who'd supposedly been on a goat killing spree before our arrival. One guy theorized they migrated in packs like coyotes or wolves. He'd followed the carnage and saw a pattern where no one else had and thought he could predict when they'd circle back around to their village." A wry smile tilted at the corner of Trent's lips.

"Let me guess," I said. "He expected the chupacabra to reappear during your stay."

"Of course. I believe his exact words were 'any day now.' I jumped at every little sound outside my tent while we stayed at the village."

"No sign of the chupacabra?" Grammie asked.

"Not one. The villagers were kind and amazing, but I was so happy to pack up and move on. Of course, the next village we went to had yeti sightings the previous week. I started to realize it was their way of having a little fun at our expense."

"It sounds like something Grammie would do."

"Without a doubt, but I'd have been the one making noises outside your tent to scare you. I had plenty of opportunities to terrorize Tucker and Braxton when they were growing up."

"Evil woman," I murmured, making Grammie laugh.

I expected Trent to join in, but he was too busy eating. He moaned happily as he looked at his food with adoring eyes. "This," he said, pointing to his plate, "is the best eggplant parmigiana I've ever had. What's your secret for getting the breading so crisp?"

"Salt," Grammie said. "Eggplant has a lot of moisture in it, so I sprinkle both sides with salt to extract the moisture then pat it dry with a paper towel."

"My sister loves this dish, so I'll have to try your tip the next time I make it for her."

"Does she live close?" Grammie asked.

"She lives north of Cincinnati," Trent told her. "She and her family are coming on Saturday to meet Tucker."

I nearly swallowed my bite of chicken whole. I made a choking sound, pulling Grammie's and Trent's attention to me.

"Did I forget to mention that?"

I carefully chewed the chicken and swallowed then washed it down with a long drink of sweet tea. "I knew you were making plans, but I didn't know when."

Worry washed over Trent's face. "Is it too soon?"

"Not at all. I have plenty of time to panic."

"Panic?" Trent asked, sounding amused. "You're going to love my sister and her family, and I know they'll love you too. My nieces are the most amazing little girls on the planet, and they'll have you eating out of their palms or wrapped around their fingers in no time."

"How sweet," Grammie said.

"You're welcome to join us, Shirlene," Trent said. If I hadn't already fallen in love with him, I would've then. Grammie was a lot to take for some people, but Trent seemed to embrace her eccentric personality—encourage it even.

"Honey, I'm so flattered you would include me, but I don't want to intrude on Tucker meeting your family for the first time. Will your parents be joining you?" An awkward silence descended in the room. "Oh, I've overstepped, haven't I? I'm terribly sorry. This is why Tucker should have an opportunity to meet them without me scaring them away."

Trent squeezed my thigh when I started to protest. "Shirlene, you didn't overstep, and you wouldn't ruin a damn thing. You have every right to ask questions about my family. The truth is I'm nearly estranged from my parents, although I haven't completely severed ties yet."

"I'm so sorry, honey. Is there any hope of reconciliation?" she asked, reaching across the table to squeeze his hand.

Trent closed his eyes and took a deep breath. "I don't think so, and to be honest, I've stopped wishing for it. The price of reconciliation is more than I'm willing to pay. I feel absolutely selfish for saying it because Tucker would probably give nearly anything to see his parents one more time."

I put my arm around his shoulders and pulled him toward me. "You're the least selfish person I know, Doc. And besides, you wouldn't sever ties with your folks without justification."

"Honey, not everyone is cut out to be a parent. Sometimes couples have children for all the wrong reasons, and the kids pay a costly price for it. I agree with Tucker. I don't know you well, but you don't seem like a man who'd make that kind of move on a whim. Tucker and I will always listen to you without judgment, won't we?" Grammie asked me.

"Absolutely," I said, kissing his temple. I already had an idea of the problems he had with his parents, but I didn't realize how deep the troubles ran. I recalled the conversation we had earlier after his phone call with his mom. I might've inadvertently pressured him to accept an invitation that wasn't good for him because of my insecurities. The idea shamed me and stuck with me throughout dinner, making me quieter than usual, but neither Grammie nor Trent let on if they noticed they were carrying the conversation.

After dinner, Trent followed Grammie into the living room to help her download some podcasts while I started cleaning the kitchen. It wasn't long before he joined me and began drying the dishes.

"Grammie believes dishwashers make us lazy," I said ruefully.

"She might have a point," Trent said. "We've become so reliant on technology that we rarely even think for ourselves anymore."

"True."

"Want to tell me why you got so quiet during dinner?" Trent asked. Of course he noticed.

"I feel like maybe I pressured you about reconciling with your mother and accepting the invitation to dinner with your parents. I shouldn't have done that."

"You didn't pressure me into anything, Tuck. I'm responsible for my own decisions—the good, bad, and downright ugly. I will call my mother and accept her invitation, but it will be on my terms, not hers. I need you to know this has nothing to do with me being ashamed of you or me not having any faith in us. Do you believe me?"

It was crazy to put so much trust in a person I hardly knew, but it felt right to give Trent everything I had. How could I think I was in love with him if the most important element in a relationship was missing?

"I do believe you," I whispered. I leaned forward and started to kiss Trent, but Grammie's sudden burst of laughter startled me.

"These two are a hoot!" she yelled from the living room.

"Think we can sneak away now that she's enthralled with Jack and Jill?" I asked. "We have wall-banging to do and whipped cream to lick."

"That sounds like a fun time," Grammie said from the doorway. "Don't let me keep you."

Trent and I both whirled around to face her. I glanced at him to see if his face was as red as mine. *Yep.*

"Right," I said, reaching for Trent's hand. "We'll just be going now."

"Thank you for inviting me to your home, Shirlene. Dinner was lovely." I wasn't surprised Trent's impeccable manners remained intact even when he was embarrassed. "I hope you enjoy the podcast."

"I absolutely will, honey." Grammie didn't budge from the doorway, so we were forced to stop in front of her. She hugged Trent tightly until the tension melted from his body. "Your turn," she said, opening her arms to me.

"Love you, Grammie."

"Moon and back, Tuck." We were almost to the door when Grammie stopped us. "You forgot your cheesecakes and whipped cream."

"I made double batches. Those are for you to enjoy."

"I'm obviously not going to enjoy it as much as you two, but I appreciate your thoughtfulness."

"Grammie," I said.

"Oh hush," she replied, shooing us out the door.

Trent and I laughed as we headed to my truck.

"I should be horrified," Trent said.

"Don't be," I told him. "It will only encourage her."

"Are we wall-banging, cream licking, or are you giving up your cherry to me?" Trent asked. "All three?"

"We can write our fantasies down on slips of paper and put them in a jar. We can take turns picking from the fantasy-fuck jar."

"That's much better than a swear jar," Trent said. "I'm in."

My pager went off just as I reached Trent's house. "Damn it. I'm sorry. This could be a short run, or it could be the beginning of a long night."

"It's no problem. I knew you were on call," Trent said. "I had a great weekend with you, Tuck."

I cupped his face and pulled him to me for a kiss. "Me too," I said. "I'll call you."

"I'll answer."

I hated driving away from him and realized I needed to start reclaiming some of my time. Everyone told me I worked too hard and volunteered too many extra hours. For once, I had a reason to work less and live more, and I was going to grab it with both hands.

Prescription:

CHAPTER SIXTEEN

Trent

EVERYONE IN THE OFFICE WAS ALL TGIF AND EXCITED TO START THE weekend, but none of them were happier than I was. With Tucker working third shift all week to fill in for a guy on vacation, I hadn't been alone with my guy since he dropped me off at my house on Sunday evening. I delivered his cheesecakes along with dinner to the firehouse on Monday evening, and he treated me to breakfast on Wednesday morning. Being able to look into his dark eyes was wonderful, but public goodbye kisses and longing glances weren't enough to douse the inferno raging inside me. Before Tuck, a solo session in the shower would've been enough to satisfy me, but no fist other than Tuck's would do, and choosing an artificial boyfriend when I had the real thing didn't sound at all appealing to me. We'd hoped to at least have phone sex together, but that was interrupted.

We needed the fine people of Blissville to stop getting sick and having emergencies.

The weekend was here, and I would have Tucker all to myself for two fucktastic nights and three glorious days. The possibilities were endless, and I vowed not to throw myself into Tuck's arms the minute he walked through the door. I mean, I wanted his dick in my ass really bad, but I also craved talking to him. I needed to sit across a dinner table from him and listen to his week and tell him about mine. I wanted to do all the things with Tucker that couples did. For the first time in my life, I felt like half of a whole, and I was flying high on all the simple ways Tucker made me so happy.

A bouquet of cherry-red carnations was delivered to my office first thing in the morning with a handwritten card that read: *I can't wait for tonight.* Tucker had added a cherry sticker to the bottom of the note. I knew exactly what his message meant. My heart galloped and blood rushed through my veins so fast I could hear it.

I tapped out a quick text message to Tucker which was basically a string of emojis—a tongue, the cherries, the eggplant, and the droplets of water we all associated with cum. Then I quickly shifted my mind to my work so I wouldn't get aroused in my office. I was maintaining my focus until a special delivery from Edson and Emma's arrived during lunch. Blood rushed to my dick as I stared at the cherry pie with a huge dollop of whipped cream on top. I thought about saving it so I could lick cherries and whipped cream off Tuck's body but made a cup of coffee and devoured it instead. Well, not before I took a selfie with the last cherry and some cream on my tongue and sent it to Tucker.

His reply was a simple, *yeah, baby.*

We'd agreed Tucker would bring pizza over around six which gave me an opportunity to see my last patient, catch up on my notes for the medical transcriber, and still have enough time to make sure I was manscaped and ready to go for my big night. I'd earned some curious glances when I didn't dart out the door after my last patient left, but I needed to stay busy so I wouldn't spend too much time dwelling on my upcoming performance. I'd topped plenty of times but never with a first timer and never with anyone I loved. I wanted to make the night perfect for Tucker. I couldn't just fall on his ass like I did the pie. I regretted my lack of insight. I should've been the one sending him a fun plug to insert and other gifts, and I would have if I'd known tonight was the night. Otherwise, I would've looked like a pushy douchebag.

I turned on the latest episode of Jack and Jill to find out the latest on Mr. Perfect, who Jack and Jill started calling the Hearts and Flowers Killer instead. I thought they were playing with fire but admired their moxie. I would've called him Wine and Dine or Swipe and Die if it were me, but Hearts and Flowers was a good nickname too.

"The police are doing their best not to release too much information about the crime scenes," Jill said.

"The last thing LAPD needs is a scorned lover who becomes a copycat-killer and uses Hearts and Flowers' MO to get even with people who hurt them in the past," Jack added.

"Plus, once they do have Hearts and Flowers in custody for questioning, he might trip himself up by using details not provided to the press. Something only the killer would know. It's a tried-and-true strategy, even if it irritates those of us dying to know."

"Let's not use the 'dying to know' phrase again, Jill. I'm curious, but I'm not willing to die for information."

"Ah, my Jack is so literal sometimes."

"Sometimes," he admitted. "Luckily for us, there's always a leak. I read that an unknown source with LAPD let it slip that the killings have become more intense."

"Like the killer is angrier perhaps?" Jill asked.

"Or frustrated he hasn't been caught? It's really hard to know with these serial killers. Sometimes they are frantic for someone to stop them and put them out of their misery. When it doesn't happen, they become more frustrated and take it out on their victims."

"He probably had cherry-teasing messages from his boyfriend all damn day that drove him to the brink of insanity. Not that *I'd* commit murder," I said out loud. Realizing where I was, I looked up and found John standing in my doorway. I quickly turned off the podcast and pulled the earbuds from my ears. "I thought you guys left."

"We did," John said, a coy smile tilting the right side of his mouth. "I came back."

"Um, can I help you with something?"

"I just forgot my phone and came back for it. Surely, you're not asking your medical transcriber to type the last bit about cherries, boyfriends, and murder."

"Of course not," I said then checked to make sure my recording software wasn't still running on my computer. "Nope. I just got caught up in...um."

"Sounds to me like you're listening to something about murders," John said with a raised brow. "Which couldn't be right after all the times you've teased me about watching the ID channel."

I shrugged casually, hoping John would move on when he realized his teasing jabs didn't land. I'd much rather verbally spar with him on Monday morning. "I'm just listening to a podcast."

"Which one?"

"John, not to be rude," I said, gesturing to my computer, "but I'm trying to finish up some work so I can start my weekend."

"With the fireman?"

"With Tucker, yes."

"Is he the one who sent the flowers and cherry pie... Oh." John's eyes grew large as he started to piece together the evidence like a seasoned, armchair sleuth. "Tonight is a big night."

"John," I said in a warning tone. "You must know I'm not going to discuss the personal details of my relationship."

"How would I know that? You've never been in a relationship since you've started working here. All I was going to say is I'm happy for you."

"Thank you."

"And if you tell me which podcast you're listening to, no one else will have to know."

As his employer, I could've been irate overs his shenanigans, but I knew he was only joking. "You're looking to blackmail a confession out of me?" I asked sternly.

"Well, it sounds tawdry when you put it like that," John said with a grimace. "Are you going to send me to Mike's office on Monday?" The hopeful look in his eyes made me laugh.

"You're too damned eager," I said. "My most recent obsession is the Jack and Jill podcast."

"Oh! They're a fun one. They have such great chemistry."

"They do, and speaking of chemistry," I said, glancing at my watch, "I need to wrap up a few more things before I head home to meet Tucker."

A genuine smile crossed John's face. "I truly am happy for you, Trent."

"Thank you. Now get the hell out of here. We'll chat about the latest podcast on Monday morning."

"Oh goody. Maybe I can be on time for once."

"I won't hold my breath."

"Nor should you," he countered. He winked then left as quickly as he appeared.

It took me a few seconds to get back in the zone after the interruption, but I finished fifteen minutes ahead of schedule, which allowed for extra time to prep my body and fuss with my hair.

I will not pounce on him.

I will not pounce on him.

I will not pounce on him.

When the doorbell rang, I flung open the door, fisted Tucker's shirt, and dragged him inside my house. He looked so fucking delicious with a scruffy jaw. He must not have shaved all week. I took the pizza boxes from him and set them on the foyer table.

"I've missed you so much, D—"

I cut Tucker off when I pressed my lips to his and devoured his mouth. I'd gone too long without his touch and taste, so pizza would have to wait.

R̲X̲

PATIENT NAME: _____

ADDRESS: _____
_____
_____

Prescription:

CHAPTER SEVENTEEN

_____

_____

Signature: _____ Date: _____

Tucker

T O SAY I LOVED TRENT'S ENTHUSIASTIC RESPONSE WAS A GROSS understatement. Sending my sexy guy surprises and receiving his responses kept me on the edge of arousal all damn day, so I made a trip to Kinky Kim's to purchase items that were both necessary and fun. I couldn't wait to show Trent the final surprises I had in store for him—us.

Trent pulled back from our kiss and said, "I missed you too, Tuck. So damn much."

Holding him against my body felt amazing, but he still wasn't close enough. I picked him up, and he wrapped his legs around my waist so I could support his weight as I pinned him against the wall. I took over the kiss, teasing his tongue with mine before sucking it into my mouth. I kissed him until his needy whimpers made it impossible for me to think about anything other than joining our bodies together.

I ripped my mouth away from his. "Is this what you want, baby? Do you want me to hold you against this wall and fuck you?"

"Yes, but we have all weekend for that," Trent replied. "I want what you've teased me with all day. Do you know how hard it was for me not to get a damn boner while eating the cherry pie?"

"Sorry?"

"No, you're not."

I grinned. "No, I'm not. I like knowing you're thinking about me as much as I'm thinking about you."

"Upstairs now," Trent demanded. "You've teased me relentlessly today until I can think of nothing else but how your ass will feel around my cock."

"Then you shall have it." I stepped back from the wall then tightened my grip on Trent's ass when he started to lower his legs. "Just hang on."

"You're not seriously planning on carrying me up the stairs?"

"It's exactly what I'm *going* to do. If you squirm and fight me, then it will only make it more difficult," I said.

Instead of trying to get free from my arms, Trent tightened his legs around my waist and his arms around my neck. "I can't wait to make you mine," he whispered in my ear. "I'm going to lick your pucker, suck it, then tongue-fuck you before I drive you wild with my fingers. Then I'm going to give you my dick." I nearly tripped going up the steps with images of Trent doing all those things to me. "I love being the only man to have you."

"Only you, baby."

Once we reached Trent's room, I set him down, and we immediately started attacking each other's clothing. Trent found the first surprise as soon as he shoved my pants to my ankles.

"My, oh my. What do we have here?" Trent asked, his fingers circling the red band around my cock and the second one secured snugly behind my balls. "Do my eyes spy a cherry-red cock ring?"

"They do. I didn't trust myself not to come too soon."

"God, you make me want to push us both to our limits."

"My body is your playground," I whispered against his mouth. "Nothing is out of boundaries or off-limits."

We finished undressing each other between kisses then stretched out facing one another on Trent's turned-down bed. I'd missed looking into those crystal blue eyes and running my fingers through his soft blond hair. Trent couldn't seem to get enough of my chest hair and rubbed his face against it while I stroked the taut globes of his ass and teased the dimples above them. Trent switched his attention from the hair on my chest to the scruff on my chin.

"This is new," he said, brushing his fingers over it. "I don't think I've ever seen you with scruff. It wasn't there two days ago when you kissed me goodbye after breakfast."

"I last shaved on Tuesday. My facial hair grows fast. Do you like it?"

"I love it. I bet you're sexy with a full beard. Right now, I'm wondering how your bristly scruff will feel on my body."

"There's only one way to find out."

Trent shook his head. "Tonight is all about you."

"It's about making us both feel good," I countered. Trent started to protest until I ran my jaw over his neck.

He shivered hard and whimpered. "God, I need to feel that everywhere."

"You *will* feel it everywhere."

I made a feast of him by kissing, licking, nibbling, and sucking a trail across his chest and down his stomach until I reached his dick. I took Trent to the back of my throat, making his back arch off the bed. He fisted his hands in my hair, pulling my mouth off him after I'd only worked him in and out of my mouth a few times.

"Huh-uh," Trent said, shaking his head. "It's been too long. I love coming in your mouth but tonight I need your tight, cherry hole to milk every last drop of cum from me." I crawled back up the bed until we lay facing each other once more. "How have I lived without someone looking at me the way you do?" he whispered.

"I was just thinking the same thing about you."

We kissed again, but this time it was slow and languorous as we savored the emotions swirling and the arousal building inside us. I wouldn't say our need for sex took a back seat or was forgotten, but we were content to slowly touch and kiss as we built up toward the ultimate connection. I inwardly smiled while waiting for Trent to discover the second surprise. He'd never been hesitant to explore my body, but maybe he worried I was jumpy about giving up my ass to him. Rather than guide his hand, I let him discover it on his own. His fingers teased the crack of my ass, inching closer and closer to where I needed him to be. My mouth captured his surprised gasp. *Bingo.* Trent broke our kiss and looked at me.

"What's this?" he asked, tracing his finger around the base of the butt plug.

I rolled onto my stomach and rested my chin on my folded forearms. "Why don't you come over here and find out."

The slow, languid feeling from before fled and was replaced with a renewed sense of urgency as Trent urged my legs apart to make room for him there. "Jeweled cherries on the handle," he said. "Very nice."

"I wanted to commemorate the special occasion."

"Sparky, you've definitely made it the most memorable sexual experience of my life, and we've only just started." Trent gave the base a gentle push, making me moan when it nudged my prostate. He leaned over until I could feel his hot breath against my stretched pucker. "I'm going to enjoy getting even with you."

"Do your worst."

"How about I give you my best instead?"

"Yeah," I said. "Let's go with that option."

Trent licked around the base of the plug, soothing the over-sensitized nerve endings. "Feel good?"

"Incredible."

He licked my crack, sucked my taint, and tongued the underside of my sac. Then he repositioned my dick so he could lick the length of it just as I'd done to him. "You're leaking so hard."

I let out a needy moan. "I've been like this all day."

Trent repeated his torturous teasing until my legs trembled and the only thing I could focus on was my white-hot need to come.

"I'm ready," I announced once I found my ability to speak.

Trent chuckled against my ass then gently gripped the base of the plug and gave it a little twist. "*I'll* let you know when you're ready." Trent placed his left hand on my lower back while he slowly removed the plug with his right. "Nearly ready," he said once it was free.

Next came Trent's tongue. He twirled it around my pucker, dipped it inside, and then tongue-fucked me like he said he would. Then Trent took his time working two lubed fingers in and out of me before adding a third. The pleasure made my eyes roll back in my head.

"I think you're ready for my cock now, baby."

"Uh-huh."

"Roll over. I want to look into your pretty brown eyes when I slide inside you." Trent moved to the side so I could roll over. I watched him slide a condom over his erection then slick it with lubricant before he positioned himself between my spread thighs. Trent leaned over me, bracing his weight on his forearm while reaching down between our bodies and lining up the head of his dick to my greedy pucker. "Tell me if this is too much."

"It's not enough."

"I haven't even started."

"I'll never have enough of you," I whispered.

Trent kept his eyes locked on mine as he slowly began to penetrate me—one glorious inch at a time. "Still with me?" he whispered against my lips.

I lifted my hands and threaded my fingers in his hair. I wanted to pull him to me for a kiss, but I didn't want to look away from him. "I feel stretched and stuffed full, but it feels fucking amazing. Don't hold back, baby." Trent's body trembled from restraint. "Take what you need. Give me all of you."

"Unh," he groaned, snapping his hips forward until his pelvis was flush against my ass.

Trent dropped his other forearm onto my pillow, bracketing my head. Sliding his fingers into my sweaty hair, he held my head still for a devastatingly beautiful kiss, allowing my channel to adjust to him. Trent continued kissing me until my hips began thrusting upward of their own volition, seeking more.

Trent broke the kiss and dropped his forehead down on the pillow. I held his trembling body tightly in my arms and wrapped my legs around his hips, needing to be as close to him as I possibly could. I wanted to fuse my body to his so not even light or air could separate our bodies. Even with the cock ring slowing down my climax, I was already on the verge of eruption. Every time Trent exhaled or inhaled, his abs created the most delicious friction against my dick.

"If I move, I'm going to come," Trent said, his voice muffled by the pillow.

"If you keep breathing, I'm going to come. I think the cock ring company oversold their product's ability," I said, making Trent chuckle. I felt the vibration everywhere, but inside my ass and against my cock were the two places that caught my attention the most. "Or maybe you're just that good."

Trent snorted. "We've reached an impasse."

"One of us is opposed to coming?" I asked.

"We're opposed to coming too fast like two horny teenagers," he countered.

Trent gasped when I flexed my hips up as much as I could, fucking myself on his erection and rutting my dick against his abs. Needing more friction and the slick glide of his cock, I shocked Trent when I rolled him to his back so that I straddled his hips.

"Jesus," Trent moaned when I began to move, slowly at first, finding the angle that felt best to me.

My mouth fell open on a silent gasp when I found it. "Right there," I said, rocking back and forth, chasing my pleasure.

Trent reached between my legs and loosened the elastic around my balls and pumped my dick in time with my hips. My head felt too heavy to hold upright, so I let it fall back on my shoulders as the most intense pleasure I'd ever felt washed over me. Stars exploded behind my closed eyelids, and I reopened them seconds before I painted Trent's chest. I had to watch myself marking him and couldn't deny the possessiveness clenching my heart as tightly as my ass squeezed his cock. *Mine*, my soul whispered.

I leaned forward and worked my hips faster and harder, needing to watch the myriad of emotions wash over Trent's face. He bit his lip but never broke eye contact. His hips rose off the bed to meet my downward thrusts, and his fingers dug into my biceps.

"Give it to me," I demanded. "Fill me up."

Trent roared my name, flooding the condom. He looked at me with wide-eyed wonder like I'd given him the most amazing gift he'd ever received. "That was..." My eloquent doctor seemed at a loss for words.

"Incredible," I said. Easing myself off his dick, I flopped down beside him on the bed, hauling Trent into my arms.

Trent nodded. "Are you sure I wasn't too rough?"

"You were perfect," I said, pulling him to me for a long, tender kiss.

Trent broke the kiss, sighed, and melted against my chest. He closed his eyes and appeared to doze. Moments later, he lifted his head and blessed me with a sated smile that made my toes curl.

"There's my guy," I whispered against his lips.

Trent slid his hands inside my hair and looked like he was about to say something momentous. It was too soon, we both knew it, so I kissed Trent instead to show him I felt it too, even if I wasn't ready to say the words out loud.

We cleaned up then ate the pizza in bed while listening to Jack and Jill. I laughed my ass off when he told me his suggested nicknames for the killer and even added a few of my own. After we finished our pizza, we cuddled in bed and got caught up on our week. Trent surprised me with more mini cheesecakes, which I, in turn, ate off his ass as I'd promised before pushing him up against his bedroom wall and fucking him until we barely had the strength to crawl back into bed. As amazing as the sex was, holding Trent in my arms while he slept was my favorite part of the night.

Damn, how I loved this man.

CHAPTER EIGHTEEN

Trent

"UNCA T! UNCA T!" MADISON YELLED AS SOON AS MERCEDES unbuckled her car seat. "Get me! Get me!" She was adorably demanding for three years old. I knew my sister and Benji were going to have their hands full with this one.

I jogged down my porch steps and sidewalk until I reached my sister's tricked-out minivan. I bent over until I was at eye level with Maddie. "I'm sorry, but do I know you?"

Maddie giggled. "You wuv me, Unca T!"

"I sure do, love bug," I said, scooping her out of her car seat.

Benji rounded the rear of the van carrying the other two heart snatchers like sacks of potatoes beneath his well-defined arms. Mercedes had ribbed me mercilessly about dating Mr. March, but her husband was no slouch. Benji worked out his frustrations in the gym so he could be the best partner he could to Mercedes and father to Madison, Brooklyn, and Savannah.

"I have two more packages for you, sir. Where would you like them?" Benji asked.

"Just set them down and get on out of here."

"Ha ha ha," Mercedes said to both of us. "You're not keeping our girls. Get your own kids."

"I will someday," I said.

Mercedes pushed her sunglasses on top of her head and looked at me with soft eyes. No one would ever look at us and think we were siblings. She was my opposite in every way—dark to my light, short to my tall, and curvy to my lean. Mercedes thought she needed to lose the forty pounds she gained from three pregnancies, but I thought she'd never looked more beautiful. I knew our mother had a lot to do with Mercedes' negative body image. Mother had never come right out and said Mercedes needed to lose weight, at least not in my presence, but she would show Mercedes pictures of her before marriage and babies and emphasize how beautiful and healthy she looked in them. Benji would be quick to remark that Mercedes had never looked more beautiful to him than she did right then. Mercedes would snort and blow off his compliment, but anyone looking at the adoring expression on Benji's face knew he was speaking from the heart.

"Hello, gorgeous," I said to her. It was true. Her dark, unprocessed hair gleamed in the sunlight, her amber eyes sparkled with happiness, and her makeup-free skin looked flawless and allowed us to see the spackling of freckles across her nose and cheeks. Mercedes had recently told me she didn't miss all the hair salon and nail appointments and hours of putting on makeup each week, which was good because she spent most of her time taking her daughters to and from school and all their activities. They had memberships to the zoo, the children's museum, King's Island, and Shirlene would be happy to know they attended weekly programs at the library. Mercedes' schedule exhausted me, but she had never been happier. Her self-care time these days was a bubble bath at night with a glass of wine and a good book after she tucked the girls into bed. My sister was the kind of parent I longed to be, and not for the first time, I wondered how she was able to pull it off with the pitiful example our parents set for us.

Mercedes smiled and said, "Hello, dipshit."

"Dipshit!" Maddie repeated.

"No, Maddie," Mercedes said. "Mommy said bad words."

"There's another quarter for the swear jar," Benji said. "I better make a note in my phone so I don't forget to collect later." He set Savannah and Brooklyn, ages six and eight, down and pulled his phone from his pocket. The girls rushed me, and I squatted down to pick them up too. Who needed a workout when I had three wriggling little girls to hold on to?

"I've missed you so much," I said, kissing each of them on the cheek.

"Baby, you're going to collect later all right," Mercedes said, leering at Benji. "Perhaps we can work out a different kind of payment system besides quarters." Then she looked over my shoulder, and I knew what made her eyes widen and her jaw drop open for a few seconds before Benji leaned in and gently pushed her chin up to close it. "Oh. My. God."

"I know," I smugly said, turning to look at my sexy man. "He's even more beautiful on the inside than he is on the outside."

"Says every serial killer they talk about on the podcast you're obsessed with," Benji remarked. I would've flipped him off, but my arms were occupied by three impressionable little girls. My narrowed look let him know I'd get even at the first available opportunity.

"You've got it bad, bro," Mercedes said, shifting her eyes back to me. She radiated joy and happiness for me, which was the balm I needed after the conversation with our mother the previous weekend. "I can see why." She leaned in and mock-whispered, "Does he give private tours of the firehouse?"

Benji chuckled and said, "You don't get to slide down his pole."

Mercedes laughed and slapped Benji's chest playfully. "Besides, I've been watching his expression since we arrived. You don't stand a chance, lady. He only has eyes for your brother. You should've seen the expression on Tucker's face when Trent picked up Maddie. He's a goner."

"How the hell did you notice all that and I didn't?" Mercedes asked him.

"A man is always aware when a potential threat is near," Benji told his wife then kissed her forehead. "I assessed the situation and immediately tagged him as a friendly instead of a hostile."

"You know I love your military jargon," Mercedes said, leaning closer to her husband. She and Benji had met at college after he'd served in the Marines for four years. She whispered something in his ear that thankfully neither the girls nor I could hear.

"Do you need Tuck and me to watch the girls for you for a while?" I asked. "There's a hotel in Goodville."

"And miss out on spending time with your guy?" Mercedes asked. "Don't be silly. I might take you up on your offer in a few weeks though. There's one weekend where the girls have zero activities on their calendar, and I could use a getaway with my guy."

"You got it," I told her. "Would my favorite girls in the whole world want to see the two surprises I have for them?"

"Yes!" Maddy, Savannah, Brooklyn, and Mercedes shouted.

"More kitties?" Savannah asked.

"A puppy?" Brooklyn countered.

"Adult beverages for me?" Mercedes asked.

"No," I said to Savannah and Brooklyn before turning to Mercedes. "I did make a special fruit punch just for the adults. The kids and designated driver can choose between regular and pink lemonade."

"Pink!" Benji and the girls said.

"I want you all to meet someone very special to me," I said, walking up the sidewalk toward the porch where my mouthwatering, mountain of a man stood smiling at me. I set my bundles of joy on the porch, and the girls looked up, up, and up, until they reached Tucker's face. "Angels, this is my boyfriend, Tucker. Tuck, these are my precious angels."

"Hello, ladies," Tuck said. I heard Mercedes make swooning noises behind me which was followed by Benji's chuckle. "Uncle T has told me so much about you."

"What'd he say?" Brooklyn asked suspiciously.

"He told me you were the prettiest princesses in all the land."

"Thank you," Benji said, earning a grin from Tucker.

"He was talking about me, babe," Mercedes said.

"What else?" Savannah wanted to know.

"He talks about how smart you are and tells me about your activities. I'm exhausted just hearing about all the things you ladies do."

"Maddie is only in baby gymnastics for now," Brooklyn said.

"Not a baby," Maddie argued. "Big girl now."

"Yes, you are, sweet pea," I said. Turning to look at me, Maddie raised her arms for me to lift her again. Having an advantage over her sisters who were still on the ground, Maddie studied Tucker closely for a few seconds before she smiled and reached for him.

Tucker's eyes widened in surprise, but he didn't hesitate to take her from me. "You're even prettier up close, Maddie." He looked down at Savannah's and Brooklyn's upturned faces. "Do you want a lift too?" They both nodded so he squatted down and picked them up like they weighed nothing.

"Don't even think about it," Benji told Mercedes.

"What? His back is still free," she countered.

Tucker's deep, rumbly laughter made my heart race as we followed him inside the house.

"Uncle T has a big surprise for you," he told them.

"Yes!" my nieces shouted.

"He worked hard all week."

"Technically, the carpenter did," I countered.

"You still planned it out and executed it," Tucker said over his shoulder. "That counts."

"Some guys just aren't good with their hands," Benji teased.

"I'm plenty good, but this was a job for two people, and my trusty sidekick had to work a lot of hours this week."

Tucker was disappointed he'd missed the opportunity to build something with me, so he dragged me through Lowe's to pick out a patio furniture set so he could assemble the table, chairs, and huge umbrella before our cookout.

"Oh my gosh!" Brooklyn exclaimed when she saw her surprise through the sliding glass door in the kitchen.

"A playground!" Savannah said.

"For us?" Maddie asked.

"For my three little ladies."

Tucker opened the slider, and we followed him onto the deck overlooking the shaded back yard.

"Whoa!" Brooklyn and Savannah said when they took in the sheer size of the wooden structure. Two forts anchored the playset with a wooden bridge between them. There were two big-girl swings for Savannah and Brooklyn, a toddler swing for my Maddie, two slides, monkey bars, and a teeter-totter. I used long pieces of rustic timber to keep the recycled rubber corralled beneath the playground so I wouldn't run it over with the mower.

"Down!" Maddie demanded, wiggling her little body for emphasis. "Go play."

"Me too!" Savannah and Brooklyn said.

Tucker set them down, and they ran as fast as their legs carried them, calling out what they wanted to play on first. Maddie struggled to keep up, so Tucker ran after her and scooped her up in his arms so she wouldn't finish last. She was still too little to do much on her own, but she had Tuck to help her. He held Maddie's tiny torso and let her pretend to cross the monkey bars. He set her inside one of the forts then walked along beside her as she ran across the bridge to reach her sisters, who hugged her when she made it. Tucker kept a hand on her back to support her while Savannah gently rocked her up and down on the teeter-totter.

"They're getting along so well," Mercedes remarked from her cushioned chair, holding a large glass of adult fruit punch in her hand.

"It won't last," Benji said.

"Hush your face," Mercedes hissed.

Benji was right. The sisterly love ended when all three girls wanted Tucker to push them on their swing.

"Maddie's hogging Tucker," Brooklyn complained.

"There's enough of him to go around," Mercedes shot back. "Take turns."

And they did. Tucker took turns pushing my nieces, each of them squealing, giggling, and chanting, "Higher! Higher!"

Mercedes put her drink down and turned to me with a serious expression on her face. "I will disown you if you don't have that man's babies."

Benji snorted. "Um, honey…"

Mercedes rolled her eyes and nudged him with her elbow. "You know what I mean," she said to her husband before returning her intense expression to me. "You do whatever it takes to keep this man in your life, Trent. I've never seen you look this relaxed, happy, and…" She paused, wondering if she should be bold enough to say what she was thinking.

"In love?" I asked.

"Yes," Benji and Mercedes said.

It was true. I was head over heels in love with Tucker Garrison, and I would do whatever it took to keep him in my life.

R~X~

PATIENT NAME: _____

ADDRESS: _____

Prescription:

CHAPTER NINETEEN

Signature: _____ Date: _____

Tucker

"**L**ET ME GET THIS STRAIGHT," BENJI SAID WHEN HE HELPED ME load the dishwasher. "You smoked the beef brisket, shopped for and assembled the patio furniture, and now you're doing the dishes. It's not even six o'clock."

"I had help," I told him with a shrug.

"With which task?"

"All of it. Trent helped me prepare the meat and start the smoker this morning, we picked out and assembled the furniture together, and now you're helping me with the dishes."

"I volunteered before my wife could," Benji quipped. "I feared for your safety."

I snorted. Sure, Mercedes flirted, but it was all in good fun. She had eyes for one man only. "She's crazy about you," I told him.

"She is," he said with a happy sigh. "I'm a very lucky man. She could've had any guy she wanted but chose me. I won't take it for granted."

I looked out the window and watched Trent and Mercedes talking together. Her head was thrown back as she laughed at whatever her brother had said. There was no denying the siblings were easy on the eyes, but their quick wit, intelligence, and compassion made them even more attractive.

"I can't imagine a day without hearing her laughter or seeing her smile," Benji said. "And, damn, she's an amazing mother to our girls. Mercedes has given me the best fifteen years of my life." A dark cloud of emotion washed over Benji's face, dimming his joy, but then he blinked, and the cloud dissipated. "It wasn't easy at first because of her parents' toxic influence, but we battled through the dark times. Mercedes found the confidence to stand up to them and hasn't backed down." He offered a kind smile and said, "I think Trent is even more scarred than she is, so I hope you won't give up on him. I promise you he's worth the fight."

I nodded because I knew he was right. This past week during our phone conversations, Trent had told me more about his parents' controlling habits and some of the ways they'd let him down. Trent recalled a great uncle who was a homophobic, racist, misogynist asshole and would spout the vilest things around them. He thought his parents would stop inviting him over after he came out as gay, but they just chalked up the old man's comments to him being ignorant or from a different era. Refusing to attend any event the uncle was invited to was Trent's first act of defiance. Even though the man died a few years ago, his parents' lack of support in the face of his horrible behavior was still forefront in Trent's mind. He wouldn't allow himself to forget it.

"Mercedes had to battle her mother's ideas of what roles a woman should have in the world. Suzanne only cared about what Mercedes looked like and the connections she could bring with her marriage." Benji snorted. "I might be from an affluent family, but my folks are

generous philanthropists who support the arts and important so-
cial issues like women's and children's rights, they advocate for the
LGBTQ+ community, support homeless shelters, and sponsor at least
one Habitat for Humanity house each year. There's no way in hell
my mother would tell any daughter of hers to choose an easy college
major because the only reason a woman should attend college was to
snag a good man."

"Whoa," I said. "That's so 1822."

"Right?" Benji asked. "Suzanne criticizes everything Mercedes
does from her hair to her weight to the activities she allows our daughters to participate in. 'Little girls don't practice martial arts, Mercedes.
Gymnastics is okay, but why not ballet or figure skating?'" Benji's impersonation of Trent and Mercedes' mother was hilarious, and though
I'd never met the woman, I had a feeling he was spot on. "When she
found out we signed Brooklyn up for soccer, you would've thought our
daughter was learning to joust." He tipped his head to the side. "What
age do they start learning how to fence?"

"I suspect you have a few years yet, but it's never too early to learn
the footwork," I offered.

"Mercedes and I don't want the status quo for our girls. We tried
explaining to Suzanne we want our girls to be familiar with martial arts
so they can defend themselves."

"How did she respond?" I asked.

"She told us it was a waste of time and money because their future
husbands wouldn't be concerned about their ability to fight or what
sports they played. Their husbands would only care about the way they
represented *him*."

"Oh fuck. That didn't go over well, did it?"

"Fuck no, it didn't. Suzanne was especially nasty to Mercedes this
week because she was mad at Trent and took it out on my wife."

"Oh no," I moaned. "I'm so sorry."

"Don't be," Benji said, patting me on my shoulder. "Trent did
nothing wrong."

"What happened?" I asked, although I wasn't sure I wanted to know.

"Mercedes asked her mom to watch the girls one afternoon this week when our sitter had to cancel because of the flu. Mercedes tried to reschedule her doctor appointment, but the next available opening wasn't for another three months. I would've come home, but she decided to take a gamble and ask her mom instead."

"Didn't pay off?" I asked.

"You might say that," Benji said, turning on the dishwasher. He turned and folded his arms across his chest. "Do you know what the witch said to my beautiful wife when she arrived at our home?" Benji's voice broke, and I felt horrible for him. "Suzanne told Mercedes she hoped she wasn't pregnant again because she hadn't lost the weight from the last two pregnancies." My eyes bulged out of my head. "It gets worse," he cautioned. "She implied my late nights at work probably had nothing to do with closing out the first fiscal quarter of the year. That...poor excuse of a woman told my wife I was most likely having an affair with a younger, thinner, and more beautiful woman."

"Fuck me."

"To make matters worse, she said it in front of our girls, and while they didn't understand the meaning of Suzanne's words, they knew what their mother's tears meant." Benji's voice vibrated with anger.

"I'm so sorry, Benji."

"Mercedes threw the heartless monster out of our house and sent me a 9-1-1 text. I don't ever want to see that kind of devastation on my wife's face again or see my daughters crying because their grandmother broke their mother's heart. I started looking for a different job. While Elon isn't quite as horrible as Suzanne, he's done nothing to protect his children from her hatefulness. I told him what happened the next day, and he just shrugged and blamed it on Suzanne's hormones and Trent's abandonment. Then he left early with his new assistant slash mistress."

"Wow. It's like *Dynasty* but worse because it involves real people. Mercedes doesn't deserve such hatefulness."

"She doesn't, and neither does Trent. I'm warning you now, Suzanne is up to no good. She already mentioned hiring a PI to check into your background. She'll be looking to pull Trent back into the family fold since Mercedes gave her the final 'fuck you' this week."

"A private investigator? Who the hell are these people?"

"To quote Trent, they are 'elitist assholes' who lack any character and decency. Their aggrandized sense of worth is appalling." I wasn't surprised that Mercedes told Benji what Trent had said since she found it so funny.

"I'm a fireman without a college degree who was raised by his hippy grandmother. I don't come with powerful connections or money. That's the worst they're going to learn about me. I've never even had a parking ticket."

"It doesn't matter what his parents do or say, because you have something *Trent* wants—craves." I quirked my brow, and Benji shook his head. "Unconditional love, my friend. Trent practically vibrates with happiness and affection when he looks at you."

I glanced back out the window and saw he was playing with his nieces on the playground. Trent was born to be a father to a bunch of kids, and it stunned me how much I wanted to be the other parent in the equation. Was our love strong enough to go the distance, to overcome the obstacles his parents presented? The part of me that was terrified of not being good enough for Trent reared its ugly head and wanted me to leave before I got in too deep. *Run. It's not too late.*

"Ready to join everyone outside?" Benji asked, interrupting my thoughts.

"I'll be there in just a minute."

Benji patted my shoulder as he walked by. "Hey, babe," he yelled when he opened the door. "You should've been much quicker to volunteer for the dishes. Tucker let me feel his biceps."

"Damn," Mercedes said, glaring at her husband.

"You owe fifty cents to the jar when we get home," Benji told his wife. Then he charged at her, swooped her up in his arms, and kissed her. Their daughters stopped what they were doing to watch and clap their little hands while Trent laughed.

My guy turned and looked at me through the kitchen window as if he could feel me watching him. His smile was brighter than the sun and chased away the chill fear had instilled in my heart. I returned his smile and winked at him. It was already too late to run; I was in too deep.

CHAPTER TWENTY

Trent

THE NEXT TWO WEEKS WERE AMAZING. TUCKER WORKED FIRST SHIFT and hadn't volunteered any extra hours, which allowed us to spend a lot of time together. Once I opened up to Tucker about my parents, I just kept talking and talking until it felt like I could finally breathe. I was heartsick over the horrible things my mother said to Mercedes and knew reconciling with my parents wasn't something I wanted. I saw what it cost Benji to be civil to my parents the last few years for Mercedes' sake, but he was done playing nice guy. He'd found a new job and tendered his resignation at my father's company, severing all personal and professional ties with my parents. While I was happy for my sister and her family, I found myself waiting for the other shoe to drop.

Tucker had told me about Benji's friendly warning, and I knew he was right. Mother was biding her time to pounce and draw first blood. After two weeks passed, I started to relax a little, which wasn't hard to do when I spent nearly every night in Tucker's arms.

Neither of us had said the L word yet, but I saw Tucker's feelings for me in his eyes and felt it in his touch. I tried to show him how much I revered him. The connection between us grew deeper every day as we learned more about each other. Exploring Tucker's home library blew my mind. His reading interests were vast and inspiring and provided insight into the inner workings of my beautiful man. I showed him the photographs I took on my trips with Doctors Without Borders.

"You have a keen eye, Doc," Tucker had said after looking through the album.

"I love taking pictures, but I know next to nothing about doing it properly. I kind of just point and shoot." Unsurprisingly, Tucker had a book about photography, and I learned a lot about light, contrast, and angles. He was my favorite subject to shoot, and I had visions of making a private calendar featuring a different shot of Tucker for the next year.

Most of our nights were spent at my house because of Natasha and Boris until Tucker bought them food and water dishes and a litter box for his house. "Might as well dirty up my sheets once and a while," he'd told me.

"And they say chivalry is dead," I'd responded.

On the nights I went to Tucker's, I placed Natasha and Boris in their carrier and packed their beds in my car. They were confused at first but seemed happy to have a new place to explore.

Things were amazing for us, and I relaxed a bit more each passing day without a call from either of my parents. Before we knew it, we were hosting the annual end-of-season barbecue for the basketball team at my house on a warm day in mid-April. Tucker and I supplied the meat and everyone else contributed side dishes or beverages.

My back yard was packed with more people than I ever expected to see, but I loved the laughter and teasing. Hailey and Braxton's sons loved the playground and didn't want to stop playing long enough to eat. Only Tucker was able to coax them away to get some dinner. He did a pretty good T-Rex impersonation as he roared and chased the little guys to the picnic tables where their parents waited with plates of food.

After we stuffed ourselves, it was time to play cornhole. Donovan wanted Jilly to rest and kick her feet up, but I recognized the competitive gleam in her eyes. She finally convinced him that tossing a beanbag at a wooden board with a hole cut at the top wouldn't jeopardize the baby. Rather than choosing teams, we paired up as couples and drew team names to see who we faced off against for the first round. After the first round, the losing teams would square off against each other to see who could get back in the win-ner's bracket. Lose twice and you're eliminated. We planned to play until there were only two teams remaining.

Tucker and I drew the Turners as our first opponent. Tucker entertained us all by swaggering about and pretending to be Captain Jack Sparrow. It was obvious he had plenty of practice annoying Will and Elizabeth.

"He's pretty agile for a big guy," Grammie said. "But you already know that." She winked and nudged me with her elbow. I looped my arm around her shoulders and pulled her into a one-armed hug. I was so happy she joined us for the cookout.

"Nice try, Moose," Elizabeth said. "You're not throwing us off our game with your silly antics."

"Yeah, Sparky," Will added. "Let's see what you got."

"Whoa now," I said, stepping into the fray. "You couldn't handle it, Will."

Everyone started catcalling and whistling at us, which is when a couple opened the rear gate and stepped inside my back yard. I felt like someone swung an ax and split my skull in half.

"Shit."

"What's wrong?" Tucker asked, pulling me toward him and kissing my temple.

"My parents just showed up," I replied. Tucker started to move away from me, but I wouldn't allow it. I turned and looked into his eyes. "I'm just going to ask them to leave and promise to call them later so they don't ruin our evening with our friends. The conversation I need to have with them is long overdue."

"Do you want me to come with you?" Tuck offered.

"I've got it. My parents detest public scenes, so it won't be hard to convince them to leave."

I pulled Tucker to me for a quick kiss then left him beside Shirlene so I could deal with the unexpected nuisance. "Mother, Father," I tersely said when I reached them. "As you can see, this isn't a convenient time for you to visit."

"Let me guess," my mother said, "you want us to go back home and wait for an invitation you never plan to extend."

"That about sums it up."

"Suzanne," my father said sternly, "I asked you not to antagonize him. He'll only refuse to listen to what we have to say."

"He has his head shoved too far up *Tucker's* behind to listen to reason anyway," Mother countered.

"Every chance I get."

"See!" she said, gesturing to me. "Trent never used to be so vulgar until he started dating trash."

"Leave now before I call the police and have you escorted off my property," I said. My voice might've been soft, but the tone was lethal. I meant it too.

"Trent, please," my father said, holding up his hands in a conciliatory gesture. "Can we please have a private word with you? It will only take a few minutes. There's something very important we need to share with you."

"I'm not interested, Father."

Even if I hadn't seen my mother's eyes widen in alarm, I knew Tucker was approaching by the way my body reacted to his nearness.

"Is everything okay here?" he asked, his deep voice sounding dominant.

"This doesn't concern you," my father said angrily.

"It sure as hell does," Mother bristled.

It was obvious they weren't leaving, and I could feel everyone staring at us. "Let's go inside. You have five minutes to tell me whatever it is you want to say. Then you will leave and never return."

"You'll change your tune when you hear what we found out about *him*."

"Mother, there's nothing shady about Tucker. I'm not interested in what you have to say about him."

"That's what you think," she countered. "Five minutes is all I need to make you see reason. Lead the way, Trenton."

"You don't have to subject yourself to this nonsense," I told Tucker when he started to follow us.

"I have a right to hear what they're saying about me."

"Would you like a five-minute rebuttal?" I teased.

"None of this is funny, Son," my father said as we stepped onto the back deck.

"You're right, Father. I don't think you showing up here to sling dirt at Tucker is remotely funny, which is why I'm trying to lighten the mood before I snap. There are many things I want to say to you and Mother, but I need to do it when I'm calm. I'm feeling anything but that right now."

Once inside my kitchen, Mother pulled out a manila folder from her oversized purse. "Here's the report Mr. Hastings compiled about Tucker's background, and while he doesn't currently have a criminal record, I suspect it will change. Apples don't fall far from the tree."

"Meaning?" I asked. What could she say about his parents who died tragically young in a car crash?

"Bad blood breeds bad blood," Mother said snidely.

"In that case, Tucker should run as fast and as far as he can. Nothing good could come from loving me."

Ignoring me, my mother continued digging her claws into Tucker's soul. "His father was an alcoholic, and his mother was a drug addict."

"That's not true," Tucker said gruffly. "My parents died in a car accident when I was nine months old." I reached for his hand, but he flinched away from me. "How could you say such horrible lies about my parents?"

Mother extended the file to him, and he accepted it. Tucker flipped through the pages of what appeared to be a traffic report. "Oh my God," he whispered hoarsely then moaned when he reached the final pages. Tucker's heartbroken sob when he saw the pictures of his parents' charred car wrapped around a tree would haunt me for the rest of my life. In much less than five minutes, my mother shredded everything Tucker thought he knew about his family. The foundation he built his life on crumbled, and he shook with it. She destroyed him, as did I, by proxy.

I snatched the folder from Tucker's hands as fast as I could, but the damage was already done. "Get the fuck out of my house, and don't you ever come back," I told my parents.

"Son," my father said.

"I am not your son. I am dead to you from this day forward. Do you hear me? Do not contact me ever again." I was shouting by the time I finished, and I knew everyone outside must've heard me. I couldn't care about them right then. I had to get them out of my home so I could help Tucker do... I didn't know. I just needed to help him somehow. "Get out!" I said, advancing on them. I looked at my parents through a red haze of rage. "Go now, or I will call the police." I reached for my phone because I wasn't playing.

"Come on, Suzanne. He needs time to think."

"I don't need to fucking think! I *know* I want you out of my house and out of my life. I'll never forgive you for hurting Tucker. Never."

Gentle hands gripped my shoulders, and Shirlene's soft voice penetrated my fury. "Breathe, sweetheart. They're leaving now. I need you to take some deep cleansing breaths. Do it with me. Big inhale; slow exhale. That's right. Let's do it again a few more times." I breathed with Shirlene until the numbness and tingling started to fade. I'd never been so tempted to commit violence, and it frightened me.

"Shirlene," I whimpered. "Oh my God. I'm so sorry." Then I whirled to face the man I loved, but I barely recognized him. Tucker's eyes looked vacant, his body trembled, and his teeth chattered. He'd seen many horrible things as a firefighter and an EMT but seeing pictures of how his parents died was far worse than anything he'd witnessed on the job. Tucker's obvious distress cleared the rest of my anger. I'd have time later to think about what my parents had done to us as a couple, but Tucker needed my medical training first.

"Shirlene, I need your help. Tucker's gone into shock. Can you please grab the blanket off the back of my couch? It might not be thick enough, but it's a start."

"Absolutely. I'll be right back."

"Come back to me, Tucker," I said, rubbing my hands up and down his arms to stimulate blood flow and try to warm him.

"Here you go," Shirlene said, returning to the kitchen. "Should I make a cup of hot tea or something?"

"That would be great." I wrapped the blanket snugly around Tuck's shoulder and guided him over to a kitchen chair. "Come back to me, Tucker." I urged him to sit down, and he did so after a few failed attempts. I just kept rubbing his extremities and talking to him while I waited for Shirlene to make the tea.

"Here you go. It's not super hot because I didn't want to scald his mouth."

"It feels perfect," I said to her after wrapping my hands around the mug. "Here, baby."

Tucker took a few sips with my help, and eventually, his color returned, and his body stopped shaking.

"There's my guy," I whispered when he finally looked at me.

Tears welled in Tucker's wounded eyes, and he shook his head. Every hope I had for a future with this man shattered on my tile floor like the mug that slipped through my fingers. "I-I can't." He couldn't what? Grasp what had happened? Love me anymore? Tucker closed his eyes and shook his head. "I just can't."

"Okay," I said weakly. "What do you need right now?"

Tucker ignored my question and looked away from me to focus on Shirlene. "How could you keep the truth from me, Grammie?" Tucker's voice sounded weak and ravaged by heartbreak. "My entire life has been a lie."

Shirlene, who had started to clean up the spilled tea and broken mug, stilled and jerked her gaze up to meet his. "Your life hasn't been a lie, Tuck." Both her tone and the expression in her eyes implored him to listen to her. "The cause of their accident doesn't change the fact that they loved you. Yes, your parents made some terrible mistakes, but they always put you first. I made the decision not to tell you about their addictions because it didn't change the outcome of their tragic deaths and it wouldn't benefit you in any way."

"Not benefit me?" The shock was wearing off and anger was moving in. "Not benefit me? Addiction is genetic, Grammie."

"Says who?"

"Scientists," Tucker fired back.

"You've never shown any signs of addiction to anything—not to alcohol, drugs, gambling, or even sex."

Tucker cast his eyes quickly in my direction, and I could tell he was internally debating the last part. Yes, we'd had our hands all over each other since the first night we decided to give our relationship a try, but it didn't mean we were addicted. "Grammie, you have no idea what I was doing as a teenager."

"In this town?" she countered. "Do you honestly think word of what happened at the weekly bonfires didn't get back to us? I knew you had opportunities to drink, smoke dope, and get into other trouble, but you never did. You fell hard for Milo Miracle and didn't care about what the other kids were doing. You better believe I knew the signs of addiction, and I kept a close eye on you to see if your behavior changed erratically."

"I had a right to know," Tucker said.

"And now you do, Tuck. Can you honestly look me in the eye and tell me you're happy to know the truth now? Is your life somehow better?" Shirlene asked. She stood up quickly then started to sway.

"Grammie," Tuck cried out and tried to stand up, but his legs got tangled in the blanket, and he fell back onto the chair.

"I got her, Tuck," I said, reaching for Shirlene. "Are you okay?"

"I just stood up too fast," she said, waving us off. "I'm fine." She swallowed hard then dumped the fragments of the teacup she still held into my palm. "Tucker and I have a lot to discuss, but I don't think it's the right time. I'll just go home, and we can talk privately."

"Of course it's not the right time," Tucker said bitterly. "Maybe we should wait another thirty-two years." The angry bite in his voice made Shirlene flinch.

"Come on, Tuck. This isn't you," I said.

"How do you know it isn't me? Maybe my bad genetics have been in remission until your parents came along and triggered them."

"I know nothing I say or do will make this better for any of us, but I truly am sorry for what my parents did to you. I would never want to see you hurting like this."

"Yeah, your apology can't fix this." Tucker stood up quickly, throwing the blanket off before he could trip again. "I need to get out of here."

"Maybe now isn't the best time for you to be driving," I said.

"Why? Do you think I can't control my anger and disappointment long enough to drive home? Fine, I'll walk." He took off for the front door. After a glance at Shirlene to make sure she was okay, I followed him.

"Tucker, please, don't go."

He stopped with his hand on the doorknob, but he didn't look over his shoulder at me. "I can't be here right now. On some level, I know it's not fair to hold you personally responsible for what your parents did to me, but I'm not in a reasonable state of mind right now." *Would he ever be in the right frame of mind to hear me out? Would I if I were in his shoes?*

"All the more reason why you shouldn't be alone right now. I understand you don't want to talk to me right now, or even Shirlene, but there's a backyard full of people who love you. Talk to one of them."

"I just need to be by myself right now."

"Please don't give up on us, Tucker," I begged, not bothering to hide my desperation.

Tucker opened the door and stepped onto the porch. "I think it's too late."

I leaned against the foyer wall for a long time after he left. I couldn't help but think he'd shut the door on more than just our conversation. I lost track of time until Shirlene's soft voice pulled me out of my brokenhearted daze.

"Honey, everyone is packing up and heading home. Do you want me to stay and help you clean up?"

"No, it's okay," I said, turning to face her. I thought I'd held my shit together until she brushed the tears off my face.

"Tucker loves you, Trent. He's upset right now, but I know he'll come around. He won't give up on you because of your asshole parents."

"I'm so sorry for what they did to you and Tuck."

"I'll have none of that," Shirlene said, hugging me. "If anyone is to blame, it's me. I could've told Tucker the truth when he was old enough to understand, but it wasn't how I wanted to remember my son and his wife. He needs time and space to absorb what he's learned before he accepts what he already knows in his heart to be true. You are his truth, Trent. I believe it with all my heart."

"I hope so, Shirlene. My chest aches like Tucker reached inside it and tore my heart out. I don't want him to give it back to me; I just don't want him to crush it."

"My boy is a gentle giant. Crushing things isn't part of his nature."

I hoped she was right, but I was too afraid to believe. I promised myself I'd give Tucker the time and space he needed and not rush him, but not knowing if he was okay killed me. I wrapped myself in a cocoon of misery in my bed that smelled like him while trying to get a grip on my tears. I hadn't gone to bed without either sending Tucker a text or rolling over to kiss him good night in a month. I wasn't going to start on this night either.

Good night, Sparky.

I didn't expect a response from Tucker, but I wanted him to know I wouldn't go quietly into the night. I would not give up on us.

R̶x

Prescription:

CHAPTER TWENTY-ONE

Signature: _____ Date: _____

Tucker

WHEN I LEFT TRENT'S HOUSE, I'D PLANNED TO GO HOME AS I told him, but I passed my street and kept driving. I drove past the sign outside of town that read: *Thank you for visiting Blissville. We hope to see you again soon.* I aimed my truck in a southern direction and just kept driving. I merged onto I-275 then I-75 and didn't stop until my warning light for my gas tank came on somewhere in the middle of Kentucky. In hindsight, Trent was right; I had no business operating a vehicle in my current state of mind.

Luckily, I wasn't far from an exit with restaurants and gas stations. Food was the furthest thing from my mind, but gas was a necessity. The idea of turning around and driving back home made me quake with too many emotions. I wasn't ready to have a conversation with Trent, and I sure as hell wanted to avoid my grandmother until

I had a grip on my anger. I might never agree with what she did, but it would be wrong to verbally lash out and hurt someone who'd only shown me love my entire life. I could at least acknowledge Grammie thought she was protecting me by keeping the information away from me. Ignorance is bliss and all that. Maybe when my anger faded and I could look at things objectively, I would better understand or even agree with her decision.

After refueling my truck, I called Braxton. "Hey, Brax."

"Are you okay? I ran by your place a while ago and you weren't home. What the hell happened at the doc's house today? Who were those awful people?"

"Those are Trent's parents who'd stopped by to save him from my evil clutches."

"Are you fucking kidding me right now?"

"No," I said. "I'm really not in the headspace to talk about this right now. I do have a favor to ask you though."

"Name it, Tuck. You know I'd do anything for you."

"I just kept driving tonight and wound up in Kentucky. I'm only a few hours away from your family's house at Lake Cumberland and wondered if it's being used as a rental this week. If not, I'd really appreciate it if I could stay a few days. I'll happily pay the going AirBnb rate." Braxton's parents, along with his two uncles and their wives, owned a stunning lake house which they rented out when it wasn't being used by the family. I'd spent at least a month there with Brax's family every summer when we were kids.

"The hell you will," Brax said. "Let me call my mom because she keeps all booking stuff in her phone. Hang tight, buddy."

Braxton called me back within five minutes. "The lake house is vacant for the next ten days, and Mom said you're more than welcome to stay there. I'll text you the code for the keypad to unlock the door."

I hadn't planned to stay there long, but a few days of peace were just what the doctor—I couldn't finish the thought; it was just too damn painful. "Tell her I said thank you, Brax."

"Tuck, no thanks are necessary. You're family. Always. You know I love you."

The careful control I had on my emotions cracked and feelings gushed out of me like water over the Hoover Dam. A choked sob escaped before I could rein it in. "I love you too."

"I can be there in a few hours, Moose."

The nickname made me laugh, and I was able to get ahold of myself. "I'm okay, Brax, but thank you for offering. I need to call Will and let him know I won't be in for a few days. I have plenty of personal time saved, but I hate to fuck up everyone's schedule with my last-minute bullshit."

"Whatever happened this afternoon was not bullshit, Tuck. You cover for everyone all the fucking time. If anyone dares give Will lip about working some extra hours, then they'll be answering to me."

"You're the best, Brax."

"So Hailey keeps telling me," he replied, lightening the heavy mood. "Say the word, and I'll be there. You said you need time, and I respect that, but please don't shut out the ones who love you. Drop us a text just to let us know you're okay."

"I will," I promised. "Talk soon."

"I'm holding you to it, Moose," Brax said before disconnecting the call.

I called Will next, and the conversation was easier than I expected. Will assured me he could cover my shifts without any problem. "You fill in for everyone else. They'll step up or be sorry," he said, echoing Brax's sentiments.

Once I had a plan set, I decided to run through a drive-thru to grab a bite to eat since it would be too late to do any grocery shopping at one of the mom-and-pop grocery stores near the lake house, if they were even open on Sunday. If they thought working on Sunday was a sin, they'd really hate the way I kicked off my morning in Trent's bed. I shoved the thought inside a vault in my mind I'd labeled: Doc. I would open the vault and sift through the memories and images of him when I was ready, but not until then.

It was completely dark by the time I arrived, but solar lamps lit the winding driveway, cutting a swath through the woods. I didn't need sunlight to know what the stunning, two-story contemporary stone, wood, and glass house looked like. I entered the code Braxton sent me and turned the deadbolt when the light turned green.

Peace washed over me as soon as I crossed the threshold. The home was the place of many happy childhood memories, so it didn't surprise me just being there eased my pain a little. I hadn't visited since the previous year, and I noticed a lot of the furniture was newer and looked more expensive than their old stuff, but it made sense they'd upgrade things to encourage renters.

The great room featured a wall of windows overlooking the lake and a huge, floor-to-ceiling stone hearth surrounding the fireplace. The kitchen appliances were also new, but the stainless steel was somehow a lovely contrast to the rustic design of the cabinets and kitchen table made of rough-hewn lumber that was sanded, stained, and varnished with love. Braxton's great grandfather built the table for his family, and they moved it from his homestead to the lake house after he passed away so the entire family could appreciate it. Pieces like the table were so much more than furniture.

Even though Braxton's folks weren't in residence, staying in the master bedroom felt wrong, so I chose one of the guest bedrooms on the second floor. Since I hadn't stopped by my house, I didn't have a change of clothes or even a toothbrush with me. I could fix that in the morning by running to a department store. The only thing I needed right then was a hot shower and sleep.

The shower was amazing, but sleep eluded me. Every time I shut my eyes, I saw the images of my parents' charred car. I saw the words "driving while intoxicated," "lost control," "collided with a tree," "burst into flames," and the worst was "dead on arrival."

My phone chirped beside me on the nightstand. I thought about ignoring it, but it would only make people more worried than they already were. I saw the text was from Trent.

Good night, Sparky.

How could three little words start a tsunami of emotion? I didn't realize until then how much I looked forward to those three words he either texted to me or whispered in my ear each night before he went to sleep. It seemed I hadn't shoved him into a vault as I'd thought. I knew I wasn't being fair to Trent and had hurt him when he'd only wanted to help me. Through my tears, I typed out the three-worded response he was used to receiving from me either by text or whispered against his lips.

Sleep well, Doc.

Then I broke. My life felt like the rubble left behind after a devastating fire. Bits and pieces of my foundation were still intact, but everything else felt charred beyond recognition and reduced to ash. I could rebuild myself on the shaky framework that remained, but I'd never be the same person. I might be able to come to terms with knowing my father's negligence robbed me from knowing my parents, but I might never look at their photos in the same way. I was sure I'd come to accept Grammie's apology, but I might wonder if she fabricated the happy family stories she'd told me. Pictures lied. Memories could become distorted and reshaped by heartache. I didn't have a time machine to travel back in time to witness how my parents were with me. I'd have to rely on trust and mine felt bruised and broken.

And Trent. I loved him wholly and completely and probably always would, but how could I look into his pretty blue eyes without being reminded of the coldness in his mother's when she blew my world apart? Trent wasn't to blame for his parents, and I knew it, but what if Suzanne was right? What if the apple didn't fall far from the tree, and he was capable of committing the same atrocities as his parents? My heart and soul wanted to reject the idea, but I couldn't.

I tossed and turned and was still awake when the sun rose over the lake, but I was too tattered and exhausted to enjoy it. I finally fell asleep for a few hours only to wake up with a throbbing head, eyes that felt as gritty as sandpaper, and a dry throat. My heart beat heavily in my chest, and I ached from head to toe. If I didn't know better, I would've thought I had the flu, but it was the aftermath of emotional trauma. I'd seen it plenty of times and knew what I needed to do.

The first step was getting to the store to get some food, beverages, clothes, a phone charger, and bathroom stuff. I could lie around and let myself heal, but I needed to make sure I ate and hydrated myself properly. It sounded good in theory, but no food items sounded good to me. I reverted to frozen items and canned soups instead of the healthy, well-balanced meals Trent and I had started making together. The realization only made me sadder, and I was a hot mess by the time I reached the dental care aisle. I was looking at the toothbrushes but seeing the nervous, dorky note Trent had left me the morning after my first sleepover at his house.

I grabbed the first toothbrush package I saw when I shook myself out of the memory, added toothpaste to the cart, and got the hell out of there. When I passed the pet area, I saw cat toys I knew Boris would glare at but secretly love. I automatically reached for them like I would have the week before then stopped myself.

The scenic drive back to the lake house normally stole my breath, but I was so locked down in misery I didn't notice. My chest felt like someone tied a cement block around it, and if I walked out into the lake, I would sink to the bottom.

I unloaded the groceries, made coffee, and sat down in one of the Adirondack chairs on the rear deck of the house. For days, I only left the chair to fix food, shower, use the bathroom, and sleep. I looked out over the lake and watched boats sail by and saw woodland creatures scamper and play through the woods surrounding three sides of the house. My only communication was the occasional text to Braxton letting him know I was okay, which I knew he'd share with Grammie so she wouldn't worry about me, and my good-night exchange with Trent. I couldn't sleep without that little bit of contact with him. He never pushed for more, no matter how hard it must've been for him.

Life went on around me, but time stood still for me. I was stuck in Trent's kitchen listening to his mother's vicious voice and seeing the words on the report. At night, I dreamed of the accident on an endless loop. Each dream was more vivid than the one before and got so bad I feared falling asleep.

It wasn't until I sat through a thunderstorm and was nearly struck by lightning that I realized no matter what I told Braxton in my texts, I wasn't okay. I needed help. I couldn't go on this way. I could either return to Blissville and try to rebuild my life or ask the person I wanted to see the most to join me. I picked up my phone and texted the address before I could talk myself out of it.

CHAPTER TWENTY-TWO

Trent

BY THURSDAY MORNING, I LOOKED LIKE I BELONGED ON THE SET OF *The Night of the Living Dead.* My colleagues, even John, gave me a wide berth. I kept my head down and spoke as little as possible to everyone except Shirlene. I'd tried to avoid her too, but she wouldn't allow it. She bullied her way into my home on Monday evening with dinner.

"Exhaustion looks terrible on you," Shirlene had said with hands on her hips and fire in her eyes. "I know you're hurt, angry, and scared. I am too, but we need to be strong for Tucker when he comes home. You need to eat and sleep."

Either Shirlene's cheesy potato soup and BLTs were made with magic, or I was hungrier than I realized. She watched me through keen eyes as I wolfed down two bowls of soup and two bacon sandwiches and drank half a gallon of sweet tea. She didn't stay long after dinner the first night, but she returned on Tuesday and Wednesday nights with more delicious food, but more importantly, she lent me a shoulder to cry on.

Anger toward my parents and hurt for Tucker spilled out of me in ugly, racking sobs. As wonderful as Shirlene was, I wanted a broader shoulder to lay my head against.

Sleep well, Doc.

Those three little words packed a wallop, and I lived for the moment they arrived every night. I was grateful that Tucker hadn't shut me out completely, but his texts weren't enough to help me sleep. I was lucky if I managed three hours of sleep nightly. I was becoming a liability to all those around me and needed to get a grip on the situation.

By Thursday afternoon, I knew what I had to do. "John, is Dr. Hinman still here?"

"She's in with her last patient."

"Can you tell her I'd like to see her before she leaves for the day?"

"Sure," he said. "Is everything okay?"

"No, but it will be."

Shirlene had told me Tucker was staying at a lake house in Kentucky that Braxton's family owned. Though it could be a huge mistake, I was going to track Braxton down and get the address from him. Hearing through the grapevine that Tucker was doing okay just wasn't good enough for me. I was barely hanging on by a thread, so I knew Tucker wasn't feeling *okay* either.

"I'll let her know, Dr. Love."

I went to my office and dropped heavily onto my chair. Leaning my head back, I closed my eyes to rest them while waiting for Dr. Hinman and drifted to sleep. My vibrating phone woke me, and I was surprised to see the text was from Tucker. He sent me an address in Kentucky followed by one word: *Please.*

On my way, I sent back.

My heart raced, pumping adrenaline through my veins. I jumped to my feet and rushed out of my office, nearly colliding with Becky.

"You scared me half to death," she said, panting and clutching her chest.

"I'm sorry, Becky. Listen, something has come up and I need to leave. I was planning on talking to Dr. Hinman first, but this can't wait. I'll call her from the road to explain. I know this is a huge inconvenience for you, but I need you to reschedule my appointments for tomorrow."

"Um, okay," she said, looking worried. "I'll start calling people now."

I smiled at her for the first time that week. "Thank you, Becky. I will make this up to all of you. I promise," I said, walking backward.

"Drive careful."

"I will," I promised.

I called Shirlene as soon as I walked outside. I could hear the relief in her voice when I told her the news. I realized she'd been putting on a brave face for me all week, and I was ashamed I hadn't tried to do the same for her.

"I'm bringing our guy back," I promised her when I stopped by her house on my way out of town to give her the house key off my ring so she could look after my cats.

"I know you will," she said, squeezing me tight. "Tell Tucker I said moon and back."

"I will, Shirlene."

My next stop was Books and Brew where Milo Miracle, aka Tucker's first crush, made me a large coffee with two shots of espresso. "I need some extra caffeine for a long trip." Milo handed the coffee to me along with a bag of blueberry scones with lemon icing drizzled over the top. They were Tucker's favorite. "I didn't order these," I said, looking at him quizzically.

"Tucker's a great guy, and I'm so happy he's found you. Now go bring him home where he belongs." Of course, he'd heard about Tuck's quick exit from town.

"Thanks," I said, accepting his kind gift. "I know he'll appreciate it."

As I was driving out of Blissville, the song "I Won't Give Up" by Jason Mraz came on the radio, which perfectly defined how I felt about Tucker. I turned the song up, sang along, and let genuine hope fill my heart for the first time in days.

It was dark by the time I reached the secluded road leading to the lake house, so my first impression of the area was trees, trees, and more trees. As a person who'd lived in a city for most of their life, I wasn't used to navigating such dark, winding roads and missed the driveway, much to my GPS narrator's annoyance.

"*Execute a U-turn as soon as available.*"

"Or I could back up and turn in the driveway," I told her, which is what I did.

"*You have arrived at your destination.*"

"You don't say?"

The driveway was at least three quarters of a mile long and kept winding up, up, up until it reached a flat clearing where a massive, two-story house sat. I parked behind Tucker's truck and killed the engine. Just knowing I was seconds away from seeing him brought tears of relief to my eyes, so I sat in the car until I had myself under control. I remembered to grab his scones from the passenger seat before getting out of my car. The cool night air smelled fresh and free of pollutants. Crickets and cicadas were the only sounds coming from the forest surrounding the house. Exterior garden lights were artistically angled to bathe the house in a soft glow and solar lights lit the walkway leading from the driveway to the front door. The area was pitch-black except for the exterior lighting and the warm glow coming from the windows. The sky was still cloudy from storms that had lingered in the area throughout most of the day, so there was no moon or starlight to soften the harsh darkness.

I'd never really been afraid of the dark before, but the only time I'd experienced anything close to this was during my trips with Doctors

Without Borders. I started to quicken my step when I thought of the yeti and chupacabra stories. I was probably safe from the chupacabra since I wasn't a goat, but a yeti could smash my skull in without working up a sweat. An owl, or so I hoped, screeched loudly, and I damn near came out of my skin.

A porchlight by the front door blinked on, and a dark, familiar silhouette stepped forward until he stood center in the circle of light. There he was: my guy. He looked as exhausted as I felt, but he was still the most beautiful person I'd ever seen. A lonesome howl split the air, and I gave up all thoughts of playing it cool. I full-out ran toward the house and didn't stop until I launched myself at Tucker's chest, squashing the bag of scones between us.

Tucker wrapped his arms around me to steady us then walked backward inside the house and closed the door. Instead of releasing me, he held me tighter. "Doc, you look as terrible as I do." A wry smile curved the right side of his mouth.

"Charmer," I said, batting my eyelashes playfully.

"No wonder you launched yourself at me," he teased. "I'm sure it had nothing to do with screeching owls or the howling wolf."

"They only encouraged me to throw myself at you faster than I had planned." I smiled up at him. "Are you sure it wasn't a yeti?"

"Positive." Tucker sniffed the air. "Do I smell blueberries?"

"Oh man," I said, reaching between us to remove the Books and Brew pastry bag. "Milo sent his *regards*."

Tucker chuckled. "You somehow managed to catch that little tidbit of information on Sunday, huh?"

"I didn't realize I'd caught it until Tuesday morning when I stopped by and saw him behind the counter. You have a thing for blonds, huh?"

"I have a thing for a specific blond," he countered.

I wanted to say, "Still?" I wisely kept the thought to myself and said something I needed to get off my chest. "I'm so sorry for what Suzanne and Elon did to you and Grammie." I'd decided I would no longer refer to them as my parents because it was a title they didn't deserve. Parents didn't treat their children the way mine treated Mercedes and me. They especially didn't lash out and harm innocent people like Tucker and Shirlene. "It's cruel and unforgiveable, Tuck. I'm a little stunned and completely awed that you could want me here with you right now."

I leaned into Tucker's palm when he cupped my face. "You have nothing to be sorry for, Trent. You're as much of a victim as I am. Rejecting and hurting you on Sunday is something I'll struggle with for a long time."

"Don't," I said, shaking my head. "There's nothing to forgive. You didn't retaliate by saying cruel things. You asked me for time to think, which was pretty damn reasonable."

"You asked me not to give up on us, and I told you I thought it was too late. This will sound cowardly, but I'm so glad I didn't see your reaction. I know it's something I wouldn't be able to forget."

"Baby, don't," I said, sliding my free hand over his heart. "We'll get through this together. One day at a time." I lifted my other hand to cup the back of his neck and bring him down for a kiss, but I was still holding the bag. "Um, can I interest you in a smashed scone?"

"Have you eaten?" Tucker asked. I shook my head. "I have some pizza rolls and chicken patties in the freezer." He'd reverted back to his pre-Trent habits.

Maybe I would tease him about it later, but Tucker's warmth seeped through my clothes, penetrating my skin. I didn't realize how cold my world had become during his absence until I started to warm up. Then exhaustion from the many sleepless nights began creeping in. "I know we have a lot to talk about, and I should definitely eat food, but right now I just want to sleep."

"Let me go out and get your things from your car," Tucker said, stepping back from me.

I gripped him harder to prolong our contact. "I only brought my phone and the scones. I stopped by Shirlene's to drop off my house key so she could look after the cats then I made a quick dash into Books and Brew for some high-octane coffee. Shirlene says 'moon and back,' by the way."

Tucker swallowed hard and nodded. "You haven't been sleeping well either," he said, rubbing the back of his hand over my cheek.

"Probably about as much as you." Encouraged by his gentle touch, I caressed the purple, half-moon circles beneath his eyes that told me he hadn't slept well either. "Will you lie down with me?"

"I want that so much. God, I've missed you."

Hearing the tender gruffness in his voice made my nose burn and my eyes sting with unshed tears. "I've missed you too."

Tucker led me to a bedroom on the second story. The bed was considerably smaller than his or mine, but I liked having the excuse to press up against him. Getting in bed beside him wasn't sexual; in fact, we only removed our shoes before climbing between the sheets. Lying beside him was like coming home after being away for months, and I fell into a deep sleep almost as soon as I laid my head on his chest.

CHAPTER TWENTY-THREE

F ALLING ASLEEP WITH TRENT IN MY ARMS DIDN'T PREVENT MY nightmares from occurring, but it was wonderful to wake up and find him beside me. I was glad he slept hard enough that I hadn't jarred him awake when I'd started to jerk in my sleep. As if Trent sensed I needed him, he moved closer, which was hard to do since there wasn't an inch of air between our bodies. At some point during the night, he'd thrown his thigh over my pelvis and fisted my shirt like he was either holding me down so I couldn't get away or offering me comfort. I realized I was gripping his ass hard enough to leave fingerprints in his flesh, so he wasn't the only one feeling scarred by our separation.

For the first time in days, I was aroused and achingly aware of how long it had been since we made love. I wanted to roll him to his back and slowly wake him up with kisses before I slid my dick so deep inside him it would be impossible to tell where I ended and he began. There were several reasons why I didn't do it. I hadn't invited him to the lake house to be my booty call. I needed to reconnect with him on a level that went far deeper than physical. He was obviously exhausted because, other than his leg, he hadn't moved since he fell asleep. I also hadn't thought to buy condoms or lube when I was at the store because I hadn't planned on needing them. Sex wouldn't magically fix our problems but neither would abstaining. I added protection and lube to the mental shopping list.

Even though I wasn't sure how long Trent was staying, I decided to relocate us to the master bedroom for the duration. As much as I loved having him pressed tightly against me, I preferred to do it in a room with eastward-facing windows that would allow me to watch the sunrise ease across the bedroom until it bathed his beautiful body in its warm glow. Then I would roll him over and make love to him.

With that image as inspiration, I gently pulled my shirt from his grip and eased myself out from beneath his leg. Another dose of brilliance struck when I was taking a leak and glanced over to see the extra toothbrush in its package. I hadn't deliberately bought a multipack, but I was glad I did.

I quietly went down to the kitchen and retrieved the notepad and pen on the counter by the phone. It took me a few minutes to find the right words to say, to begin mending the hurt we both felt.

Trent

Here's an extra toothbrush. I didn't get it on sale, because I'm not as consumer savvy as you. I bought a multipack of toothbrushes because my subconscious knew what I needed even if I was too stubborn to admit it. You should know this toothbrush comes with strings attached. I don't want just last night; I want all your nights. I want to share all the good times, the bad, and the stuff in between. If you accept this toothbrush, you're agreeing to take a leap of faith with me.

Your Sparky

I tiptoed back upstairs, but it wasn't necessary. Trent was sprawled in the middle of the bed completely unaware I'd even left. I set the note on the bathroom counter next to the extra toothbrush then scrubbed my teeth with my own. I studied myself in the mirror for the first time since I arrived. Up until then, I'd avoided looking at my reflection because I was afraid of what I would see. I looked just like my father, so would I turn out just like him? Reckless and impulsive without regard for anyone else? When I looked at my reflection, I didn't see a reckless, impulsive man staring back at me. I saw a guy who dedicated his life to helping others. I saw a man who was loyal and who loved with all his heart. I wasn't perfect—far from it—but I was a good guy who deserved a good life. I couldn't have the future I wanted until I got a handle on my demons. The man sleeping in my borrowed bed—the man I loved—deserved the best version of me, and I was committed to giving that to him...if he accepted the toothbrush.

I started a pot of coffee then made the phone call I should've made on Monday. She answered on the second ring.

"How's my boy?" she asked.

"Moon and back, Grammie," I said. It was typically the way we ended conversations, but I wanted her to know I received her message.

"Moon and back, Tuck. I'm glad Trent made it safely. I've been worried about my boys this week."

"He's exhausted and sleeping right now."

"That's exactly what he needs. How are you?"

"I'm better," I said, "but I'm not where I want to be yet. I'm ready to listen if you're ready to talk."

"Of course," Grammie said. "Where do you want me to start, honey?"

"Did the drugs and alcohol start before or after I was born?"

Grammie took a deep breath, and I knew it hurt her to remember. I almost told her never mind, but I needed to know, and I *did* trust Grammie to tell me the truth. "Your father started drinking in high school. Your grandfather and I tried talking to him and getting him help, but he insisted he didn't have a problem. It was just a few beers on the weekends with his friends. By the time he went to college, the few beers turned into hard liquor. His drinking got so bad he flunked out of school for missing too many classes. He came home with his tail between his legs and no zest for life until he met your mother one day when he visited me at work." Grammie giggled. I knew the next part, but I let her retell it because she needed to remember the good stuff too, and I needed to hear it. "Suddenly, your father became the most prolific reader in Delaware County." She giggled some more.

"They fell fast and hard for one another, and he stopped drinking for a while. I thought what he'd experienced was a phase and he'd outgrown it. They got married and everything was going great. He'd found a good factory job while your mother worked part time with me and went to school full time to be a teacher." Other than the early alcohol abuse, I knew the rest. They got married before Mom graduated because of an unplanned pregnancy. "They were so excited about you, Tuck. I promised them I'd do everything I could to help them so your mom could finish school, but her parents pulled their financial support." They severed ties with her completely because they didn't think my father was good enough for their daughter. "It was a tough emotional time for her, but I'll never forget her tears of joy when she heard your first cries."

"When did Dad start drinking again?"

"After you were born, he got laid off from his job. I told them they could move in with your grandfather and me until they got back on their feet, but your father was too proud."

"He turned to the bottle to drown his feelings of failure?"

"Yes," Grammie said, her voice gentle and cautious. "It gets worse, Tuck. Are you sure you want to hear more?"

"Want to? No, but I need to know."

"Your mom went in for a routine dental checkup when you were only two months old. She had a bad tooth that required a root canal.

The dentist prescribed her pain killers, which she became addicted to. Over the next four months, her addiction switched from pain pills to illegal drugs and your father lost himself further and further in the bottle. By this point, you were already living with me full time. Your parents might've been caught up in their addictions, but they'd put you first when they asked me to take care of you. I filed documents to become your legal guardian, and my petition was granted the week before they died."

"What happened that night?"

"Your mom overdosed. Rather than call for help, your dad decided to drive her to the hospital. You know what happened next. Grandpa and I decided we needed a fresh start and moved to Blissville," she said. "I should've told you when you were old enough to understand, Tuck. I should've had a conversation with you about addiction, but as I said, you never showed any signs of addictive behaviors. Will you ever be able to forgive me?"

"I already have, Grammie. Will you forgive me for the way I talked to you?"

"There's nothing to forgive, Tucker."

We talked for a few more minutes until I heard Trent moving around upstairs. I promised to call her later then got busy making a grocery list while I waited for Trent to appear. I heard him come down the steps and pad across the floor, but I pretended to be engrossed with my task. His arms circled around me and settled at my waist, and he pressed a kiss between my shoulder blades.

I turned in the circle of his arms and looked down at Trent's smiling face. He looked so much better after ten hours of sleep. I lowered my face and kissed him—tentatively at first so I could relearn the shape of his lips. Then I deepened the kiss, tasting the minty freshness of his mouth.

I pulled back and looked into his eyes. "Does that mean you accepted my offer."

"Yes, I will marry you," Trent said.

"What?" I asked, grabbing the counter for support. "Marry me?"

"Isn't that what you meant when you said you wanted to spend all your nights with me?"

I blinked at him for a few seconds. I had said that, and in hindsight, I could see where he might make the leap. The idea of marrying him didn't scare me, but I was worried he thought a dorky note left in the bathroom was the best kind of proposal I could conceive.

Trent's eyes widened in alarm. "I was just teasing you, Tuck. I accept and welcome all the strings that are attached to your offer." He rubbed his stomach and looked around the kitchen. "Do you mind if I make a few chicken patties? I'm starved."

"I can do much better than that," I said. "Let me take you to my favorite restaurant. I could really use a serving or two of Mama Cass's sausage gravy and biscuits."

"That sounds awesome."

Awesome was watching Trent enjoy them for the first time then taking him to buy a few outfits and toiletries before stopping at the grocery store on the way back. Perfection was joining Trent in the shower to relearn his touch and taste before leisurely making love to him. Breathtaking was preparing a meal together in the amazing kitchen then cuddling beneath a blanket while roasting marshmallows on the fire pit with twinkling stars as our only witness. Heavenly was looking into Trent's smiling eyes the following morning in our sun-dappled bed.

How could I have feared looking into those baby blues and seeing anything other than love, compassion, and kindness?

"There's my guy," I said, brushing his messy hair off his forehead.

As always, he leaned into my touch. "I love you, Tuck," he whispered.

I'd known how he felt about me and didn't think I needed to hear the words until they were spoken. I needed his love like I needed air. I was too choked up to return his sentiment immediately, but Trent didn't look alarmed. He knew I was crazy in love with him too. He deserved to hear the words and know my heart's testimony. "I love you so much it scares me. To love you and lose you…" Emotion rose swiftly, choking off my words.

Trent didn't make false promises he couldn't deliver. He understood my fear was deeper and more complex than worrying about a breakup, so he said something that meant more to me than well-intentioned but impossible assurances. "All we're guaranteed is this moment right here, baby. We can focus on the uncertainty of a future moment we might never have or live for this one. Be present in this moment with me, Tuck."

"Yes," I said, rolling him to his back. There was no better way to live in the moment than kissing every inch of his golden skin before making love to him.

Trent

"**D**ON'T COME YET." I NIPPED THE SHELL OF TUCK'S EAR THEN leaned back so I could watch his pucker flex and tremble around my bare cock. We'd both gotten tested after returning home from Lake Cumberland, and after two weeks, we still hadn't come down off our sex-in-the-raw high. Everything felt much more intense without the thin barrier separating our flesh, even if I realized a lot of it was psychological. I couldn't really feel Tucker's cum painting my channel, but I could feel the heat of him inside me and visualize him marking me. And making love to Tucker, feeling his tight heat clamp around my dick… Let's just say I insisted on a lot of practice so I could build up my stamina.

"You're just going to have to spank me then because I…can't—" Tucker's hole clenched and pulsed around my cock. "Unh."

"This is your payback for teasing me at the gym this morning," I said, sliding my dick fully out of him so I could watch his pouty pucker twitch and beg for more. I fisted my dick in my hand and circled the crinkled rim, making Tucker groan.

"You better fuck me," he demanded, but his voice was muffled by his pillow. I loved having my big, strong man submit to me with his ass up in the air.

"Or what?" I drove my dick inside him, pegging his prostate at the same time I slapped his taut ass cheek.

Tucker grunted. "Fuck!" His ass clamped down and spasmed around my dick as he lost control and spurted his release on the sheets beneath him. "More."

"This?" I pistoned my dick in and out of him, nailing his gland while chasing my own orgasm.

I roared his name when I filled his ass, drawing out my pleasure with slow strokes. I eased my cock out and said, "Do it." Tucker squeezed some of my cum out of his ass. "Mine," I said, spreading it around his rim before pushing the rest back inside him.

"Yours."

I started to lie over his back, but Tucker rolled so I landed in the wet spot instead. I quickly turned onto my side and glared at him as he rose from the bed. "I'll get you for this."

"I'll be home by seven. Do your worst," Tucker tossed over his shoulder as he headed to the bathroom. *Home by seven.*

We hadn't formally discussed moving in together when we returned from Lake Cumberland, but "all your nights" implied we no longer wanted to sleep in separate beds. Tucker had only gone to his house long enough to grab clothes, a few books he wanted to read, and Owen the orchid. According to our research, Owen didn't pose a threat to Natasha or Boris, and since my kitchen window was shaded by trees, Owen's new home was the end table near the picture window where he flourished from rocking out to Queen every night.

I loved seeing our mixed clothes in the laundry basket, finding

Tucker's books lying around the house, and listening to a variety of podcasts while preparing dinner. Our lives became more entwined every single day, and it made me happier than I could ever express.

"Are you joining me?" Tucker asked from the doorway.

I forgot all about orchids, Queen, and cats when I raked my eyes over his nakedness. As much as I adored his body, my heart raced at the happiness I saw in his eyes. His sexy smile almost made me forget he'd had another nightmare a few hours ago.

"I know the pleasure you get from my body turns your legs to noodles, but you better get out of bed before you fall back to sleep and are late for your rounds at Goodville General this morning."

I dragged myself out of bed and zombie-shuffled to the bathroom. Tucker was already beneath the hot spray and watching the water cascading over his body never failed to stop me in my tracks. I was envious of those water droplets until I realized those poor bastards only got one chance to touch him where I got to glide my hands over his body as much as I wanted. Wasn't that addictive?

I jerked at the thought, grateful I hadn't spoken it out loud. Tucker hadn't said much about his parents' addictions. He'd recounted the story to me but hadn't said how it made him feel. I'd taken several psychology classes because I found the subject intriguing, so I recognized that Tucker was burying his feelings, and it was probably the source of his nightmares. I felt like I stood on shaky ground with him, so I was cautious about what I said. Okay, I tiptoed around Tuck when he was particularly quiet, or when I wasn't certain of his mood. I felt powerless, which in turn made me angry. We worked off our frustrations in the gym or between the sheets. In the short run, our methods worked for us, but I feared we would explode in the long run if we didn't do something. It was hard to convince myself to speak up when Tucker nuzzled my neck and kissed me long and passionately while we showered and dressed.

"Be safe today," I said when he kissed me goodbye in the driveway.

"I always am."

"I love you, Sparky."

"I love you, Doc."

We never went to bed without saying good night, and we never started our day without saying I love you. It was dorky and sappy, but it was us.

During my twenty-five-minute drive to Goodville, I listened to a new true crime podcast Shirlene had discovered. Tucker teased me that I'd created a monster, but it was wonderful to talk to someone who shared my same passion. Tucker enjoyed listening to them too, but he was never caught doing a little jig in the kitchen when he received an alert that new episodes were available to download. That was all me.

The newest episode was especially entertaining, so I was in an extra good mood when I began my rounds. Not even seeing Dr. Steller's sour face could diminish my joy. Both my pneumonia patients looked and sounded so much better than they had when they were admitted. Their families were relieved when I signed off on their release and promised to follow up with me or Dr. Hinman in ten days.

I had just left the second patient's room when I was paged up to the mother baby care unit. It seemed that my newest patient arrived a week early. I headed upstairs and congratulated Greg and Stephanie Morrison and met baby Abigail.

"What do Garrett and Grady think about Miss Abigail," I said, accepting the bundle of joy from Stephanie.

"Grady thinks she's wrinkly like his toes after he's been in the bathtub for too long," Stephanie said.

"Garrett thinks she makes funny faces, but he guesses she's okay," Greg told me.

"That's a ringing endorsement," I said, gently placing Abigail on her infant bed. "I bet you'll have prettier digs at home, sweetheart."

"Pink explosion everywhere," Stephanie said wryly. I glanced over my shoulder, and she tilted her head in her husband's direction. Greg just shrugged.

I declared Abigail a beautiful, healthy baby before handing her back to her mother. "I think she's hungry," I said when Abigail started sucking on her tiny fist.

"I was just about to feed her when you arrived," Stephanie said.

"I'll see you in a few weeks," I told them. "Don't you grow up too fast, Abigail."

Stephanie and Greg thanked me, and I headed out to give them some privacy. I didn't have any other newborns on the floor, so I decided to head back to Blissville. I was halfway there when a call from Shirlene interrupted my podcast. I assumed she was calling to talk about the episode until I heard the worry in her voice.

"Tucker's been hurt." Those three words wrecked my world, and I had to pull over on the side of the road.

"What happened?" I asked.

"I don't know many details besides he's conscious. I'm still listed as his emergency contact, so Will called to let me know there'd been an incident and Tucker's being transported to Goodville General for evaluation and treatment."

"I just left there," I told Shirlene. "I'll turn around and head back so I can meet the ambulance."

"Will you keep me posted? Braxton is sending Hailey over to pick me up and take me there, so I won't be too far behind the ambulance."

"I absolutely will, Shirlene. He's going to be okay," I told her. "Will would've told you if Tucker sustained life-threatening injuries."

"I know you're right, but he's all I have left in this world." Shirlene had lost her only son and then her husband a few years later. Tuck was her entire universe.

"You have me now too."

"Yes, I do. Oh! Hailey just pulled in. I'll be there in less than half an hour."

"I'll be waiting for you. I'll call once I know more about his condition. I love you, Shirlene."

"I love you too, honey."

Ahead, I saw the flashing lights of an ambulance speeding toward me. "I have eyes on the ambulance. I'm going to hang up now so I can follow them."

"Be careful," Shirlene urged.

"I will."

I disconnected the call and tried to tamp down the rising fear and panic as the ambulance got close enough that I could hear the sirens. *I cannot lose him. I cannot lose him. I cannot lose him.* The nearer the ambulance came, the more I shook. Doctors are taught to push their emotions aside, stay calm, and focus on the science, but it was nearly impossible to do when it involved someone you love. When the ambulance passed, I swung my car into a U-turn and followed behind it, not caring that I was driving twenty miles over the posted speed limit.

I pulled into the hospital parking lot right behind it but had to park in the ER lot. They had already unloaded Tucker and were headed inside the hospital by the time I caught up to them. His face and what I could see of his clothes were covered in soot and smoke. An oxygen mask covered his nose and mouth.

"Hey, Sparky," I said weakly.

Tucker opened his eyes, and his gaze locked on me. I was relieved to see he was conscious, and his dark eyes looked alert. One of his arms was pinned against his body from the gurney strap while the other lay across his chest covered in bandages. He tried to reach for me with his injured arm, but one of the EMTs barked, "Don't move, Moose."

"I'm right here," I said. "Stay still and listen to what they tell you."

Will snorted behind me. I turned to look at him, and he looked haggard. "Listening isn't something Tucker feels like doing today." I knew there was a big story there, and I definitely wanted to hear it, but not until I was assured Tucker was going to be okay.

I stayed out of the way while the ER doctors and nurses did their jobs. I kept my eyes on Tucker's while they moved around him, assessed the burn on his arm, checked his oxygen flow, and ordered X-rays to look at his lungs.

"Can I see you outside?" Will asked me.

I tore my eyes away from Tucker's to look at Will. I didn't want to leave Tucker's room, but something in Will's eyes told me I needed to. I looked back at Tucker, but he wasn't looking at me; he was glaring at Will and shaking his head, which only bolstered my decision to speak to Tucker's captain.

"I'll be right back," I told him. Tucker shook his head and reached for his oxygen mask. "Touch that oxygen mask and I will force Owen to listen to all my Taylor Swift albums on repeat when you're not around." I was a huge Taylor Swift fan, but Tuck was not. "Her country albums," I added.

Tucker relaxed against the bed, giving up the fight.

I followed Will out of the room and down the hallway. "What's wrong?"

"I'm putting Tucker on administrative leave pending a psychiatric evaluation. He's a danger to himself and his brothers who rushed into a situation to save his ass."

"What?" I asked, taking a step back. "This is the first time I'd heard anyone imply Tucker takes reckless risks on the job, Will."

"He never has before, but he's been off since he returned to work. He arrived on the scene before the trucks and went into a burning building without the appropriate equipment or assessments to see if the building was safe enough to enter. I'd specifically instructed him to wait when he called to let me know he was already there."

I heard a scuffle behind me and knew Tucker was tired of waiting for us to come back. "Come on," I said to Will. "We can talk about this later, but right now, we need to make sure he doesn't hurt himself worse."

"You go on," Will said. "I love that man like a brother, but I need to get my anger under control so I can talk to him without screaming."

When I walked back into Tucker's room, his eyes were glassy, and I realized they'd injected him with something to calm him down. I walked over to his bed and ran my hand through his ashy, sooty hair. The acrid smell burned my nose, but I didn't pull away from him. I dropped a kiss on his filthy forehead and whispered, "I'm here, baby. You're going to be okay."

We're going to be okay. Anything else was unacceptable.

R℣

PATIENT NAME: _____

ADDRESS: _____
_____
_____

Prescription:

CHAPTER
TWENTY-FIVE

_____
_____

Signature: _____ Date: _____

Tucker

*B*AMB! *B*AMB! *B*AMB!

"It's dead, Tuck," Andy Mason said dryly.

I looked at the nail I'd driven into the piece of lumber and noticed the divots left behind from my hammer. "Nailed it," I yelled, imitating the contestants on the baking show Grammie and Trent loved so much.

"I thought you were going to drive it clear out the other side," Andy said with a grin. "Doing okay?"

"Yeah, I'm okay." I wasn't, but I was trying my best to get there. I stepped back and looked at the frame for the detached garage and was impressed at the progress we'd made since we arrived on the job site that morning.

The fire department had put me on paid leave until I was cleared for duty by an approved psychologist. *Reckless. Impulsive.* Words I never associated with myself even if Will suddenly did. I needed to stay busy and feel useful during my stalemate with Will or lose my mind. I'd spent too much time comparing my personality to my father's and not liking the similarities. The solution to my problem had come from the guy who'd once hated me because I had the audacity to date the boy he'd cast aside to make it big in college baseball. Milo had cared for me a great deal, but his heart had always belonged to Andy. It just took Andy a while to realize it.

Andy's carpentry business kept growing year after year, and he needed to hire seasonal help for the summer. He ran into me at the hardware store after I was first put on leave. I looked like hell and was doing my best to stay busy by fixing little things around the house. Being told by Will that I was a threat to my brothers broke my heart. They were my family; I'd never hurt them. I'm sure my father would have said the same about my mother and me if someone asked. Will had pointed out that my careless behavior nearly got me killed because the structure of the house I'd rushed into was far worse than I realized. I was a few feet from the door when the structure started to cave in. A smoldering piece of wood from the second story came down on my arm and burned me, but it had luckily missed the unconscious woman I was carrying to safety. Will was furious that I hadn't waited for the appropriate equipment, but if I had, the Saunders siblings would be without their mother. I refused to regret or apologize for my decision, and given the choice, I would do it again.

"How handy are you with tools?" Andy had asked me.

"Hand or power?"

"Both," he'd said.

"Not bad. Are you looking for help?"

"I am. Do you know of anyone who needs to stay busy while he works through some demons?"

"I do," I had admitted. "Where and when do you want me to start?"

A month later, I was still swinging hammers and chasing demons. "Ready to head out for lunch?" Andy asked the crew of five men.

"Sure thing, boss," Andy's foreman, Tyler, said.

We put our tools up and headed to the diner. I'd worked up a full appetite and was ready to tear into a pulled pork sandwich with cole-slaw on top until I saw Braxton, Will, Donovan, and Carl sitting in a booth in the back. I'd distanced myself from them after Will delivered his verdict in my hospital room. It hurt too much to be around them and not be a part of them anymore. For so long, my job defined me. It felt like someone had severed my limbs from my body, so I kept my distance.

"I just remembered I'm meeting my grandmother for lunch," I said to the guys. "I'll meet you back on the job in an hour."

Andy looked to the rear of the diner and back at me. He knew I wasn't being honest but didn't call me out on it. "Tell Shirlene I said hello."

I'd decided to go home and eat a bologna sandwich and chips. I stepped outside the diner and realized I'd ridden over with Tyler and Joe. Our house was in walking distance to both the diner and job site, so it was no big deal.

"Moose, wait up," Braxton said from behind me. I should've known he'd follow me outside.

I stopped on the sidewalk and let him catch up to me. "Hey, Brax. What's up?"

"That's it? 'Hey, Brax. What's up?' Is that all you're going to say to me?"

"How's Hailey and the kids?"

Braxton's expressive eyes showed his hurt and disappointment. "Is this the way things are going to be now after all these years? Will makes a decision he thinks is for your best interest, and you cut the rest of us out of your life like we're cancer?"

"I don't think you guys are cancer," I said sadly.

"Talk to me, Moose. This is me, Braxton. I'm the same person you came out to when we were like twelve years old and you got your first woody for a player on the Reds team."

I chuckled at the memory. Brax had taken the news well even if he didn't understand why Hailey Benson's boobs didn't make me want to write poetry. I'd told him some men wrote poetry about boobs and others wrote it about penises. Brax teased me endlessly about reading penis poetry anytime he caught me with my nose stuck in a book. For the record, he was probably still writing poems about his wife's boobs, except they weren't Benson's boobs anymore; they were Hilsop's Hooters.

"It was the Bengals, Brax."

"Whatever, dude," he replied, rolling his eyes. "I know you're upset, but we miss our brother."

"Are you sure this doesn't have something to do with summer league softball signups?" I teased. "The timing is quite suspicious."

"I hadn't thought of that, but now that you mention it."

"Too late," I firmly said. "I already agreed to play centerfield for the Blissville PD."

Brax gasped and covered his mouth. "No. You wouldn't."

"I'm not a firefighter anymore, so why not?"

"Bullshit, Moose. You're always going to be one of us."

"Not according to Will. He thinks I'm a headcase."

"Don't you fucking put words in my mouth, Garrison," Will tersely said as he walked up behind me. Sneaky fucker. I knew I shouldn't have turned my back toward the diner. I narrowed my eyes at Brax because he could've warned me. "Brax, can I have a minute with Tucker?"

"Um," Brax said, looking back and forth between Will and me.

"It's okay," I assured Brax. "We'll talk later."

"That's what you said last week," Brax said. He reminded me of a bulldog with a bone. He wasn't going to let up.

"I mean it this time."

"Don't make me sorry for believing you," Brax said, hugging me tight.

"Shut up, or I'll rub my sweaty pits in your face."

Will remained silent until Brax walked away then he turned to me. "Headcase? Really, Tuck? After all these years of friendship, you're going to lie about the conversation we had."

"You told me I need to see a shrink."

"No one talks like that anymore, Moose. I said you needed to see a psychologist because your inability to assess risk makes you a liability to yourself and everyone on the team. You were minutes, seconds even, away from dying. I get what it means to you to save kids from losing their parents, but it's also a big red flag. How would you have felt if Braxton followed you into the fire and had died? Hailey would be a widow at thirty-fucking-two years old, and their sons would've lost their father. Everyone goes home on my watch, even the ones who are too boneheaded to know when they need help."

I'd nearly bit a hole in my tongue during his spiel and was grateful when it was my turn to defend myself. Instead of coming up with a resounding rebuttal, all I said was, "I'm doing fine."

"You don't look fine. Are you sleeping?"

"I'm sleeping fine." I was lucky if I slept five hours a night, but I blamed Will for some of that. The nightmares involving my parents were occurring less frequently but being torn away from the job I loved was wreaking havoc on me. I felt a sharp, stabbing pain in my chest every time I heard the sirens blaring when the life squad or fire trucks went on runs.

"How are things with you and Trent?"

"Great," I said too quickly for him not to notice. Trent was tiptoeing around me more than usual, and that only added to the pressure pushing down on my chest.

"Uh-huh." Will pulled a business card from his wallet and extended it to me. "Your paid suspension is up at the end of next week. Meet with this psychologist, show me you're trying, and I'll go to bat for you." I took the card from him and slid it inside my pocket. "We miss you and want you back, Tuck."

I swallowed hard and had to look away from his piercing hazel eyes. He sounded so sincere, and I wanted to believe him. I just didn't want to acknowledge that I might not be able to handle my issues alone. That was on me, not Will. "I'll think about it."

I was still thinking about it a few hours later when Trent came home from work and found me at the kitchen table staring at the card.

"That better not be some hot dude's phone number," he teased, dropping a kiss on my head.

I scooted back the chair and tugged him onto my lap. "You're the only hot dude I want in my life, Doc. I love you."

"I love you too." Trent ran his hand over my hair then dropped a sweet kiss on my lips.

"I want to be the best partner to you that I can, and I'm just not cutting it right now."

Trent briefly stiffened in my arms. "What do you mean?"

"Doc, you know about my nightmares, but we don't talk about them because I don't want to do or say anything that will make you feel guilty. Nothing that happened with Suzanne and Elon is your fault, and we need to stop pretending it didn't happen. It's like we apologized to each other, made love, and expected everything to go back to normal, but it didn't."

"No, it didn't," Trent admitted. "Even though it was the sweetest lovemaking on the planet."

"No one is questioning that, and I'm not doubting that we belong together."

"Then what are you saying?" he asked me.

"You tiptoe around me because you're afraid of saying something that will trigger my nightmares." I could see he wanted to argue with me, but having the conversation was hard enough without prolonging it with silly side trips. "Like that one time you were making porn noises while eating a pint of ice cream. You said something about becoming addicted to it then nearly choked because you thought it might set off some inner trauma."

"Guilty as charged," he admitted.

"You're not wrong. It does make me think of my parents' addictions, and I do start thinking of how they died. I won't ever get over it, but I need to find ways to accept and move past it."

"It sounds like you have a plan figured out."

I tapped the business card on the table. "I do. I made an appointment to meet with the psychologist Will recommended. My first appointment is next Thursday."

"Is this because you want to return to the firehouse?" Trent asked. "Or are you doing this for yourself."

"I'm doing this for me, for my career, and for us."

Trent's smile lit up the kitchen. "I'm so proud of you, baby."

"I have a favor to ask you."

"Anything," he said eagerly.

"I would like you to come with me."

"Of course."

"Doc, I don't just mean I want you there for support. I think you could benefit from meeting with Dr. Rhudemen too."

"You think I need to see a psychologist?" Trent didn't seem offended or alarmed; he seemed surprised.

I nodded. "You're battling a lot of things right now. Anger is at the top of the list, even though you're pretty good at hiding it. You've had years of trauma inflicted on you by those people. You can't tell me you won't benefit from a few meetings."

He thought about it for a second. "You're right. I am carrying around so much garbage, and it seems to get heavier every day. I don't want to drag us down."

"I'm glad you feel that way because you have an appointment right after mine."

"Okay," he agreed.

"And there's more."

His eyes widened, and he said, "You made an appointment for Mercedes too?"

"No, but that is a good idea. I asked Dr. Rhudemen to recommend a couples therapist for us also. She gave me the name of a few we can choose from."

Trent's mouth fell open, and he stared at me for a few seconds before pulling himself together. "Let me get this straight. You've refused to meet with the psychologist for a month, but suddenly, you made an appointment for you, me, and you also want us to attend appointments as a couple."

"I know this is a sudden reversal, but talking to Will today was the catalyst I needed." I told him about the conversation outside the diner. "I'm not just doing it to get my job back, although it's a big part of it. I want the best for us."

"I want the best for us too. Let's do this."

"What if the couples therapist tells us something we don't want to hear?" I asked.

"Like?"

"Our relationship is co-dependent, and we moved too fast."

"Do you think either of those things apply to us?" Trent asked me.

"No, but I'm not an expert."

"They're an expert on the way the brain functions and can help us learn how to cope and recover from trauma. That doesn't make the couples therapist an expert on *us*. He or she is going to make suggestions about what's best for us in *their* opinion, but it's up to you and me if we want to implement them. If we don't like one of their suggestions, then we can discuss how we feel with her to see if we can come up with something that makes all of us happy."

"You sound so wise," I told him.

"I just think we need to go into this with an open mind and not start assuming this couples therapist will want us to break up and live separate lives."

"You're right," I agreed. I exhaled a deep breath. "I feel lighter than I have since all hell broke loose on that fateful, Shitfest Sunday."

Trent laughed. "Me too. This is a good thing we're doing for ourselves and each other. I'm proud of us."

"I am too."

"Now that we know what we're doing next Thursday, there's a decision we need to make for tonight," Trent said.

"Top or bottom?"

"No," he said, tweaking my nipple. "What's for dinner?"

"Easy. I have pork chops marinating in the refrigerator. I'm going to grill them in an hour."

"Sixty whole minutes?" Trent asked, repositioning himself on my lap so he straddled my thighs. He thrusted his hips forward, rubbing our groins together. "Whatever will we do to pass our time."

"I say we consult the jar."

Trent fist-pumped the air. "Yes! It's my turn to pick from the fantasy-fuck jar." Some of the fantasies were funny, and others were sexy enough to scorch your underwear—if you wore any—but they were always memorable. "I'm telling you right now, Sparky. No matter what any of the therapists say, the fantasy-fuck jar stays. This is a hill I would die on."

I threw my head back and laughed. "I won't let her take your fuck jar away, baby."

"My hero," Trent said, kissing me.

"I don't see myself that way, but I'm charmed you do."

Trent made a big production of pulling out a strip of bright yellow paper then laughed when he read it. He turned it around for me to read it.

Villain captures hero and does naughty things with him. Tools/props: Blindfold, rope or cuffs, and a cape.

"Sounds fun to me, but I think we need to flip a coin to see which one of us gets to be the villain and who gets to be the hero," Trent said.

I waggled my brows. "If I'm your hero, then I'm at your villainous mercy tonight."

And there was no place I'd rather be.

Prescription:

CHAPTER TWENTY-SIX

Trent

Labor Day weekend...

"**M**ERCEDES, DO YOU THINK TUCK IS ACTING ODD?" I ASKED my sister who was helping me assemble a platter of ingredients for s'mores.

"Not that I've noticed," she said casually. Almost too casually. "Girls, quit running in the house," she said to Brooklyn and Savannah, who streaked by as fast as their little legs would carry them. "I'd hate for your friends to ban you from the lake house after hurricanes Madison, Savannah, and Brooklyn blew through it."

"Relax; they're fine. They're having a great time. Isn't this place the best?"

"It's stunning," Mercedes replied.

"And nothing like the vacation spots we went to as kids," I told her.

"I'd choose this lake house over any of the trips we took with Suzanne, Elon, and our nannies."

I'd come a long way in therapy over the past three months—both individually and as Tucker's partner. While I still got angry over some memories from my childhood and early adult years, most of the time I was able to view them as what they were—Suzanne and Elon's failings. I started my closure by officially severing ties with them through a letter. It took several drafts, but I finally came up with one that felt right. Even though I told Suzanne and Elon not to contact me, they blew up my phone and flooded my inbox until I was forced to change both my cell phone number and my email address. I planned to have them removed from my property if they showed up uninvited again, but they never did.

Tucker was making great progress and was due to return to his firehouse after the holiday. I wondered if that was why he was acting weird.

"Mom!" Brooklyn hollered from the sliding glass doors leading to the deck. "Uncle Tucker said to hurry up. The movie is going to start. Don't forget the popcorn and sodas!"

"Like she needs anymore sugar," Mercedes said, shaking her head.

Tucker had come up with the idea to move one of the big TVs outside so we could have an old-fashioned movie night similar to a drive-in. He promised me we could sit in the back row and make out, but when Mercedes and I walked outside, the only two seats available were two chairs up front or one in the back by Benji.

I pouted at Tucker, but he just shrugged. "Benji beat me to it."

"That's right," Benji said proudly. "Bring it on back here, baby, and give your man a kiss."

"Um, I'm taken," I told Benji.

"Not you, jackass," Mercedes said. "He means me."

"Uh oh," Brooklyn said. "Mommy said a bad word."

"Our girls have one heck of a start on their college funds," Benji said.

"Jackass is an animal," Mercedes said. "It doesn't count."

"You weren't singing that tune when Brooklyn called her soccer coach a jackass last week," Benji countered.

"I called him a dumbass, Daddy," Brooklyn said.

"See!" Mercedes said.

Tucker shook his head then tugged me down into the seat beside him. Shirlene leaned over from my right and said, "I absolutely adore your family, sweetheart."

"Me too. I'm so happy you came with us this weekend."

"I wouldn't have missed this for the world."

I'd set my cell phone on the arm of the chair, and it lit up with a new podcast notification. I was prepared to ignore it until I saw the title. "Jack and Jill Episode 245: Mr. Perfect Arrested."

"Oh my God, Shirlene. They arrested Mr. Perfect!"

"Really?" she asked excitedly.

"Who's Mr. Perfect, Daddy?" Brooklyn asked Benji.

"I am. Just ask your mother," Benji told his daughter.

"He's a serial killer," I said without thinking of the audience.

"What's a serial killer, Daddy?" Brooklyn asked.

"Um," Benji said, thinking over his answer while I tried to sink lower in my seat. I could feel the heat from Mercedes' gaze on the back of my head. "It's a person who eats a lot of cereal, sweetheart."

"Mommy eats a lot of cereal," Savannah said. "She's a cereal killer."

"Trent," Mercedes said between gritted teeth. "Paybacks are hell."

"Movie time," Tucker announced seriously.

What was his deal? Were we about to watch a film on fire safety or something? He hit the remote and the black screen turned blue. "I don't recall you telling me what movie we're watching."

"You're about to find out."

I started to roll my eyes, but the title of the film popped up on the screen. Prescription for Love. It looked kind of cheap and cheesy and so was the music that started playing. "Babe, did you grab the wrong DVD? This looks like a movie you meant to play just for me later?"

"Just keep watching," Tucker said, sounding crankier by the moment.

The music shifted from cheesy porn to Jason Mraz's "I Won't Give Up." It was my ringtone, and Tucker knew it reminded me of us. Then the credits started rolling on the movie. A Sparky Loves Doc Production. Happily Ever After Studio. Starring Tucker "Sparky" Garrison and Trenton "Doc" Love. All porn jokes and thoughts of Mr. Perfect fled my mind. I'd even forgotten that we were surrounded by the people who loved us most. I was only aware of the man beside me holding my hand and the television screen in front of me.

As the music continued to play, one picture of us after the other appeared on the screen. There were goofy selfies we took with our own phones as well as photos taken by others. Some snapshots showed us doing silly things like washing the car and some were taken at special occasions like the first wedding we attended as a couple. My favorite was the one Shirlene had taken when we officially moved in together. Tucker had sold his house and moved his things to ours. We'd had a cleaning party, and at the end of the day, it looked like all the dirt and dust from the house ended up on us. There was so much hope and love in our eyes as we smiled at Shirlene on the front porch of our house. In the background, Natasha and Boris, watched us from the window with expressions that said, "These two fools."

My lips trembled and happy tears ran down my face as I stared transfixed at the progression of our love story, our prescription for love as he called it. After the photo collage ended, Tucker slid to the deck in front of me. I sniffled when I saw he held a velvet box in his hand. Suddenly his nervousness made sense as did Mercedes' elusiveness and Shirlene's sweet comment just before the movie started. They were all in on the surprise. I was beyond moved Tucker thought to include our family on our big night.

"Trent—"

"Yes!" I said, answering him before he could ask his question. My exuberance made everyone laugh. "Wait a minute. There better not be another misleading, dorky note in that velvet box." More laughter, even though they couldn't possibly know about the notes unless he told them.

"Open it and see," Tucker said.

I took the box from him and opened it. Even in the dim light, I could see two platinum bands.

"Now can I ask the question?" Tucker asked. I nodded.

"Trent, will you do me the honor of becoming my husband?"

"I will."

I kissed my man amidst exuberant cheers and clapping until the rest of the world drifted away and it was just the two of us. When I pulled back, I slowly opened my eyes and realized we were the only two people left on the deck.

"There's my guy," Tucker said, tenderly caressing my cheek.

"Here I am." *And here I shall always be.*

The End!

Want to be the first to know about my book releases and have access to extra content? You can sign up for my newsletter here: http://eepurl.com/dlhPYj

My favorite place to hang out and chat with my readers is my Facebook group. Would you like to be a member of Aimee's Dye Hards? We'd love to have you! Go here: www.facebook.com/groups/AimeesDyeHards

OTHER BOOKS BY
AIMEE NICOLE WALKER

Only You

The Fated Hearts Series
Chasing Mr. Wright, Book 1
Rhythm of Us, Book 2
Surrender Your Heart, Book 3
Perfect Fit, Book 4
Return to Me, Book 5
Always You, Book 6
Any Means Necessary, Book 7

Curl Up and Dye Mysteries
Dyeing to be Loved
Something to Dye For
Dyed and Gone to Heaven
I Do, or Dye Trying
A Dye Hard Holiday
Ride or Dye

Road to Blissville Series
Unscripted Love
Someone to Call My Own
Nobody's Prince Charming
This Time Around
Smoke in the Mirror
Inside Out

The Lady is Mine Series

The Lady is a Thief

The Lady Stole My Heart

Queen City Rogue Series

Broken Halos

Wicked Games

Standalone Novels

Second Wind

Coauthored with Nicholas Bella

Undisputed

Circle of Darkness (Genesis Circle, Book 1)

Circle of Trust (Genesis Circle, Book 2)

ACKNOWLEDGMENTS

First, I need to thank my husband and children for their constant support and encouragement. It's not easy living with a writer who often disappears into a fictional world for long periods of time. They do so many things to help me out so that I can realize my dream. I love you guys more than words can ever express.

To my creative dream team, thanks seem hardly enough for all that you do. Miranda Turner of V8 Editing and Proofreading, thank you for your tireless work, feedback, and many laughs while editing. Jay Aheer of Simply Defined art is an incredible artist, and I love how she brings my words to life. Stacey Blake of Champagne Formats is also an amazing artist who does incredible interior formatting, illustrating, and designing for e-books and paperbacks. Let's not forget Judy Zweifel of Judy's' Proofreading. She does an amazing job of finding the tiniest details that make a book shine.

To my lovely PA, Michelle Slagan. I'm not sure how I ever did this without you. I love you to the moon and back!

Lastly, I am so grateful for my beta readers and the honest feedback they provide me. Thank you for all that you do, Racheal, Kim, Dana, Jodie, Michael, Michelle, Brittany, and Laurel.

ABOUT

AIMEE NICOLE WALKER

Ever since she was a little girl, Aimee Nicole Walker entertained herself with stories that popped into her head. Now she gets paid to tell those stories to other people. She wears many titles—wife, mom, and animal lover are just a few of them. Her absolute favorite title is champion of the happily ever after. Love inspires everything she does, music keeps her sane, and coffee is the magic elixir that fuels her day.

I'd love to hear from you.

You can reach me at:

Twitter—twitter.com/AimeeNWalker

Facebook—www.facebook.com/aimeenicole.walker

Instagram—instagram.com/aimeenicolewalker

Blog—AimeeNicoleWalker.blogspot.com

Made in the USA
San Bernardino, CA
17 May 2020